RETRIBUTION

Richard Anderson is a second-generation farmer from northern New South Wales. He has been running a beef-cattle farm for twenty-five years, but has also worked as a miner and had a stint on the local council.

Richard is the author of one previous novel, *The Good Teacher*. He lives with his wife, Sue, four dogs, and a new cat.

RETRIBUTION

RICHARD ANDERSON

SCRIBE
Melbourne • London

Scribe Publications
2 John St, Clerkenwell, London, WC1N 2ES, United Kingdom
18–20 Edward St, Brunswick, Victoria, Australia 3056
3754 Pleasant Ave 1100, Minneapolis MN 55409, United States

Published by Scribe 2018

Typeset in Garmond Pro by the publishers.

Printed and bound in the UK by CPI Group (UK) Ltd, Croydon
CR0 4YY

Scribe Publications is committed to the sustainable use of natural
resources and the use of paper products made responsibly from
those resources.

9781911617709 (UK edition)
9781925713404 (Australian edition)
9781925693201 (e-book)

CiP records for this title are available from the National Library
of Australia and the British Library.

scribepublications.co.uk
scribepublications.com.au
scribepublications.com

To my father, Jim, and my son, Matt

1

The dogs were barking. He didn't like it. The sound of a dog barking with intent could carry clear across the warm plain on a still night like this. Any local who heard that sound would know it wasn't the rhetorical yelp of a dog on a chain.

In the dark distance, the random lights of scattered houses broadcast an unneeded reminder of the risk he was taking. Even though it was midnight on Christmas Eve, the best night of the year for stealing, you never knew who might have stepped outside for a leak, or a leg-stretch, or an attempt to cool the blood after too many servings of 'family'.

Sweetapple commanded the dogs to drop, and in the weak light of the skinny moon he could just make them out, squatting, unconvinced, as anxious as he was. Then he sooled them on, and, padding lightly, fast and slow, snapping at heels, they guided the heavy, black steers over the remaining short span of tussocks, through the gate into the steel cattle yards that were perched on the boundary fence, with the loading ramp aimed at the road as if they had been especially designed for Sweetapple's Christmas.

He climbed the railing fence and stepped down in behind them. All he could see was the steam from the steers' nostrils; all he could smell was the rich stink of their manure; all he could hear was the sound of them snorting and stomping against each other, the dogs panting softly, now resigned in the background. He ran the steers through the yard, hissing at them. There was no light for them to run towards, and no way for them to know what was up ahead. He just had to keep them moving away from the sound of him, up the loading race into his little truck.

The stock float rocked as they jostled each other, one way and then the other, like they'd been crowded onto a too-small boat. They were big. If they decided to jump or fight, they were big enough to smash the structure of the creaking float and then leap back out onto the road. But 'big' meant money—more than a grand each.

This time, there was no bike or horse to load. He'd taken the chance: either the dogs could bring in a mob on their own or he would let it go. He clipped the back gate, let Whiteface and Smiles jump up into the cab, because there was no time to put them in their boxes, and followed them up into the driver's seat.

He turned the key, but the motor didn't respond. Sweetapple held his breath and tried again. This time it half-heartedly complained, not ready to be reawoken, making only a weak, squealing noise that tortured his insides. He tried again, and the same resistant sound rattled out into the dark. Being stuck with a broken-down truck at the wrong loading ramp was something he didn't have a contingency for. He would have to jump them off and let them out, and then what? Hope for some magic to make the truck start? In an old truck like this, the problem could be any number of things. Could he find it and fix it before daylight?

But he was panicking. He tried to calm himself, to think his way through the problem. The battery was good, and there was plenty of fuel. It couldn't have been much more than an hour since the truck was running well. He tried again, but it was no keener. He could feel his heart start to go. Something flashed in his rear-vision mirror. Headlights in the distance? A single car could give the whole game away. He turned the key again, willing it, wishing it to start, knowing he was asking for supernatural help that he didn't believe in.

Then it fired and, after a few coughs, continued to fire. His lungs worked again, his pulse no longer banging along the insides of his arms.

He pushed the truck into gear, kept the lights off, and pulled out onto the coarse-gravel road, feeling the weight of the steers as they tried to hold their feet on his tired tyres and suspension. The truck groaned, even in the lowest gear, but gradually built momentum as though it were a giant lumbering machine that, once started, could never be stopped. There was no cough or smell from the clutch. He peered into his side mirror, saw that the float was holding, and then looked back at the rear tyres, knowing it would be a very bad time for one of them to blow. It was a risk he hated taking, but one he had to. Bald tyres didn't leave tread marks.

As the truck eased into its rhythm, and the yards faded behind him, he almost began to hum to himself at the wheel. This would make for another good payment. Soon enough, maybe a year on, there would be no more duffing, and that would be a relief, even if he didn't care for the landowners he stole from: self-righteous, two-faced bastards, proud cockatoos of honesty until it didn't suit their needs.

Suddenly, far back, a tiny set of headlights appeared from behind a rise in the road, and Sweetapple felt adrenaline's surging return. If anyone saw him driving with cattle on board at 1.00 am, Christmas day, nowhere near home, the conclusion would be obvious. And, worse, they would be able to place the time and location of the truck.

His truck couldn't outrun them. He'd be caught — if not now, then in a week or two, when old man Alcorn worked out that he was missing cattle, alerted the Stock Squad, and they joined the dots.

Sweetapple consoled himself with the idea that the vehicle probably belonged to revellers of some sort, finally finding their way home after Christmas. Possibly, hopefully, they had over-indulged, and were tired, maybe even drunk, forgetful, and not very observant. Or maybe it was a pigger, restless and bored, filling in the night. Or perhaps a traveller with no family who wanted them, driving for the sake of driving. Sweetapple knew all about that, too.

He could take a risk that if they were piggers, out on a night like this, they might be up to no good themselves: cutting fences and sneaking into properties to chase porkers, using the festive season to their advantage, just like he was. They might not give a bugger about what he was up to, but they would know pretty quickly that he was up to something, and he wasn't keen to chance it and give anyone that kind of leverage over him.

Up ahead, a sign pointed to a large ramp that said: 'Pine Hills — truck entrance'. The lights behind him were getting larger. The vehicle, whatever it was, was moving at a hell of a clip, which meant it probably wasn't conveying a Christmas family.

He took the entrance, accepting it as as close to an instance of divine intervention as he was ever likely to get, and coasted up the road, his lights still off, as if it were perfectly normal for him to be doing what he was doing. He drove until he was far enough off the main road that the vehicle's lights couldn't pick him up—but not so far that he would alert the property owners—parked within sight of the pale reflection from the Pine Hill sheds, and killed the motor. The homestead was probably seven hundred or eight hundred metres in the distance. There were no lights on. He was pretty sure this was the McKinnons' place: Ted and Janice, wasn't it? And their son, Peter, who he knew to be a good guy. It didn't matter. If they heard the truck and came looking, they would be unforgiving. Everyone hated a thief.

The night was warm and still, except for the throaty sound of the vehicle approaching at pace. Within minutes, a ute, the owner of the headlights, sped past, trailing music almost as loud as its motor. He breathed out in relief. The only threat they offered was to themselves.

Sweetapple started the truck again, and then eased it forward and manoeuvred it around, trying to use as little throttle as possible. If he could get across the couple of hundred metres to the road without being detected, he would be safe. It was a long way, his ears tuned for any sound, his eyes scanning for a light. He was out of Plan Bs. All he could do was make a run for it; at eighty kilometres an hour, it wouldn't be a long run.

Halfway to the road, one of his bovine passengers started a window-shaking bellow, loud enough to rattle the sleep of the McKinnons, as well as neighbours two properties away. The McKinnons probably didn't even have cattle in this paddock. They would wake to the noise, and immediately know that something wasn't right. He slammed on the brakes, hoping to knock the beast off its feet and its song, and then sped up, racing to the ramp and turning out onto the road, pushing the truck as fast as it could go and hoping desperately that old man kangaroos would resist the desire to jump blindly onto the road.

About ten kilometres away from the Pine Hill turn-off, he turned his lights on and, despite the sensation of being a little blinded, began to relax. He was gone from the crime scene and was now just driving a lorry on the road, minding his own business, bothering no one. His home was still forty kilometres away, but they were kilometres he could do in his sleep, on a road he knew as well as anyone. And now there were no cars and no kangaroos to worry about. Even the ghost-faced barn owls had given up for the night.

Sweetapple dared to turn the radio on, and was ignoring the early-morning fill-in talkback when he rounded a bend and saw in his high beam a ute on its bonnet, newly squashed against a tree, its wheels still spinning. He felt fresh, sickening fear. The gravel near the crash was carved with the fishtailed swerves that had sent the ute sling-shotting upside down into the tree.

He pulled the truck over, grabbed for his torch, leapt down, almost sprawling, righted himself, and ran to the wreck. Contents from the back of the ute—swags, bags, and a spare tyre—were strewn cyclone-like among the sticks and trees. Two kids, twenty-ish, a boy driver and a girl passenger, were in the front of the ute, still strapped in their seats, upside down. Music was blaring, as if nothing was wrong and they were waiting to drive off.

He got the driver's door open, leant in and down, and felt for pulses and arteries. What else did you feel for? He turned the music off. They were both breathing. Then the girl groaned, and the boy whimpered.

What was the next thing he needed to do? He knew that vehicles didn't normally blow up — that was a TV myth. *Back injury*. They couldn't be moved until he was sure.

The girl was breathing deeply, not yet panicked as she ran a hand over her legs and arms. She nodded and looked at him, her eyes clear in the dark.

The boy appeared to be trying to work out what had happened. The air around him was heavy with alcohol. 'Shit. My leg. My ribs.'

Sweetapple stepped back out and dialled an emergency number. An irritable woman began asking him what part of the state he was in. When he explained, she asked him again. He cursed her and hung up. He would deal with that when he'd got these kids out. The phone would have to be dumped, too. Lucky it was a cheap pre-paid.

He went around the other side of the vehicle, reefed the door open, then held the girl as best he could as she undid her seat belt and flopped down onto him, onto her side, and he dragged her out. She lay on the ground and sobbed, maybe twice, and then caterpillared herself up into a sitting position. Sweetapple went to the driver, who had his seatbelt off and was bawling in pain as he tried to fold his legs down.

'Are you all right?'

'It's broken. Down here.' He was pointing below his knee.

Sweetapple could hear the girl on her feet, shuffling behind him. He guessed she was coming to help, but when he turned to look he saw she had stumbled over to a bag that had been thrown clear. She knelt and rummaged through it. Then she extracted a small suitcase and, still limping, carried it warily away into the trees, and put it down flat.

He stopped watching her because the boy was scrabbling to get out. Sweetapple did his best to help him, to take some of his weight. Then the girl was suddenly by his side. They pulled the boy clear, and he sat on the ground, almost holding his thigh and cradling his chest, breathing like it could control the pain.

'You know first aid?' Sweetapple asked. He wondered if the girl was capable of helping. She nodded, and bent down to inspect the boy. He watched her look into the boy's eyes, and then feel his leg and search the parts of his body that were covered in blood.

'You got a phone?'

She looked up at him as though he had said something strange. 'A phone?'

He made a signal with his hand. She nodded and reached into a pocket, pulled out a phone, examined it, turned it on, and handed it to him.

Sweetapple rang the emergency number again. This time, a different woman came on the line, one who seemed to pick up very quickly where he was and how long an ambulance would take. He clicked the phone off and handed it back to the girl.

'The ambulance will be here in an hour and a bit.' Lucky they weren't dying.

He walked over, and retrieved a swag that had been launched into the branches of a whitewood shrub. He unbuckled it and spread it out on the ground, away from the ute.

'Can we get him over here? He needs to rug up for shock or … whatever. So do you.'

As the girl put the boy's arm over her shoulder, Sweetapple stepped in under the other side, and they swung him across to the blankets. The boy was strangling a scream. Sweetapple got them to sit down close together, and covered them.

'I've got some painkillers in the truck.'

He found some old tablets in the glovebox. They wouldn't do much, but the thought might help. As he shut the cab door and closed the dogs in, sniffing and licking at him, the steers shuffled restlessly in the back, rocking the truck as though it were a little overloaded boat. When he returned, the boy and girl were sitting, dazed, murmuring nothing intelligible, wrapped in the blankets.

'Here.' He offered them the tablets and a water bottle.

Sweetapple sat down in the spiky grass next to them. The night was black and unbroken; hardly a cicada sang. The girl swallowed some tablets with the water, and helped the boy do the same. Then they sat still again, shocked.

Sweetapple thought it was best to talk.

'Ute's too old for airbags. You hit your heads?'

'No.'

He tried to see if there was anything out of kilter about them, some injury he hadn't picked up.

'Where're you from?'

'He's from round here.'

'You?'

'Nowhere, really.' It wasn't glib; it sounded somehow disappointed, as if belonging somewhere was something she had never been offered.

'Pleased to meet you. What's your name?'

'Anna. Yours?' She had straight hair, probably blonde, right down to her shoulders. A nose ring caught the light. She looked fit enough in her unremarkable shirt and jeans. She could have been anyone's daughter.

'You'd better ring your parents.'

'My parents? I'm not going to do that.'

They sat in silence for a while. The boy couldn't stifle an occasional groan. 'You been to a party or something?' Sweetapple really didn't want to talk to them. He wanted to leave. The longer he stayed, the greater the risk that the police would turn up, alerted by Emergency Services, and the better the chance that, in the future, the boy and girl would remember him and his truck full of steers on Christmas morning.

'I got a lift with him yesterday, so I could get the lift today. He's taking me south. I had to go to their Christmas family piss-up. Got a bit out of control.' She sighed heavily. 'You think the police will come?'

'Eventually. You're supposed to report it anyway.'

She looked at the boy. 'I don't think this one ought to be breath-tested.'

'What were you doing, letting him drive?'

She shrugged again, and shook her head. Sweetapple pulled at the dry plains grass under his legs. It crackled in his hands, crisp against the dull murmuring from the boy. How many times had he seen or heard of kids in car accidents?

'Must have been important.'

'What?'

'Whatever it was that was in your bag.' He couldn't see her face well, but could make out her eyes.

'I just had to check something. It was only a few seconds.' There was discomfort in her voice. She paused. He couldn't tell if she was thinking or just calming herself. 'Anyway, there wasn't anything I could do to help right then.'

He looked at his phone and stood up. 'I've got to go.' He saw her looking at the phone, and put it back in his pocket. 'Do you think you two will be all right? The ambo's only about quarter of an hour away. You could ring and check.'

'You're going to leave us here?'

He realised how bad this sounded. 'Ah, yeah. Got a bit on. Got to get back.' It didn't make sense, but he wasn't going to jail because two kids had decided to drive too fast, full of grog. 'Keep the water bottle.' He didn't think there was anything in the bottle that could link him to it.

'Thanks.' She said it like she meant it. 'For everything.'

He strode towards his truck, telling himself it was self-preservation. There was nothing more he could do. The ambulance would arrive soon, and they would be fine. Maybe he could drive back through at daylight and make sure.

As he opened the cab door, he heard her ask, sharp as a dog's bark, almost to herself, 'Your cattle, are they?'

He stopped and held on to the door. Then he said, clearly enough for them both to hear, 'I didn't have to stop, you know.'

'Wait'.

He saw her stand, painfully, and then walk determinedly to the place in the trees where she'd left the suitcase. She picked it up carefully, came back, and stood in front of him, holding out the small bag.

'I need you to look after something for me.'

'You don't even know who I am.'

'I know you're a thief.' There was no reproach in it. It was just a useful fact.

She pushed the suitcase at him. It was heavy in his hands.

'What am I supposed to do with it?'

'Don't open it. Get rid of it. Don't burn it, it's … explosives.'

'A bomb?' She didn't look like she could ever have got hold of a bomb, or would know what to do with one if she did. He held the package a little further out from his body, thinking that to throw it away might cause it to explode, and then pushed it back at her. 'You're kidding.'

'It's not a bomb yet.' She pushed it back. 'I had to remove it so someone didn't use it as that.'

He was trying to decide if it was worth throwing the bomb as far as he could and then diving for cover behind the truck.

'What if it blows up me and my truck?'

'It can't do that. The detonators are quarantined—the computer has to provide a number to make it go off. The computer tells the bomb when it's a bomb.'

It probably wasn't a bomb; most likely something else precious to her that needed safekeeping. It wasn't the time and place for a game, but it didn't make him feel any safer.

Sweetapple held her gaze and weighed up his choices. She knew what he was up to, and that this bag meant as much to her as the wellbeing of her friend, if not more.

'Why don't you just leave it in the scrub?'

'Someone'll find it sooner or later.'

'Maybe they'll find it at my place.'

She was still, a two-dimensional image suddenly granite-hard. 'But that will be your problem.'

Her resolve chilled him. 'Are you a terrorist or something?'

'No. That's why I'm giving this to you, to get rid of it.'

He could call her bluff—drive off and leave her there. She didn't even know his name. But all she had to do was describe the truck to local cops, and when the cattle were found missing, they'd track him down and maybe even pin the bomb on him.

He put the suitcase onto the passenger seat of his truck carefully.

'Last time I stop at a crash.' Then he walked around and swung up into the cab, behind the wheel, and kicked the motor into action first time.

It was still dark when, blurry-eyed and feeling his fatigue, he crossed his own ramp. He had spent the first part of the trip rigid with panic that the bomb sitting next to him on the seat would launch him suddenly into the night sky. And then he got used to it near him, and started to believe that it wasn't a bomb, and that even if it was, it was as safe as she had said. It had already travelled this far and been in a car accident. It couldn't be too unstable.

He figured those stupid kids would be fine. Lucky. But that girl, Anna, was scary; nothing like what he had first thought. Why would she have a bomb? Was she a religious nut? She had that kind of certainty.

The bag, with its supposed bomb inside it, was still on the seat. Years ago, before the time of terrorist threats, his dad had done a farm-explosives course and afterwards taught Sweetapple what he'd learned. For a while they'd blasted holes and blown up tree stumps together, and then a miscalculation had caused a crack in the concrete at the sheds, so his mother's insistence that they give it up finally had its effect. But because of that time with his dad, he'd always felt he knew a bit about explosives.

Now he was close to his house, and the lights were on. The television would be blaring, and the timer would have just made the kettle boil. He liked to have it set up so that at any time, if anyone happened to come snooping around, they would think someone had just left, had just been having a cup of tea and watching television. You couldn't be too careful with security. The Stock Squad were pretty good at their job, but only if they got help from suspicious neighbours or could track backwards from a dodgy sale. So far, he hadn't aroused suspicion and had never been caught.

Sweetapple drove past his house and his yards — the yards he used for show — and continued to where the scrub started on the rise at the back.

He motored in amongst the box trees, old giants and skinny saplings, and almost thanked them for their protection. His second set of yards, the ones he used, where no one could see what was loaded in and out, was up ahead. From there, he could walk the steers up into the scrub paddock and leave them till the fuss died down. They would do well up there. It was rested, and the feed was fresh.

Sweetapple backed up to the loading ramp, and unloaded them. One by one, he pushed them up the race and put their heads in the bail, cut off their lifetime identification tags, and put them in a bag. It was still dark, and his only light came from the torch.

The steers didn't have any earmarks or brands, so, with their tags out, he'd have no trouble reselling them. He let them out onto water with their genetic mates. Sweetapple had gone to the trouble of buying culled cattle from Alcorn through the yards. It had taken some time, but he'd managed to pick up some tailender heifers that were too weak and malnourished for anyone else to bother with.

It was a strategy that was worth the trouble. If the police decided to pay him a visit, it was important that they didn't find any incriminating cattle DNA stuck to fences and yards. Alcorn had a pretty closely bred herd, which meant that any DNA testing of hair, or hoof, or even steer slobber would give clear-cut results. The cops would want to know where the paperwork was for the cattle that matched the DNA. The cull heifers gave him paperwork and an alibi.

He drove back to his house, showered, took the phone off the hook, and went to bed. When he woke at midday, sweaty in the bedclothes, his first thought was of Anna and the suitcase. They had both invaded his dreams, talking to him and taunting him. Somewhere, too, Carson was involved, laughing at him, teasing.

Sweetapple got up and walked outside, letting the dogs go, checking garden taps, and turning on hoses—anything to clear out the dreams and remind himself it was just his head making stuff up.

When he felt calmer, he ate a large breakfast, and listened to Kenny Chesney crooning and young galahs outside wheezing dissonantly about the heat. Then he washed up his breakfast things, wiped down the benches, took some frozen meat out of the freezer for dinner, and went out to work on the truck. But once outside he realised that, before he could start on the truck, he had to deal with the bag. He would not be able to think straight while it sat there in the truck, warm and possibly glowing like it had in the dream.

He pulled the suitcase from the front seat, wrapped it in several bags, and then took the bike far up into the scrub through the apple trees, kurrajongs, and shiny bush, before stopping and walking along a rocky wallaby track above the dry gully to a stand of remnant box trees, huge-girthed and imposing in the landscape. The heat had its own weight, squashing the smell of eucalyptus out into the air as the sweat ran down his ribs under his shirt. He shoved the parcel deep into the grey hollow of one of the larger trees. There was no need to mark the tree or remember the track; the trees were solid in his memory, more permanent than family or love or desire, or anything else that had imprinted itself on him.

He walked back to the bike, dusting his hands and feeling that the problem was now dealt with. A kookaburra raised the possibility of rain, and, in the distance, one of his new steers bellowed in confusion about its new surroundings.

Now he had things to do: the good tyres had to be put back on the truck, and the white truck doors had to be replaced with his trademark brown ones. He could forget about last night.

2

On Christmas Eve, Ginko, raw-smelling and wrapped in unexplained beach towels, was giving Luke a lift into town from the protest site to the bus, shaking his head at the windscreen as if Luke's condition were terminal.

'We'll miss you, buddy.'

His driving was even more rhapsodic than normal, a sure sign that Ginko was feeling the weight of the moment — his foot on the accelerator unable to commit to its task, pushing and then sliding off, while the steering wheel functioned mostly as a support, only occasionally as a directional aid. There was no explanation for the towels; perhaps he planned to swim at the council pool, or shower at the caravan park, or maybe he just couldn't be bothered with pants.

'Won't be the same.'

Luke adjusted his long legs in the crowded space of the car, wondering about Ginko's assertion. Even though protesters came and went from the picket all the time — young, old, foreigners, ideologues, farmers, radical activists, students, lost souls, opportunists—creating little ceremony, Luke's farewell had been emotional, even before the bag search, as if they were losing one of their own. He had said 'Goodbye' and hugged the whole group (they'd been through a lot together), with special attention to his gang: Wedge, Panda, Smoky, Gina, Hope, and, of course, Anna, who ended up getting out before him. Some of them were a little more animated than usual—Glenys, the retired school teacher; Penny and Susie, the tennis mums in search of a cause; and that painting contractor from Dubbo—but he couldn't really push them away. You had to accept their loving pungency, and to hope they suffered some of yours.

They had celebrated early, on the day before Christmas Eve, when the mine was due to be shut for three days and many had already headed home. Wedge, with his usual organisational skill, had got them together to share their triumph and the warmth of mutual belief. There were drinks and a Christmas picnic that featured chicken among every kind of salad. Some had made presents: carved wooden sculptures, knitted beanies, and feathered dream-catchers. He had almost enjoyed himself and felt part of a community, even though that was never true.

By now, Luke would have been unsettled by the pulsing throttle under Ginko's foot, or questioned the towels, or angrily relived the bag search, if he could have thought of anything other than a hot shower, a genuinely cold beer, and a porcelain toilet. Maybe even real soap, toilet paper that didn't rasp, and a mattress without lumps. If you were going to dream, dream large. His dreadlocks were getting heavy, and beginning to feel like they were carrying enough animal life to require their own protest picket.

'Won't be the same.'

Ginko clung to the wheel of the green, squeaking jalopy, as the levels of smoke and noise from the engine broke more laws than he ever had. Beads, Rasta trinkets, feathers, and pieces of stick covered the dashboard. On the floor of the back seat were stones that Ginko had found and treasured. If you accidentally asked about them, he would take you through the collection (or as far as he could get) one by one, explaining their significance and how they reminded him of a bird, or maybe a favourite aunt, or the rocks off Byron.

Ginko was the sort of idiot who needed to talk about a concept several times before he could understand and retain it. Then he would bring it to any discussion he found himself involved in. Whether the weed had made Ginko stupid, or whether he had always been stupid, Luke hadn't decided. He was some sort of throwback to hippier days, a 'feral' who liked to resurrect slogans such as 'subvert the conventional paradigm' from the internet. There weren't many on the picket like him, no matter what the media said. The picket held the full spread of humanity.

Unsurprisingly, Luke was glad to be free of them. Despite the camaraderie of Christmas, the intensity of the group was draining, and their need to be 'supportive' managed to make him feel claustrophobic in the most open of spaces. The constant reinforcing of their rightness made it difficult for him not to say something cynical or inappropriate.

He had been surprised to see Anna leave. He had thought she was the sort to stay to the bitter end, turning up on the news time and again, yelling at police, or being pushed into a paddy wagon. She had been particularly upset by what had happened, although she refused to say that was her reason for leaving.

Old sweat and older incense leaked from the seat covers. Luke wound his window down.

The hardcore members freaked him out a little, too: the ones who were keen to smash equipment, or set booby traps, or attack incoming mine workers. For some of them, it was just a contact sport, their cause a secondary thing that legitimised extreme behaviour. Not that Luke had anything against extreme behaviour, but it was impossible to know what they might come up with next; and in his situation, that was dangerous.

Ginko was muttering his way through a song, bobbing his head in a way that suggested it was loose on its moorings. The dust rose like a bushfire behind them.

At least the sex had been abundant. Luke had taken advantage of it whenever he could, mostly with Anna, but as often as not with whoever made themselves available (not men, even though they tried); he had even had a crack at Penny, in the shadow of the Square Rock, up past the old fencer's hut. She was way too into it, making all sorts of passionate but unrelated noises. Luke was happy enough to be part of someone else's fantasy, but even as he humped away in the soft light, dappled by the eucalypt leaves as the birds he couldn't name sang sonatas, he couldn't stop himself imagining Penny's salesman husband (the last man in the world he would normally feel sympathy for), working sixteen-hour days and living on planes to keep his wife in the manner to which she was pretending not to be accustomed.

So he'd only been with her the one time—probably all she wanted—but from then on she treated him like a 'special friend', notably when Susie was around. It made him keen to return to Anna, who was smart, steely, and seriously focused on everything she attempted. When she left, Anna had gone to some trouble to say, 'Goodbye.' She'd said she'd had a 'good feeling about him', and hoped they'd meet up down the line. He couldn't see that happening.

For four solid weeks, they'd camped in the scrub on private land, the Fieldings' farm, just off the mine lease. Before that, they'd been coming and going every day from the caravan park in town for two months—setting up camp, making tripods, battling security, arguing with the workers, painting banners, dressing up for weird stunts to entice the cameras and hopefully provide them with a moment that might go viral or catch fire on the nightly news. They had been a small group, but he had to admit to having had some fun. A few celebrities had drifted through, and gradually the protest's profile had grown.

In the slow times, they talked of a new world where mining companies and big business didn't hold all the power; a world where people fought for what was right and were listened to; where renewable energy was the only energy source. It was rubbish, of course, but a nice game to play, and he thought he'd played it well.

And camping amongst the gum trees was okay, but the camp was so rudimentary it felt like some sort of punishment. Not to the others. They didn't want cushy; they wanted to be at one with the environment they were defending. Every hardship encouraged and sanctified them. Even the caravan park had been six to a tiny cabin and a shower-block shower that was reluctant to stay hot. He had to work really hard to disguise his dislike of his fellow travellers.

Something crawled in Luke's armpit, and he ignored it. He had become accustomed to independent movement on his skin.

'I'll drop you at the bus, and then get the food and the other stuff. You might be late otherwise.'

'Thanks, man.' Perhaps Ginko had been awake all night planning this trip.

Now out of the hills and the forest, they bumped through the river country with its sparse, massive red gums, if that's what they were, and fat cows and large tractors appearing at intervals. It was an attractive landscape, much prettier than the scrubby hillsides they were trying to defend. He wondered if anyone else noticed.

Ginko seemed to have presumed that Luke was leaving reluctantly and was dealing with remorse at letting the side down. As if he wasn't just another ring-in, like the rest of them on uni holidays, bussed in for the action.

'Don't worry, brother. I reckon we've got them on the run. Public support is coming in behind us. If we can just stick it out for a few more weeks, we'll be able to put some real pressure on, knock the share price, and pressure the government. It'll be downhill from there for the bastards. All over the world, universities, banks, and even governments are divesting themselves of their coal interests. The end is nigh for these fuckers.'

He hadn't heard Ginko string so many words, half-coherently, together at any one time, and almost looked to see if he was reading a cue card. Then he remembered that Ian, the public servant with the tight pants, had said something similar the day before.

'Hope you're right.'

It was possible. According to the media, there had been a rise in public support for them. Social media had played its powerful part, but it had been a long time coming. There had been marches in the city, which had to mean something, even if people in the city seemed to like marching for its own sake. Public opinion could have an effect; everyone said so. But governments didn't shut coal mines if there was any way they could avoid it. The boom might be long gone, but money was money.

'Bomb thing was mad, eh?'

Luke nodded sagely. Mad as.

'Stupid shit. All of it. Peaceful resolution is supposed to be our thing. Non-violent, eh, brother?'

From somewhere, the hardcores had come up with a bag of explosives, or so the gossip had it. They were going to blow up the coal loader. The camp know-it-alls were claiming that the explosives had been stolen from the mine with the intention of creating the beautiful justice of blowing up the mine with their own bombs.

Luke didn't believe it. Breaking into the mine's magazines through constant, observant traffic and past multiple cameras would involve skills and precision of the highest level. If you managed to steal the explosives, the company would know very quickly what was missing, and the alert would be out statewide, even nationwide.

He also didn't believe them because bombs weren't a part of the protest ethos, but wild rumours certainly were. Around the camp fire at nights, the group was keen to agree with each other about the importance of holding the moral high ground and how the public would instinctively know they were in the right. The public didn't trust big companies, especially mining companies, so it didn't take much to play them as the baddies. Let them do the violence and make the mistakes. Even the whiff of a rumour of a bomb in the picket group wouldn't fit with this ideal.

'That why you got out?'

'Nah, but it helped.'

Then Ryan, one of the hardcores that Luke almost trusted, told him that a small amount of explosive, a 'sausage pack', had been sourced from in the mine. An operator in the mine had discovered it when it failed to go off, put it in his crib bag, and smuggled it to the protestors. No one had ever met him or asked him to do what he did. It was against every mine rule, and a huge safety risk. Apparently, not every miner supported the company. At first, the hardcores didn't believe the bomb was real. Who'd take such a risk? And then someone, somewhere, with a knowledge of explosives assured them that it wasn't such a risk, because this type of explosive was very stable and extremely hard to set off without using computer codes.

The hardcores didn't know what to do with the sausage pack, and Ryan suggested they weren't going to do anything. But the power of having the bomb, of knowing it was in their possession, was something they couldn't let go of.

And then the shit had really hit the damn fan: somebody had stolen the pack.

'You know who nicked it?'

'Nah.'

Ginko gave a solemn nod, appropriate to an extremely profound answer.

'I would have, if I had the guts.' Luke was remembering Anna's face and the way it responded to things he'd said.

'Mmm, brother.'

The hardcores went berserk, blaming everyone, ripping

through people's gear, threatening, smashing; it was out of control. It was why Luke called it in. That sort of madness could uncover things accidentally. The group split, and everybody began to suspect everyone else. Luke had to stop himself giving in to paranoia. It was definitely time to get out.

After things had settled down, he had gone to find Anna, to share a drink and maybe talk about all the shit that was going down. Anna had a tent on her own near the gully that delineated the edge of their camp. The position on the outer perimeter gave them a chance to spend time alone together, which in the picket group was difficult to achieve. She was tidying her area, which was always spotless: everything ordered, clean, and folded like an army recruit's. But she wasn't really tidying anything, just moving things around. At the time, he'd thought the sight of Anna in slight disarray in the middle of her ruthless tidiness was funny. He asked her, teasingly, if she was all right. She collected herself and frowned at him.

'I'm fine.' Then she said, 'Why wouldn't I be?'

'No reason. You look a little tuned up.'

She turned her back to him, put a shirt in a bag, and over her shoulder said, 'Have you been on your own for the past hour or so?'

'Yeah.'

'Would people have seen you on your own?'

'Probably. I was reading my book. The others were making some scarecrow thing for tomorrow.'

'Scarecrow?'

'Apparently. Don't ask me.'

'So you can say you've been with me for a couple of hours, yeah?'

'If you want. Why?'

'That vegan dude was getting a bit keen. I told him you were going to be around. Beer?'

Luke had not bothered to attribute any significance to the moment. It had made sense. Anna was slim, blonde, and looked like she might be a real challenge. Guys were always hitting on her, and she was forever thinking of polite ways to deflect them so as not to upset the harmony in the camp. Harmony was only important because the protest needed it.

'You and the vegan stole the bomb?'

'Funny.' She zipped the bag, grabbed two beers from a cool bag, and passed him one. 'I wouldn't know how to get rid of a bomb. If I hid it around here, or on the farm somewhere, I'd be terrified it would go off at a random time and hurt someone.'

She gulped her beer. The sound of her drinking had something inappropriately indulgent about it, and there was nothing indulgent about Anna. Her only affectation was a small stud on the side of her nose.

'So then I would have to take it with me, and I don't like the idea of carrying a bomb around.' There was laughter some distance away, coming from the scarecrow-makers. 'I was thinking you might have it.'

'Why would I take it?'

'Oh, there's something about you.' She stared into her beer can. 'It's like you're not really afraid of anything.'

'I'm afraid of bombs.'

'I doubt it. You're not wired that way, are you? It's what I like about you.'

'I don't think I'm wired any particular way.'

They hadn't really talked about the bomb after that, and

within the week they were both gone. Did Anna become friendly with Ryan during that time? She'd talked to him a lot. Ryan was very upset, making accusations about everyone. What he thought was the group's most powerful leverage had disappeared overnight. Had Anna told him she thought Luke could be the thief? Luke had imagined she was trying to talk Ryan down. And that's probably what she was doing. For him to start being suspicious of Anna now was paranoid and stupid. He'd never had any questions about her when he was with her every day.

It was only a few days later, after Anna had left with some farmer ex-boyfriend in a scuffed-up ute (the bloke who always came to her rescue, she'd said), as Luke had put his bag into Ginko's car to leave, that Ryan and Kyle had grabbed the bag and dumped it on the ground. Kyle had gone through everything: toiletry bags, undies, clothes, shoes, books, and coats, as if Luke might have cut the explosives up into small pieces and spread them through his bag. Kyle had found nothing. Luke hoped he'd never see Kyle again, for fear of what he might be unable to stop himself doing to him. Stopping himself doing things was his life's work.

As they bumped along in the loose gravel, Luke remembered his mother's opinion that he had been born with a bear inside him. When he was little, she called it his 'grouchy bear'. She regularly warned him to put his grouchy bear away, or else he'd get into big trouble. Later, she tried to talk him through managing his anger and channelling his negative energy to productive use. She'd read about this in one of her half-finished self-help paperbacks. He'd thought he hadn't listened, but later, when he'd left home, found himself echoing some of her techniques to avoid and outsmart the more-than-grouchy bear.

The outskirts of town, marked by tall, pale grain silos, was suddenly upon them. Luke felt a layer of skin lifting; in no time, he would be emerging as a shiny new version of himself. He couldn't imagine a better feeling.

'What are you going to do now?'

'Go and see the oldies. Mum's not great. Need to spend a bit of time with her. Then I might go up north.' It was possible his mum was sick. He had no idea.

'Picket the Basin?'

'Yeah, probably. Need to make a bit of money first.'

Ginko grunted at this, as if it was some sort of common disease that he was thankful he hadn't yet contracted, and then guided the car into a side street where the local council had erected a covered waiting area, probably sponsored by the coal company.

'Here you go. Should only be about ten minutes' wait.' The local bus timetables were something Ginko was an expert on.

Luke got out, grabbed his bag, and walked to the driver's window. He shook Ginko's hand, gave a thumbs-up, thanked him again, and wished him luck. As Luke took a step away, Ginko asked, 'So you really don't know who got the bomb out?' It wasn't a probe or an accusation; it was an expression of incredulity at his ignorance. Luke turned back to him.

'You know?'

'Yup. Can't believe you don't.'

'Who?'

'If someone hasn't already told you, then I definitely can't.' Ginko disappeared, noisily, with a wave out the window, the word 'Namaste' left behind like litter. Luke watched, momentarily slack-jawed. Ginko knew who'd got the bomb out, and he didn't? What else had been going on that he didn't know about?

He shook it off. He was out, finished with that adventure, and what did he care who did what on the picket, or what any of them did for the rest of their lives?

When Ginko was out of sight, Luke shouldered his bag and crossed the road, and walked down two avenues to the back entrance of the Steamroller Motel, a large L-shaped building that had taken on Australiana as its décor. It was clumsy, poorly thought through Australiana: there was a large plastic wagon wheel in reception, alongside shiny plastic rabbit traps and cheap broad-brimmed hats. His phone said it was midday and a bit early to check in, but he knew they'd been forewarned.

The older lady behind the counter, under hair that was too dark, smiled at him with a smile that needed more effort to make it believable. No local liked a greenie or a protester.

'We did your room early.' The Christmas decorations around the window already looked tired.

'Thanks.'

'Neil …' She began to write in her newspaper of the day before stopping after scribbling two letters, not looking up … 'put your bag in there this morning.' After a calculated pause, she spat out, 'Christmas Eve, mind you.'

She shook the pen as if it might help her think, frowning at the newspaper, her pencilled eyebrows unaware they should be joining in.

'Still, Zill Park are good clients for us. We do what we can for them.'

She dropped the pen and gave him another appraisal.

'Never seen a miner with a hairdo like that, though.' Her hair bobbed up in the direction of his, while the rest of her enjoyed the moment. She was wrong. Even Luke knew there were plenty of dreads on mine sites.

'Charlatan.'

'Beg pardon?'

'Four across,' he said. '"Charlatan". Nine letters: "Person falsely claiming to have a special knowledge or skill".'

They read a lot of newspapers on the picket.

3

The day Carson felt an unexpected hand on her arse, she could have sworn she also heard the sound of doors slamming: bang, bang, bang, bang.

When the hand first touched her, she ignored it, treating it as an accident. She was in an aisle, showing Mr Statham, Bob Statham, the new brand of pipe fittings. It had been an okay day, with a steady stream of customers, none of them with complaints or difficult requests. Another reasonable day that almost papered over the constant dread she felt of where her life might be heading.

When Bob had asked her to show him the fittings, she hadn't thought anything of it. It wasn't what she'd expected — pipe fittings were as straightforward as you got, and didn't need to be 'shown' — but the boss talked a lot about 'service' and being friendly to customers, and Bob was a nice-enough older guy who was one of the company's really big customers. It never occurred to her that she might be putting herself at risk in the aisle of a rural-produce store.

But when the hand on her arse progressed to a little squeeze of ownership, a horrible rush of understanding flooded through her. It wasn't just one man's hand. It was the hand of men everywhere, waiting their turn at what they thought was a right, their part in a deal. She had to face the immediate and undeniable knowledge that she had allowed herself to be put in a position where all her options were bad ones. The soundtrack to this epiphany was those doors slamming: bang, bang, bang, bang.

At any other time in her life, Carson would have wheeled round and flattened him, screaming blue murder without a thought for the consequences, without acknowledging that such a thing as consequences existed. But there, in the aisle next to the fittings, across from the electric-fence gear and alongside garden chemicals, she had taken his hand and returned it to him, looking at him squarely, reproachfully in the eye, but saying nothing. He had just laughed boyishly, confident that it was all part of the game they had both played many times — maybe cat and mouse, boss and maid. If she had called out, he would probably have liked it even more.

Carson could have yelled, screamed even, and reported his actions to her boss. That's what any independent woman would have done, wouldn't they? No doubt her boss would have asked Bob not to do it again, probably with a wry, knowing smile. He would tell Carson he had dealt with the problem, and how he felt it was unacceptable from a customer, and he wouldn't tolerate it from anyone. She could trust him on that. Then Carson would be out of a job as soon as they thought the heat was off. She was meat, plain and simple. And no one knew it better than her.

Carson locked the doors to Ponsford's Rural Produce,

breathed a shoulder-heaving sigh, and looked around. It was 5.30 pm, Christmas Eve, and there wasn't another human being in sight. On the road that ran past the front of the store, a seemingly driverless car purred its way down the hill and disappeared, and then there was nothing. She stood and listened. There was not one sound: not a squeal from children at play, or the popping wheeze of a struggling lawnmower, or the clack of a coal train. Nothing. You could have sworn the town had been evacuated. *Peaceful*, she told herself. *Peaceful or dead.*

She was supposed to go to her mother's place for Christmas, but she had already texted her that her car had broken down and that there was no one around to fix it. Her mother was pissed off, but not for long. Nothing ever really lasted with her mother — tempers, boyfriends, jobs, and ideas all disappeared as quickly as cash did. Carson would miss Christmas morning with her little stepsisters, but she wouldn't miss the ugly afternoon that would surely follow. When the drink and the drugs took hold, there'd be arguments and accusations over nothing much, spurred by their endless need to blame someone else for everything bad that had ever happened to them. In their dark moments, her mother and her boyfriends needed excuses, and often enough it was the people closest to them who had to provide them. Carson had learnt long ago to avoid being that source.

Her car started first go, and she pulled out blindly, knowing there was no risk of traffic.

It was weeks ago now, but she knew that by sleeping with Mark Jameson she had created the problem, or at least had allowed Mark to come up with the scheme. A supposedly well-mannered guy like Bob would never have done something like that without assurances from someone. At least, that's what she thought then. It seemed Mark and his mates had presumed that Carson would be happy to be turned into someone they could use, to be passed around among them. There might even have been money involved. Could you blame them? She couldn't argue that she'd slept with Mark for love, could she? Or in the hope of any sort of lingering relationship. Did Mark find a new girl every year — school leavers who didn't know any better, who were happy to put up with a wrinkled old cock for the chance of being introduced to a bigger world? Maybe she was just as bad as they were.

Carson drove out of town, past houses messy with tinsel and as many versions of Santa Claus as the human brain could conjure. Occasionally, music thumped through the peace, bassy and persistent. Some of the houses had more Christmas lights snaked and wrapped through their front gardens than their small trees had leaves. It was all to win a street competition, or to claim bragging rights in an endless one-upmanship game, or maybe to simply piss off the neighbours with enough festive light streaming through their front windows to wake the whole lot of them. Most driveways had either no cars or several in them; and when it was several, they lined the street, covered the lawns, and filled the garages and the entries. She felt no envy or disappointment. She was going to have a quiet night — eating a pizza she planned to make herself, taking in a couple of movies, and downing a few ciders. On Christmas Day, she had arranged to meet up with Sweetapple, because he was alone, too, and because she liked to be around him, even if she went to some trouble not to show it.

A B-double truck approached, its horns blaring, with Jimmy

Taylor in the driver's seat, waving madly at her from his high cab. He probably wanted her to stop for a chat, or God knows what. Any dude in his truck at this hour, on this day, loved his truck more than his wife—that was for sure. Carson swerved across in front of the truck, and saw its clowning driver suddenly turn shit-scared as he swung his rig out of the way, running out onto the gravel on the side of the road. Carson steered back to her side of the road, laughing to herself, laughing at everyone.

On that day, some weeks ago, when she had returned the squeezing hand to its grinning owner, she had marched to her boss's cubicle at the end of the room, and pushed her way in.

'I'm really sick. Going to chunder, I think. All right if I go home?'

Barry had looked up from paperwork and said, 'Yeah, fine,' as his face said, *No, it's not all right.*

He'd probably want her to produce a doctor's certificate or something. But after a held moment, he conceded, 'You do look a bit pale.'

She was in her car before anyone could intervene or change their mind, went home, and drank bourbon till she really did throw up all around the bathroom.

In the morning, she tried to tell herself it was just a hand on her arse, nothing sinister, nothing nasty meant, the sort of thing that just went with the territory—the old bloke was just having a bit of harmless fun. If she couldn't handle Bob Statham, what could she handle? It had happened before in many other places, so much worse than just a squeeze on the arse. What was the big deal?

But she couldn't sell it to herself. Any idiot knew when they were at the wrong end of this sort of crap. You knew when you were being bullied; you knew when you were being used; you knew when someone was taking advantage. Ignoring it, you were the one who lost. Carson had the feeling that she was always the loser. She saw then that the good-natured smile and friendly chat from Bob Statham wasn't pleasant at all. He did it because he knew he could. It was a means to an end, and she was that end. When she saw him again, she would have to control her building rage against him.

After that, if Carson was alone with a man in the store, she made sure there was a barrier between her and the customer: a counter, a hay bale, a pallet of dog biscuits, a human being, anything.

Of course, you could fight the harassment stuff, in the courts maybe. Some did. You saw them in the media, bravely, determinedly fronting the reporters; their supporters behind them, their mouths hard. They never hung on to their jobs either. And Carson's job was important, because there wasn't another job to go to, except numbing bar work in one of the empty pubs.

She took a wide turn and came down off the hill. The heat was still snaking off the pale plains, the only signs of green hiding at the base of tanks, leaking troughs, and tended gardens. It would be cooler soon, and it was always good to get out of town, into space and away from the small whispering of voices.

Carson had missed the chance to get out. All her dumb friends had gone to uni, got into trades, and had good jobs. The rest were pregnant or brain dead. She was smarter than them, but now she was stuck, and that fact was never more unshakeable than when Bob Statham reached over and put his gnarled hand on her arse.

The do-gooder teachers had liked her in her early years, praised her intelligence, and encouraged her to try harder. By her final years they had given up, annoyed that their faith in her, their suggestions and solutions, had been rejected. She was a lost cause, and liked to joke that she was an 'outlaw' — nobody's bitch, for better or worse.

But Carson had always thought that she would be the one to get out: travel, work in all sorts of exotic places, make a career in the city or somewhere beautiful on the coast. She hadn't known what she would make it as, or how, but she knew she was less afraid and much cooler than pretty much everyone else in her school.

But it hadn't worked out. After the final exams, she had taken her bag and jumped on the day train to the city. She had no plans, but Ewan, an older brother of Jess, a boy at school, had said he could get her some bar work. She had her certificate and had worked in the pubs in town, so she was confident she was ready for the world.

Ewan had been true to his word. There had been a couch to sleep on, and ready shifts at a very busy, kind of glam inner-city pub. But that was all. She had worked hard on long shifts and made good money, but in the city you never had enough money. It bought her clothes, nights out, and a shared unit, but nothing more. When she moved into her own place and started paying rent, there was hardly enough left over for a night out. Travel and an exotic life weren't even worth daydreaming about.

And then she got an offer to do topless bar work, with the possibility of some 'personal service', for big money. Enough money to get her out and into the life she had dreamed up. Enough to solve all her problems, make her a different person, maybe even get her to where she could take the first steps to an interesting somebody's sort of life.

Carson walked past that bar many times. There was nothing to be seen from the outside, but she knew it was dimly lit and not seedy, a clean, expensive place, posh even. The girls were babes, too, hot-bodied, and she knew she would be nervous alongside them. It would be a good job. The guy who wanted to employ her claimed to look after his girls well. He said he could only charge the big bar prices if the girls were of top quality, and to keep top quality he had to look after them extra well. It was the break she was looking for. She was on her way.

And then she did a bit of half-hearted research in a bar that specialised in the topless thing and some unlawful bottomless (if men were prepared to put the money out). It wasn't as sophisticated as the place she was going to work in, but it was similar, so she was there, sipping on a drink, looking over the top of her glass at the pretty girls smiling, laughing, wiggling, touching a hand. They were good at it, and it didn't look like hard work. She was convincing herself that she could do it, be it. It had to be easier than most other jobs. Then, some time between spying and sipping, the realisation arose in her that this was the sort of thing her mother had been doing all her life.

When she was a little girl, there had always been men coming and going from their house, or providing them with a house. Sometimes they were helping out; sometimes they were in the bedroom with the door locked, and sometimes with it not locked. It was how Kelly got through life, trading on her looks for everything: money, love, help around the house; help with her car; at the welfare office; in the street; in trouble; to get her through. She said she was just like a model or an actress using a natural talent to get ahead.

To Carson, Kelly had always been beautiful and so much younger than the other mothers at school. She was a sort of princess of the parents. The mothers wished they could be her, and the fathers laughed too much around her and watched her in a special way. When she was little, Carson liked to leave the school walking close to her mother, knowing everyone was watching in awe.

But as high school went on, Carson began to see the way people thought about Kelly, and at home felt the isolation created by Kelly's run of useless boyfriends. Carson still held to the idea of Kelly as beautiful and sexy, as far as she understood that idea. She treated other people's attitudes to her mother as a sort of jealousy, which it was: dowdy mothers in their sensible shoes, saying nasty things to get back at someone more naturally blessed than they were.

But making money off how you looked, especially how you looked without any clothes on, didn't seem like a dream that Carson had ever had. She didn't mind guys admiring her body, and she'd slept with her fair share, but turning it into your job, your one talent, seemed wrong, and wrong in a way that could be damaging. Other girls could handle it, like water off a duck's back, but not her. She wasn't anywhere near as tough as she'd always thought. She had prided herself on being tough, not intimidated by anyone, never crying or playing for sympathy when something didn't suit her. The times her mother's boyfriends came on to her (and they all did), she didn't make a big deal out of it. She just got over it and carried on. But now it was all looking like an act, because she couldn't handle wiggling and smiling for a few old men. *Some outlaw*. She needed to be out of this place, and this city, and this pathetic dream.

Suddenly, in that bar, she was crying into her drink, her tears obvious and embarrassing, washing down her face: a hick chick lost and terrified in the big city. She couldn't stop, nor even say what started it. Before someone, a manager or maybe one of the bar girls, could come over and suggest she might be 'more comfortable elsewhere', Carson had got herself out. Under a dim light in a nameless street, she knew that the options for a different life, an interesting life, that she had thought existed, didn't. You had to work in a menial job—as a nurse, or bar staff, or an office worker—until you scraped some dollars together, or met a guy who had bothered to scratch a few together himself, and then you got a tiny house you couldn't pay for, had some kids, and the cycle began again. She didn't want to be Kelly, but she felt maybe now she understood her.

So Carson didn't take the job. The girls she worked with said she was mad. If they'd got the offer, they'd have taken it in a heartbeat. And what was she going to do, they asked: stay working at the pub, pulling beers for the rest of her life? Go back to her dead-end existence at the back of beyond? She didn't have any answers for them or herself, and could never decide whether she had done the right thing or if she was just weak, shit-scared.

She stayed on at the bar for a few more months and then headed home, which wasn't home—just the town she grew up in. There was no house there for her, and no family. Kelly had already moved away with Jake, another of her totally out-of-control choices. It was a new start, but not a fresh one. Jake had been talking about a job in an abattoir, but it was pretty obvious to everyone, except her mother, that Jake couldn't stick with a regular job for more than a couple of weeks. Carson barely knew Jake, but it was a fair bet that soon enough there would be an argument, or a fight, or a failed drug test, or a drunken 'incident', or Jake would nick something. Maybe all of it would happen at once, and Jake would find himself back at home, taking drugs he couldn't afford and blaming Kelly for his misfortune.

Carson rented a house in her old town and took a job in merchandise, telling herself it would only be for a while. She would resit the final exams and go to uni, or get a trade of some sort. Hairdressing couldn't be that hard, could it? That was three years ago. She had played netball, slept with a few local men, gone to parties, done drugs, and just passed the time. It hadn't been so bad, because in the back of her mind it was just a stop-off for a while. Soon enough, she told everyone (almost believing it), she would head back to the city or to school, or go to uni. But she didn't, and they did. They made it look so easy — even offered, quietly, to help her out with places to stay, people they could have a word to, and so on. Carson always rejected them, saying there was no need to worry, she was organised. She had held that worry at bay right up until she felt the hand on her arse.

The farms looked hot and summer-dry as she turned and crossed a broken ramp, and ran down the hill to her cottage. When she had decided to move into a farmhouse out of town, on her own, her mother and her friends had been all finger-wagging and

OMGing. It was dangerous and stupid, apparently. How would she get home from parties in town? She might get stalked and attacked, and no one would even know. Carson was asking for trouble. They were probably right, but she was never going to concede that. She bought a dog for security—a huge, lean, hairy greyhound-cross called Stretch—and was given a duck (as an alarm system). And now as she pulled up, Stretch was running and jumping back and forth, barking mindlessly, while the duck honked to join in. It felt like home, and she loved it: a tumbling-down cottage with weedy garden beds, a broken fence, and a passionfruit vine that half-covered the western roof. The rooms were basic and didn't leak much. All the bits in the kitchen and bathrooms worked okay, and if she needed help she could ring one of the Hopper family, who owned the place, and they would come and fix things for her. Stretch slept on her bed and growled at male visitors, even though he had no idea of follow-up.

It was still special to take a chair out onto the cracked path under the vine and eat her meals in the quiet, with only the sound of small birds and insects and the Hoppers burning around on their machinery to invade her space. It didn't make sense. She was happiest in the quietest, loneliest place, and spent the rest of her time mad at the boring sameness and smallness of the world she had returned to.

Carson got out of her car and felt relief to be away from the town, and wondered what Sweetapple could be doing, floating around on his own planet. Stretch tried to jump up on her, and she pushed him off, scolded him, and took her things inside. The house was still hot, so she opened some windows, grabbed a cider from the fridge and her tablet from the bench, and went outside to her seat in the shade.

4

The shower was even better than Luke had hoped. His skin was wrinkled by the time he lay on the bed, turned on the television, and fell asleep. Within the hour, he was awake and back in the bathroom.

He pulled the bin close, took a bare razor blade from his bag, and began hacking at his hair. It fell in brown tails, as though he was docking so many small animals. He used his scissors to cut it right back, and then attacked his head with a disposable razor. When he was finished, both bins from the motel room were full, the razors were blunt, and he was white-headed and weird-looking. He put on his freshest shirt and pants, selected a cap, and went out to buy some beer.

In a dark bottle shop at the back of the nearest pub that was just closing, he bought two six-packs, asked for coins in his change, and then went next door to the Chinese restaurant and ordered takeaway. You could always rely on a Chinese restaurant to be open.

While the order was being cooked, he went in search of a

pay phone. It would have been easier to just send a text, but the rules they had given him were that he must only make contact by pay phone. They might message him on his mobile, but he had to use a pay phone. As if it were a top-secret operation. But they still put his motel room in the company's name. Stupid. And even more stupid because pay phones were so hard to find. He had to walk almost to the centre of town to the post office before he found a small bank of them, glowing yellow and unloved, set back from the street. They were so little used that the graffiti needed updating—he guessed that the writer of 'Nelly Hot 4 Ned' was no longer hot for anything.

He put money in, listened to the coins clunking through the machine, and dialled. When a man's voice answered, Luke said, as ordered, 'I'm out.' He felt ridiculous. Maybe he should have said, 'I'm in from the cold,' or even, 'The eagle has landed.' The voice said, 'I'll be there in an hour.'

Luke put the handpiece back in its silver cradle, pushed out the sticking door, and walked back to the Chinese, where his order awaited him at the cash register. Did the small, busy woman behind the counter realise he was an important figure in a covert operation? He sniggered. Somebody in the coal company was watching too much television. They monitored everything: the television, the papers, the volume of comment on social media, everything their employees did, every internet reference, every government opinion, and God knew what else. The city PR company they used was always coming up with new ways to buy social-media support. And the company most likely got their exploration and mining licences by bribing government ministers. Who was going to be shocked to find out that they kept an eye on the picket protestors?

He walked back to his motel swigging on a beer and feeling pretty happy with himself. The relief of being out was greater than he had expected.

Halfway through his Mongolian lamb and into his third beer, there was a knock at the door. It was the man who belonged to the voice, Peter Morris, in mufti: no hi-vis shirt, no company logos. He stood in the doorway looking furtive and slightly sheepish. It made him almost unrecognisable. Peter was a company man — practical, straightforward, oblivious to nuance and contrary points of view — who never appeared to doubt his mission. Luke let him in, and they shook hands awkwardly, as if someone had insisted they do it.

'Merry Christmas. You got out alive, then?' It was as human as Peter got. He was the guy who preferred the tough exterior thing, wrapped in the protection of company rules and purpose, rejecting everything but the hard line as 'soft'.

'Beer?'

'No.' Peter pulled over the only chair in the room and sat down. 'Thanks.'

Luke wasn't going to offer to make him a cup of tea.

Still holding the Mongolian lamb, Luke said, 'Mind if I finish my dinner?'

Peter made hand gestures that suggested Luke could do what he liked.

'So. What did you learn?'

Luke sat down on the bed, fantasising about tipping his meal over Peter's arrogant head. But to get the money they'd promised him, he had to play his role. It would take self-discipline, but he could do it. Luke had been working on discipline for some years now. After he'd burnt down the sports-equipment shed at school and not been caught (even though he'd done it on an impulse, and any half-decent cop could have figured it out), he had resolved to gain some control of himself. He was not going to be one of those morons who let one flash of stupid anger put them in jail for the rest of their lives. The protest site had been a significant test of his new control, and he had passed without error. But every day was a new challenge.

'Not much. They're pretty harmless. True believers. Zealots, maybe. Good people, mostly.'

Peter snorted at the last reference: it was an impossibility to him. Luke remembered the unshakeable viewpoint of the company: they had a legal, paid-for right, with all the hoops jumped through, to mine their patch of ground, create jobs and energy, and anyone who disagreed with that was a ratbag.

'Good people with explosives?' Sarcastic now.

Luke had let them know, in the only brief report he was able to despatch, that explosives had appeared amongst the group. It was a small amount, but enough to blow up machinery. He had expected the company to come in with the police, guns blazing, but there had been no response.

'Well, I'm pleased to hear you got my note.' Luke put his food down. 'Anyway, I think they got out of their depth.'

Peter was waiting for something less obvious.

'When the rumour went round that they had a bomb, there was a huge blow-up—they fought about it, some of them got really pissed off, it nearly destroyed the group. Then the bomb, which no one was sure existed, disappeared.'

'Disappeared?'

'Yup. Someone stole it.'

Peter gave no indication as to whether he thought this was

dangerous or ridiculous.

'They weren't tricking you?'

'No way. The group believes in passive resistance. Except for some of them, who went berserk when they found the explosives were gone. Kyle somebody. He went through everyone's bags, their stuff, abused everyone, accused everyone. Went off their heads.'

'Were they our explosives? Nitro pril?'

'A sausage pack, I was told. Smuggled out of the mine after it didn't go off. So they said.'

'They hadn't rolled you? Didn't guess what you were up to? Decided you couldn't be trusted, and put on a little play for you to see where the information would turn up?'

Luke stood up. This was now a question of competency, and maybe even the company's way of getting out of paying him. Ginko's earlier insinuation that he didn't know some of the very important things that had gone on at the picket made Luke suddenly nervous about that competency.

'I'm not an idiot. If you don't want my information, fine. I was very careful that they didn't suss me. And I expect to get paid for a thorough, professional job done.' Luke gripped his fork tightly and breathed through his nose. He tried not to picture swivelling the fork into his fist and bringing the tines down hard into the company man's meaty shoulder. Instead he ate, still standing, knowing he hadn't thought up any insurance against not being paid.

'You'll get paid.'

They were silent. Peter watched him as you might a child, and Luke felt childish. With his last mouthful, he decided there weren't any alternatives. If he didn't report, they wouldn't pay him.

'Pretty much all of them thought it was a step too far. Too

dangerous, making them too much like the bad guys. There was a lot of argument. Harmless, I reckon.'

Peter wrung his hands. 'So someone in the mine, an operator maybe, smuggled it out?'

'That's what they told me.'

A dusty print of a cat on a cushion hung on the brick wall behind the bed, looking down on them. 'Prick.'

'Bloody gutsy, though.'

'Gutsy? This isn't the fucken Wild West—dynamite going off if you sneeze. Those explosives are as safe as houses. This guy's a treacherous prick, that's all.'

Luke knew all the stuff about sausage packs—there had been a lot of talk about them on the picket. He had thought the guy was gutsy, because if anyone caught him he would lose his job, get charged with heaps of offences, and probably be kept under surveillance as some sort of terrorist. The police were very touchy about bombs these days.

He remembered Peter talking about the company's attitude to the protest: they thought it was helpful, because it let people think they had a voice, gave them a chance to air some frustrations without actually affecting anything. As long as the protest was kept under control, the company was happy for it to run for as long as the protestors wanted to. But when the movement posed an actual threat, the company got very nervy.

'Seem like a normal thing? Something they'd done before?'

Luke laughed out loud. 'No. No. It completely freaked most of them out. Peaceful is their thing. Most wanted anyone involved kicked off the picket.'

'You'll write me a proper report with everything you saw

and heard—all the dates and names, especially the names of the hardcores?'

Luke was bored now. To write a report was to repeat everything he'd just said, and then elaborate like he used to in a school essay.

'The problem is the dude they got the stuff from, not the mob I was with.'

'You didn't steal it?'

'I thought about it, but it I wouldn't have been able to get it out without anyone knowing. I would have had to bury it in the scrub somewhere.'

'Did you?'

'No.'

'Don't bullshit me.'

Luke almost laughed out loud again. Bullshitting was his thing. 'Should I have?'

'Maybe.' He shrugged in a way that meant *Yes*. 'We'd like to know where it went. I was pretty sure you'd be able to inform me.' Peter now looked at him with the kind of certainty that only the two-dimensional possessed. 'We already know most of what you've told me. We've got professionals who do this stuff.'

It was another put-down, even if Luke was a long way from being a 'professional'. He'd got the job through an old uni mate who worked in the government, in security, who had put him on to someone else who gave him a phone number. There'd been little training, no 'covert ops' instruction, and certainly no trading of tax details. But there had been checks: background, security, education, mental health. They'd rung old flatmates, schoolteachers, and even girlfriends, posing as a government department that Luke had applied to for a job. The sports-shed fire never rated a mention. Apparently, they normally used a labour-hire company for this sort of thing, but that company had recently had operatives busted on a whaling protest, so management wanted a 'cleanskin' (their word).

'I don't know where it went. I didn't take it, and I never heard any hints that someone else might have. It was a tight operation.' Luke was ignoring the memory of Ginko's parting words. He really didn't know who had got the bomb out, and giving Peter his best guess was pointless.

Peter stood, and reluctantly stuck out a hand. 'All right, then. Thanks for your work.'

They shook briefly, inconclusively. Something was unfinished, and Luke couldn't stop himself pointing it out: 'Do much of this?' The sneer was not withheld.

'You mean sneaking around at night dealing with low-lifes and liars?'

'You're a real fucken professional, Peter. It's not like I instigated the spying. That's a company specialty. Cause you're such a moral entity.'

Peter turned to leave.

'Make sure you pay for the room.'

Peter stepped away.

'Peter?' Luke stopped without turning. 'Just so you know, I've got nothing to lose.'

Peter nodded again, as if he didn't need reminding, but Luke knew he had to make it clear. 'I don't have a reputation to damage, a business to destroy, a mortgage to default on, a wife to embarrass, kids to shame: nothing. Publicity might even make me a media star. So you play this how you want.'

Peter was gone.

Carson didn't really care for movies. The romances, comedies, and blockbuster action movies that everyone seemed to enjoy were little more than time-wasters for her. She felt like she didn't get what everyone else got. The only movies she enjoyed were the ones where women triumphed, where women beat insurmountable odds. She played her favourites over and over, reliving the moments when everything seemed lost and the heroine doomed, and then, through courage and perseverance, they turned the tables. In her worst times, those movies could lift her from feeling hopeless and worthless to a place where she felt like she might be strong, someone who could fight back, no matter the odds, just like the movie heroines did. But there weren't many of them. Mostly it was men who beat the odds, with women looking sexy and helpful beside them.

And now, bored by the movies available, the carols on the television, and the yearly repeated goodwill stories, Carson opened her computer and flicked past the many Christmas messages to her favourite project: the scam.

From the internet, she had learned that a Nigerian-style financial scam needed hundreds of thousands of recipients, maybe even millions, as a starting point. But more interesting was the fact that scammers actually wanted a large failure rate. They wanted to weed out the sceptical and the suspicious, and latch onto the vulnerable, the desperate, and the dreamers, so it was important that the people who were never going to be taken in were eliminated early on.

She remembered going to a hypnotist's show at the RSL, and seeing how the hypnotist tested the audience and then chose his participants from the most suggestible in that group. The scammers used a similar sort of process: there was no point in trying magic tricks on people who were never going to believe in magic. It wasn't a process that fitted with her plan. She only had a couple of hundred recipients, and they weren't really the gullible type.

However, in her favour, these types of scams relied on greed and the prospect of love. They didn't seem to be using sex — not up-front anyway. Sex, attainable sex, was going to be her weapon. She would have to write the perfect letter of introduction. And the right photo would be crucial: certainly not her own photo, nor that of anyone she knew, but she guessed the web would be able to provide her with what she was looking for.

To create her own scam, Carson had taken the time to steal a phone and email list from work. She had sifted through it, removing small farms, female-dominated businesses, town customers, and younger families. The list was much shorter now, consisting of large operations run by men whom she knew, or guessed to be, older types. Many of them had several contact addresses, including a city number. It was a rough-and-ready process, but Carson felt she had a pretty good handle on the types she was seeking. She had decided she would send her 'letter' through mobiles so there was less chance of wives or office staff seeing it. It was the longest of shots, but it satisfied something that screamed inside her. It was getting back at somebody, at least in a small way. Or maybe it just distracted the part of her that badly desired some sort of vengeance.

One of her friends had given her a copy of an email he had received from 'Olga'. He had printed it rather than sent it to her, because he guessed it carried lots of viruses.

The email started: '*How do you do? Hope, you are fine! I am fine because I can write first message to you.*' It proceeded to introduce 'Olga' in broken, chopped-up English, pointing out that she was companionable, had many interests, was looking for love, and was asking the recipient to please write back. You had to wonder how many million copies of this email would have to be sent out before someone was taken in by it. Carson didn't have that sort of luxury of numbers. Her girl would need to be modest, pretty, a little vulnerable, almost innocent, and sort of accidentally hot — a nice girl who could be manipulated.

She skimmed through photos, looking for demure and natural, sexy as all get-out, but almost unaware of the fact. She didn't want cleavage or anything revealing, not much make-up, if any, and no 'big hair'. Almost every photo, even from social media, had been posed, Photoshopped, and glamorised somehow. She kept trawling.

And then, on a Christian site, she found a slim, blonde girl with straight hair, disarmingly unaffected, in a light turtleneck jumper of some kind that covered her large breasts. This was not a provocative photo, except that the girl was so well-endowed. She seemed to be saying, 'I'm ready for something, but I'm not quite sure what it might be. Can you help me?' It had exactly the right incongruity that Carson had been looking for. She copied the shot several times and Googled the girl's name. Nothing came up. She saved the photos, and hoped she wouldn't need to send any others.

Making her girl Russian or foreign had some value: it leant an advantage to the men. Someone who might be ignorant of the local culture and language could be guided, educated. It would be easy to think you could put one over a girl like that. It was about power, after all. But it also sounded much too much like she might be one of Olga's friends. Someone from the other end of the globe did feel like the right choice.

Carson opened a file where she had several drafts of the letter she was working on, and changed the name of the girl and the country, and then continued writing, pausing, and rephrasing:

Hello. My name is Felicity Sven.

The name had a cool Scandinavian ice-blue sound to it.

I am a third-year Finnish Agricultural Science student travelling in Australia.

Would a Finn seem too cold and not amorous enough?

The Australian Faculty of Agricultural Sciences has suggested you might be a suitable contact for someone like me. You have a very good reputation for business management, innovation, and vision. I am very impressed with your success and the way you have conducted your business ventures. It seems to me that you have succeeded where so many others have failed.

It was pretty generic, but flattery always worked on men, didn't it?

I am looking for a close mentoring relationship with someone of your skill set.

'Skill set' seemed a step too far.

> I am looking for a close mentoring relationship with a
> man of your skill and character.

Maybe that wasn't something that Felicity might say, but it would do.

> I don't have any contacts in Australia and would very like
> to gain some experience in agriculture and business in
> your beautiful part of the world. Would it be possible that
> we could communicate with a view to meeting?

She thought the last bit sounded like someone who didn't speak English naturally.

> If you thought it was possible that we could do some-
> thing together could you please contact me on this email
> address?
> I very much look forward to hearing from you.

Carson moved words around and erased others. She wanted to suggest loneliness or openness, but too much would be a giveaway. Instead she inserted, 'You have a very nice picture!', and left the letter at that.

Her troubles had started—any moron could see it—because she had followed a spark, out of boredom, pretty much, looking for trouble. Mark, who was one of those brown-skinned, still lean forty-year-olds who had a smile that could entice almost anyone, had asked her to track down a part for his shearing plant. He'd claimed his shearing gear was old but of the best quality, and even though parts were hard to find, they were still available — you just had to look in the right places. Instead of suggesting he look them up on the net himself, she took the bait. So when, after only minutes of searching, she found the parts he needed, she rang him. He was so thankful, he insisted on buying her a drink. She had sniggered at him. There was no way a girl her age could have a drink in a pub in this town with a man his age without creating a story.

Mark had responded with a throaty laugh, suggesting, 'At my place.'

So it was on. He was married. Lucy. Carson had seen her about, but never met her. His place wasn't safe ground, so why even go? Was this the thrill she had been chasing? A family dinner? Maybe with little kids? Carson imagined herself sitting straight-backed at their dining table, trying to speak nicely and make sweet conversation — the last thing she would want to be doing. But she had decided to go anyway, expecting to stay a short while and have a sneak peek at his house and his life.

When she turned up (at 4.00 pm, as suggested) in her battered little car, at his front gate that marked the border of an expansive green lawn, he strolled down to meet her in white linen like some sort of billionaire host from a movie — a good-looking man presented as well as he could be. He was all smiles and grabbing hands, welcoming her with a kiss on the cheek that you wouldn't give a relative.

'Anyone else coming?'

'Nope. Not even Luce.'

She felt a light, pathetic blush fill her cheeks.

'In the city with the girls.'

She didn't ask which girls. Carson had considered saying, 'Just us? What's your game?' to tease him and put him on the back foot, if that was ever possible, but instead she played along. If it was an adrenaline rush she was seeking, she had certainly found it. Carson had worn a simple top and shorts, imagining Lucy would be present, but he still licked his lips and said how nice she looked.

They sauntered up a winding gravel path, around a rose garden in full, white bloom, to a wide timber verandah shaded by a luminous grapevine. He had glasses, ice, and drinks set up on a small timber table under the leafy eaves. Perfume rose out the many-flowered garden beds. It felt like she was in *The Great Gatsby* or maybe a reality-TV version of the story.

They drank, laughed, and ate small, expensive-looking cheeses, dips, and salami things. After that and a few more drinks, he took her to the kitchen and cooked her a tasty stir-fry, quickly, with ease, chatting, charming all the time. Despite her natural reluctance, she was taken in by the whole performance, by a player well practised.

So they ended up in his bed, a massive mattress with fresh sheets. She imagined him quickly washing them after she was gone, and then imagined living in this house, this bed, surrounded by the garden; having friends over, owning nice things, travelling, painting, doing whatever she liked. She knew that some women actually lived like this. Her mother could have; all you had to do was pick the right man.

It went well after that. He was a skilled lover, but she wasn't really into it. She enjoyed it, but it might have been a ride on an older roller-coaster: ups and downs with few genuine thrills. The look on his face when they'd finished suggested it had been more than that for him: a triumph even.

Afterwards, as he dozed, she looked around the bedroom for the first time, and realised it wasn't quite the magazine-feature place she'd thought it was. It was worn: paint peeling in the corners; cracks in the wall; the dresser and the wardrobe bumped and scraped over time. In fact, the bed was plain rickety. Mark was a player and a bullshit artist. Everything was for show. Lucy would not be leading the life Carson had fantasised about. Lucy probably worked her arse off, looking after the kids, looking after Mark, working part-time, keeping the garden going.

Carson needed no more confirmation that this was a game that Mark had played many times. She didn't mind. It had been a fun day out, and she certainly didn't want to be Lucy. The dilapidation was almost endearing. Even the sight of his skinny legs on his way to the bathroom didn't put her off. When they agreed it was safe for her to drive, well after midnight, she headed home, calm and pleased with herself.

Mark didn't ask her again, and she wasn't sure if she should be insulted, even though she would have said, 'No.' But he was friendly with her and familiar when he turned up in the store; he didn't pretend that he barely knew her or didn't think she was worth talking to. She thought they'd got it right—both were happy, and no one had got hurt.

And then, in a backhanded kind of way, he started introducing her to his friends. He'd come into the store with them—as though it was a coincidence that they'd just met up—they'd buy things, and then, in passing, chat to her, and Mark would make a sort of formal introduction. Later, his friends would return on their own, and strike up casual conversations that often ended with a description of their beach house they were about to visit, or a flight somewhere interesting they were about to take. No direct offer was made, but there was always a message conveyed that these were lovely places to go to, and that someone like her should make an effort to visit them too. She would really enjoy herself.

Carson knew who they were: all wealthy men in the area, some of them farmers, and the rest businessmen who owned farms just because they could. She shrugged them off, but didn't feel any threat. Something was going on, but she decided to ignore it, and hoped no one else saw anything in it. Some of the men returned several times, as if they thought she hadn't got the message or they felt sure that their particular brand of confidence, or cash, or looks would convince her. She was sweet to them, and played the role she didn't want but couldn't avoid. Thankfully, they did no more than chat, and she was able to pretend that perhaps they were just being nice; perhaps they were thinking of employing her later on, in some fantastic job, in their companies. Maybe Mark had told them how quickly and efficiently she had found the parts.

So in the week when her old schoolmates were home from uni and distant apprenticeships, and the dread reality that they were getting out of there and she wasn't was getting harder and harder to avoid, she felt that hand on her arse. In her chair, in her peaceful garden, she remembered it with a body-shaking anger — the kind that never disappears until an opportunity provokes its re-emergence.

5

Carson had met Sweetapple in the Bowlo. He had been sitting at a table with a couple of the older men, much older than him, having a beer and talking quietly, not paying attention to the women in the place.

That night, Carson, with no particular excuse, had had too much to drink. She had organised to stay with a friend in town so they could go out and have a few drinks, but her friend had fallen ill and decided to stay at home. Carson didn't want to sit around watching TV with a sick friend, or go home to a quiet house, so she went to the Bowlo on her own. It was a Friday, and Macca and the Thomsons had bought her drinks and were daring her to do crazy things, obviously thinking it was the way for one of them to get her into bed. She took the opportunity to be loud and silly and a tease to the men in the bar, slapping her arse and pretending she was about to take her top off. Eventually the barman, Ted, got sick of her carry-on and threatened to kick her out. She ignored him, and he got more annoyed, so she went and hid at the nearest table of unknowns and pretended to be their friend. Sweetapple happened to be one of those at the table.

At first she didn't really see him or the other men with him, and just sat quietly, trying to stop giggling. Then, when her amusement faded, she decided to engage with the men, thinking that their seriousness represented another opportunity for ridicule. When she asked, 'How's your night going?' the other men at the table gave her a 'pain in the arse' look, but Sweetapple turned to her, saying, 'Not too bad,' and adding, 'but I think you might be having more fun than us.'

She sniggered, and looked at him for the first time. He was dark-skinned with too-large brown eyes under black eyebrows, his hair short without deviation, his hands and arms lean and strong. The alcohol allowed her to focus on him without inhibition, and she perceived that he carried a powerful maleness about him.

'Oh, I don't know. I think I could have some fun over here.' She perched on her elbows and looked closely at him.

'So what's the occasion?'

'Nothing. Never any worthwhile occasion in this town, is there?'

'That's a bit harsh. You a local?'

'Born and bred. You?'

'Same. You want a drink?' Sweetapple figured he had never encountered an energy source like this one. But she had the sparks of big trouble around her.

'Probably not.' She slumped a little.

'Soft drink or something?'

'Being a bit too nice, don't you reckon? I mean, if you want to get into my pants, you should be getting me sozzled, shouldn't you?'

'Every punter in this place would like to get into your pants. Including Fanger and Ticker.' He nodded towards two bent-over men sipping beers next to the bar, their walking sticks leaning with them.

'Not you?'

He looked at her intently. 'Of course me.' The game of shock had been turned around. She was unsettled by his forthrightness.

'Ah, you're smart for a cowboy.'

'I'm not that.'

'So what do you do?'

'Got a place. Buy and sell a few steers, that sort of thing. Look after horses for people.'

'So you're a cowboy.'

'Not sure what I am. What about you?'

'Just a girl. Girl about town.'

'Okay.' He drank his beer and looked away. He sensed that some of the guys in the bar were watching him with this girl. They were both quiet for a while, and he guessed she had moved on, his novelty already worn off.

'How about you give me a lift home?' He must have looked alarmed, because she quickly said, 'No funny stuff. I'll catch up with you another time.'

He drank the last froth of his beer and stood up. 'Come on, then. No funny stuff.'

She got up and followed him out, with catcalls snaking through the crowd behind them.

In his ute, she said, 'I live out of town. Probably should have told you.'

'Whereabouts?'

'Pilgrim Road, out past the silos, in one of the Hoppers' cottages.' She still intended to stay in town, but wanted to see how far she could push him.

'Okay. I can go home that way.'

He started the vehicle and she said nothing, letting him pull out from the curb and head down the street.

'I'm kidding. You don't have to take me home. I'm staying in Francis Street. Sixty-seven.'

'Righto.' Sweetapple was disappointed. He thought the fifteen-minute drive would have given them a chance to talk a bit more. He knew her face, had seen her around town, but he remembered her as a schoolgirl.

He took the turns towards the place she had named. 'You still in school?'

'Good one. I'm twenty-three. You married? Kids?'

'Nope and nope.'

'Gay?'

'Not that I know of.'

'I think you'd know by now.'

She pointed at a white house at the end of the street.

'Then again, maybe you've had so little action, you don't have a clue.'

She was taking off her seatbelt as he pulled up, then produced a phone from her bag as she got out. 'What's your number?' He told her, and asked for hers.

'Nah. I'll do the ringing. Thanks for the lift. Night.'

He watched her walk across the grass and the path to the house, and felt like the blood might burst out of him.

Carson remembered ringing him a week later, and his response on the phone was cautious and halting. Maybe he thought she was setting him up for something, but she liked his scepticism.

'I thought I'd bring some lunch out. What do you think?'

'That would be good, but I'm capable of making a meal.'

'Yeah, right. I'll bring out some fresh stuff: rolls, chicken, salad, and we can have a little picnic.'

He gave her the directions.

Sweetapple had watched the car arriving, still concerned there was some sort of trick involved. Then the car stopped on the road, maybe for a couple of minutes, and it occurred to him that maybe it wasn't her, just someone lost. He wouldn't have been surprised if she didn't show. She hadn't shown much interest on the night they'd met, and he'd wondered if the alcohol had confused some of the interest she did show.

Now, six months later, on Christmas morning, as Carson crossed his ramp, and the heat ratcheted its way up the thermometer, she remembered that first visit; the good feeling she had about his farm, how it was neat and well kept; there were even flowerbeds and mown lawns around the house — not what she had expected from a guy who lived on his own.

She hadn't intended to ring him at all. There were plenty of guys about. No need to go chasing them down. But there she'd been, crossing his ramp with a cooler bag of picnic foods, like a desperate woman, like a woman who hadn't had the experiences she had — as if she wanted to be used and manipulated by some other older man.

So she had stopped right there on the road and considered her options. It would have been smarter to meet in the pub and play it safe. He might have turned out to be a complete bore or any sort of violent deviant, and out here she was at his mercy.

But if they met for a drink in town, the gossipers would pick it up, and word would spread. Carson wasn't worried about people knowing she was with Sweetapple, but she didn't like opinions being formed about her. Who knew what Mark and his mates would make of it? She didn't want that sort of invasion, and her gut had told her that Sweetapple was all right. So she had kept going.

They had spent the next few days and nights together.

Time had moved quickly, and her desire for him had gradually increased to a level where she had to hold herself back from visiting him every second day, every day, and revealing her feelings for him. Carson had vowed to make sure she was in control of the relationship. She visited him when she felt like it, holding off when she was expected, knowing it drove him crazy and deepened her own desire.

He was like so many other guys she knew: quiet, certain about what he thought was important and what wasn't, and annoyed by fuss. But he burned inside: an unexplained brightness that made him interesting, attractive, and worth being around. She wondered if the fire didn't come from something like hate, but she never saw any actions arise from an emotion like that: he didn't ever direct anger or violence at her or anyone he knew, and certainly not at one of his animals. Carson had the feeling that he did wild, unexpected things that he didn't tell her about. Sometimes she wondered if she wasn't just hanging around to find out what would happen.

But now Carson could see he was waiting for her, strolling around his little garden, freshly showered, out of paddock clothes and into something she might like. Carson giggled. Sweetapple knew nothing about women or clothes, but he looked like he was trying.

On his front door he had hung an aged Christmas wreath. There was new tinsel over doorways, and a neat little pine Christmas tree in a bucket in the corner of the TV room.

He had a supermarket Christmas cake that he was shyly proud of. They ate it with cream, on unchipped plates in the kitchen with the air-con blowing, and then he brought out a small box that had been gift-wrapped elsewhere and put it on the table in front of her. Inside was a tiny silver bracelet. Carson was shocked. The windcheater she had given him, still in the bag it was bought in, had been a casual, even careless, gesture, which she had thought was appropriate but now felt rude. She knew she should kiss him, but didn't.

'So what did you get up to last night? Quiet one?' Carson had her suspicions about him, but it didn't actually concern her. Everybody had secrets, most of them not very surprising.

The day was warming, but still comfortable. His house was set well back from the road, so the view from his table only took in Sweetapple's country and some of the flatter country of the neighbours'. It was peaceful and safe, and everywhere she looked she felt like he had had a hand in it, checking, guiding it, caring.

Sweetapple enjoyed her being caught off-guard by the gift, and wondered about telling her the truth about his night. It was dangerous to tell anyone, and even more dangerous to tell someone like Carson. In a rage, she might use it against him somehow, maybe share it with someone else. But he knew that telling her would provoke and maybe fascinate her, and he had a persistent fear that she would suddenly be bored by him, with his contained life and his limited needs. The idea that he might be able to excite her was too powerful for him to discard.

'I stole some steers.' He watched her laugh off the statement and then take a second look at him, cocking her head.

'Steers? Where?' She wasn't going to show any sign that she had been taken in by his silliness.

'They were in a paddock next to the road. I've been checking them out for a couple of weeks — yards and loading ramp right on the road. All I had to do was back the truck up and run them in. Job done.'

'Seriously?'

He couldn't help the start of a smile as he nodded firmly. She wriggled in her seat.

'You steal cattle?'

He inclined his head a couple of times.

'Wow. You're not worried about going to jail? You don't care you're doing something wrong?' She was reaching across the table at him, staring into his eyes, in search of something she hadn't seen before. Outside, the heat was starting to slow everything down as every moving thing sought the shade.

'I need the money, and I'm worried about going to jail. I don't reckon it's the wrong thing, though. I'm only taking from people who've taken from someone else. They've got it coming.' His last sentence sounded so cool to her. So many of them had it coming. The flush of her face told him she agreed that they really did deserve it, and she didn't even know who he had stolen from. It aroused him and he looked away, feigning coolness.

'Have you done it before?' The edge of disapproval had gone, replaced by a hope for complicity.

'A bit.'

'Only cattle? Sheep? Pigs?'

'Sheep. Goats. No pigs.'

'You are so out there. A bloody cattle-rustler!' Carson sat back, slapping the side of her chair and hooting at the air. His admission might have been her greatest Christmas present. 'Are you going to do it again?'

'Yes.' He was feeling hot-skinned in the suddenly small room. The duffing, the thing he despised, had delivered this to him. Nothing ever made sense. You never got what you deserved.

'Can I come with you?'

'Never.' He hadn't thought she'd want to be involved. It drained some of the pleasure.

'Why not?'

'One person in trouble would be enough.'

'Oh, but the rush.'

'Rush? It's just being shit-scared.'

Carson was suddenly unrecognisably reticent, the energy submerged, not gone.

'I made a website.'

He didn't know what to say to this revelation. His knowledge of websites was contained by a few favourites to do with the weather, stock sales, sport, and a couple of recent jewellery additions.

'The guys you steal from have given me some shit over time.'

He didn't like the mention of 'steal'.

'So I came up with this way to get back at them. A scam thing.'

'You write crap about them on the internet?'

'No. I send them letters saying I'm an innocent young woman interested in business and agriculture, and looking for a mentor.'

'Using yourself as bait?'

'I made this girl up. Finn. Big tits. Got a cool photo of her and everything.'

'You know how to do that?'

'Sort of.'

'I've had stuff like that on my phone before.'

'I bet you have.'

'Funny. Any luck?'

'Not yet.' She didn't seem put off by this. It was just a matter of time.

'What'll you do?'

'String 'em along. Maybe ask 'em for money after a while. If they get sexy, print their texts.' Carson shrugged. She had thought about it, but not much.

'You really hold a grudge, don't you?'

'You can talk. Anyway, I think it'll work. Those old creeps can't help themselves — always looking for a bit of young stuff, someone they can use and manipulate.'

He looked across at the fire in her dark eyes. If he had seen anything more beautiful, he couldn't remember it.

And then, awkward under his scrutiny and ever keen to smash a special moment, she stood, reached out, and put his plate on top of hers and took them to the sink.

'So what's planned for this afternoon?'

He almost laughed. She would rather he hit her than mention love.

'You want to go for a ride on the Statham horses?'

The name made the muscles in her stomach clench, even though she knew Bob Statham was Sweetapple's neighbour and that Sweetapple looked after his horses. As she forced herself to relax, she realised it was the first time he'd suggested horses. It seemed an intimate proposal.

'What if I can't ride?'

'I'll teach you.'

It wouldn't occur to him that there was anything difficult about horses. 'Let me finish my drink, and you're on.'

Sweetapple looked after Bob and Caroline Statham's horses. They didn't know anything about horses, and didn't seem to care much. They probably just liked to tell their friends they had horses, and Caroline always maintained she wanted horses that her friends and their children could ride when they came to stay. Sweetapple couldn't think of any time when the people who came to stay at the Stathams' wanted to ride horses or take any notice of the country. They were usually blowhards who drank the whole time and rode the motorbikes too fast.

Bob was some sort of multi-millionaire who had investments in all sorts of things, including the nearby mines. Local gossip had him involved in electricity projects, clothing stores, fast-food outlets, casinos, travel spots, and many other things that Sweetapple didn't listen to. Every now and then, Bob would come down to the stables and have a chat, and tell extravagant stories about what he'd been up to. It was as if he was trying to impress. Sweetapple couldn't understand why Bob would bother, but he guessed Bob was the sort of wanker who liked everyone to be impressed by him.

Caroline was a politician, or had been up until the most recent election, always in the news, loved and then hated. Towards the end she'd done something wrong by her electorate—Sweetapple didn't pay enough attention to politics to know what, but whatever it was, it had smashed her career.

He couldn't help liking her, and guessed that now she'd been voted out he'd be seeing her a bit more. But Bob and Caroline weren't his sort of people. They were privileged, self-assured, and confident of their place in the world. That they had more money, opportunities, rights, and influence than most other people was something they would never question. To suggest to them that their success might be based on resources owned by all the people, or the result of the hard work and ingenuity of many poorly paid people beneath them, would be to suggest that the moon was a balloon. Winners and losers. That's what it was about.

Carson saddled her own horse to show him she had some idea of what to do. Even if she didn't, she would never have let on; she would have got on the gelding without help or guidance, no matter what.

They rode quietly out through the grass country. It was hot, and the air was thick with fine insects.

'Stupid time to be doing this. Should have come out at seven.'

They were in tandem, but he set the pace.

'I want them to get a good sweat up, so when we wash them, their coats'll get a real clean-out.'

'My coat's going to get a good clean, then. I'm bloody soaked.'

They cantered down towards the creek as Carson marvelled at the smoothness of the canter and the control she had over the gelding. Her riding experience had been on cantankerous old ponies that only responded to direction when there was no other option. Despite the ease of the ride, alongside Sweetapple she felt like she was ungainly, bumping out of the saddle, barely in contact, but he made no observation about her style. He was simply serene. It might have been his perfect day. Christmas.

It didn't stop her feeling annoyed that she was at such a disadvantage, so completely contained in a world that he was master of. When they slowed to a walk, she started to push past him and slapped a hand down hard on his horse's butt, thinking to scare him or the horse and to provoke an unexpected response. A section of the horse's skin moved independently, but the rest of the animal ignored her, not even being drawn into an absent-minded tail flick. She had registered as a fly.

They cantered again for what felt like a great distance and then slowed, turned, and walked towards home. The horses were snorting and blowing, their bodies wet with sweat, the salt crusting on the edges of the saddle blankets as they cooled. As she and Sweetapple reached the stables, they saw a white ute bumping towards them from the homestead. It pulled in alongside as they dismounted.

A middle-aged man got out of the vehicle, his head large and round, his clothes loose on him, smiling as though he knew everybody needed to be his friend. He walked quickly, and stuck out a hand at Sweetapple, almost whispering, 'Merry Christmas.'

Sweetapple introduced him as Bob, and he looked her in the eye and issued a warm, 'We know each other.' Carson's skin rippled and spiked in the presence of a deadly enemy. Now she couldn't see the nice older bloke she thought he'd been; she only saw his awful grin of confidence, the sense that he could have what he wanted and that it would never be any other way. She knew he had already looked her over again; it was his accepted right, so deeply ingrained that he didn't even know it existed.

He had no idea what a prick he was.

'Glad I caught you, Graham. Do you think I could have a word?'

Carson moved away to unsaddle her horse and begin the washing. She wanted to kick the horses now because they were his, but couldn't because they were only his in name.

Sweetapple looked after the horses because he was paid to do so and because they were fine, expensive horses, and he knew they wouldn't be properly cared for if he wasn't around. There was nothing more to it than that. So when Bob came around for his little chats, he listened politely and put up with them. He didn't want any favours, or junkets, or special deals.

On this day, Bob was as close to nervous as Sweetapple had ever seen him. He laughed a little too loudly and quickly at the blokey jokes he made, which weren't really even jokes. He stood close to the horse and Sweetapple, rubbing the mare's neck repeatedly in a way he never normally did. He went on about presents, families, and Santa Claus, and asked Sweetapple what he had done for Christmas morning. Sweetapple pretended not to hear. He considered asking Bob if everything was all right, presuming he might be trying to fire him, but Bob got to the point before there was any need.

'I've got an idea I'd like to put to you. A lucrative little contract.'

He put out a hand, and gestured down the road where he thought they should walk. Sweetapple accepted his direction, and they strolled away from the stables, stupidly walking towards nothing. Sweetapple wanted to turn back to Carson. It was too much like a child's game, but again Bob broke in.

'It's a very sensitive area I want to talk to you about. I really don't want you to get upset, which you might. So if I just come out and tell you my plan, feel free to ignore me, and we'll just go on as usual, no damage done. Okay?'

'Sure.'

'The thing is, there's this horse, a really fucking good horse, and I want it.'

Sweetapple kept strolling. He didn't want anything to appear a big deal. Why Bob would want a 'fucking good horse' Sweetapple could only guess at, but if he was going to ask him to help with horse buying, maybe on a commission basis, that could be a good thing.

'Problem is, it's not for sale.'

Sweetapple pretended that the direction of the conversation was of no significance to him. Bob might change the topic and talk about something else at any moment.

'I really want this mare. She can get me access to some very important people.'

Bob stopped and went very still. He was no longer jittery, and Sweetapple suddenly knew what was coming.

'I need someone to steal her—a good horseman, a skilled bushman, who can carry off something like that without anyone knowing.'

Sweetapple stopped, too, and looked away at the paddock and then back at Carson, who seemed preoccupied with the horses. Did Bob know about his night-time missions?

'I would pay this person a lot of money—$50,000 cash. No one would ever know.'

'What horse?'

'She's called Retribution.'

Sweetapple looked at the ground. He'd heard of Retribution.

She was a perfectly bred cutting horse that had won everything, and supposed to be worth upwards of $250,000. It was an awful thing to do, to steal a horse. But it was a huge amount of money. Especially for one night's work.

'What would you do with her? You could never use her, never show her, never breed …'

'That's my worry. I just need someone to do the job. Someone I trust. Would you consider it?'

Sweetapple scraped his feet and tried to slow things down. Bob was the sort of player who could manoeuvre you into doing things you didn't want to do before you even realised it.

'What if I decline, and tell someone of your plans? What if Retribution goes missing, and I tell the cops about what you've just said?'

'I approached you because I know a bit about you.' Bob was relaxed now. Negotiating nasty deals was probably something he did every day. 'I know things are hard for you, and money is difficult to come by. I'm aware you still carry your father's debt and … sometimes that means you have to cheat a bit.'

Sweetapple shook his hands loose, and took a step closer to Bob. If this was blackmail, he would settle it now. But Bob was quick to keep talking.

'I don't care what you get up to. As far as I'm concerned, you're an honourable man. I have no desire or need to manipulate you, but this is dangerous business, and I have to protect my interests. If you don't want the job, nothing more will be said.'

The air was still and empty. Bob's eyes were fixed on him, pushing for a decision.

Sweetapple considered asking for a few days to think about it, but he knew it would send him half-mad with the indecision.

Stealing was stealing, no matter how you said it, and he had done plenty of it. But stealing a horse felt like a much bigger crime, a serious crime. It might even be too much for him to live with. He thought about the money, about the other things he would have to do, that he didn't want to do, to make that much. The weight of at least another year—of sneaking around, covering tracks, lying and deceiving—against one more night made up his mind for him.

'I'll do the job. But I want half up front.'

Bob stuck out a hand and smiled grimly. 'Deal.' They shook.

'You'll have to have the mare at your place for a little while, and then you'll deliver her here. But I believe you've got the facilities for something like that.' Bob pushed his eyebrows upwards. 'Amazing what you can see from a chopper.'

'You're handing me the risk? I steal the horse, then when the shit hits the fan, she's at my place?' Sweetapple was beginning to feel he was out of his depth again.

'Any one of the local rodeo boys could steal a horse for me. This guy who has the mare doesn't have any security, no cameras, nothing. It's what happens after the mare's been taken that's difficult and risky. I'm not paying fifty thou for a pickpocket.'

'Are there other catches I don't know about?'

'Not catches. There will be a vet dropping in now and then to check that she's going all right.'

'The local fella?'

'No. Someone I can trust.'

'What if I change my mind?'

'Don't play games with me. If you don't want to do it, tell me now. Otherwise we're on.'

Sweetapple stared back at Bob. It was just another horse,

owned by some other rich guy, who had probably made his money by ripping off someone else.

'We're on, then.'

They shook hands again, and walked back to the ute without saying anything. The horses were already washed and had been let out, cantering away together.

Bob said to Carson in parting, 'Nice to see you again,' got into his ute, and gave a happy wave goodbye, a man without cares.

'What did he want?' Carson bent and removed a burr from her sock as she said it, as if the burr was of more significance to her than anything Bob might want.

'I can't tell you yet.' He didn't know what he thought about the offer, so he wasn't ready to explain it to someone else.

'If it's something to do with him, it definitely stinks.'

'Let's forget about him and enjoy our Christmas, eh?'

6

Luke wrote in a file on his computer everything he could think of that had happened on the picket. He embellished a little as if it were a school assignment, spell-checked it, and then sent the file to Peter.

Later, after knocking off as many beers as he could, he passed out, fully clothed, on the bed, in front of *The Tonight Show*, as if someone had king-hit him and laid him out cold.

In the morning, he stayed in bed for as long as he could, pulling the sheets over his head, squeezing his eyes shut against the light. Christmas Day. There were family phone calls to face, but nothing else. No shops would be open, and there would be no buses.

He had told his mother he was working, and had apologised for not being able to make Christmas. They were upset, but understood 'working'. Expected it. Working had always been their thing, above all else, no matter what.

Later, he took a walk through the hot, empty town, and felt a sort of revulsion at everyone's boxed-off comfort. All these people with their small cubicle worlds of huge TVs, internet nonsense, stacked fridges, and meaningless jobs. And their acceptance. You could hate them for their acceptance. In the afternoon, he sat next to the air-conditioner drinking beer, flipping through the internet.

Next morning, he showered in quick time, dressed in a black T-shirt and jeans, packed up, checked the room, and left. In reception, the same woman looked at him with hardly hidden alarm, raised an eyebrow, and said, 'Haircut?'

'Something like that. My bill paid?'

'Yep. But don't think I won't add to it later if anything's broken or stolen.'

'Cheers.'

He walked back to the bus terminal and saw that a bus heading for the next town, a pensioners' community-service bus, was waiting. He climbed on board, muttering something about being disabled, and took a seat right up the back. The passengers were mostly ancient men, some with sticks, engaging in fitful chatter about not much.

One of them turned to Luke and affably explained that they were off to a Boxing Day lunch where there would be lots of food and good talk. Luke had been confident that his newly shaven head and bloodshot eyes would be enough to put any old-timer off. Not this one.

'I had a haircut like that once.'

'Really? Someone held you down and cut off your hair, too?'

The old man turned back to the front, mumbling to himself. The rest of the passengers looked at each other and looked away.

The ride took fifty minutes through flat farming country, expanses of crops and irrigation channels, occasionally broken by small, treed hills. A text on his phone said, 'Money in.'

The driver announced there were three stops in town, but as soon as the bus halted, Luke got off. He could almost hear the whoosh of relief following him out the closing doors.

He walked up to the main street, and turned into the first pub that advertised accommodation and meals. It had just opened, and was dark, sticky-carpeted, and thick with sporting memorabilia. The pokies tinkled and glowed from an adjoining room, adding to the colours provided by the card machines and the jukebox. It was just how he liked it.

He booked in and went to his room, where a skinny woman in a pale-blue uniform was hurriedly making the bed. Her long, dark, greying hair was almost contained by an elastic band: a few wayward strands hung down over her face, which was lined with gritty exhaustion.

'Just making the bed. Won't be a minute.'

Luke dumped his bags in the corner. When he went to leave, she stopped and said, 'The sheets are fresh and the bathroom's done, but I haven't emptied the bins or tidied up.'

'That's cool.' Luke wasn't sure why he needed to be told.

'It's just that I've still got ten beds to make and the washing-up to do. I wonder if you wouldn't mind if I did the rest of the tidying-up later on?'

He wondered if he should use the moment of power: demand she do her job properly, and tell her he wasn't interested in her excuses. It was something Peter would probably do. 'Don't worry about it. Looks tidy to me.'

He thought she might hug him or cry, so he moved out the door and she followed, not to thank him but to get to the next task, and the one after that, and whatever else awaited her at home.

In the bar, the large, round barman was friendly enough, if only because there was nothing else to do. Luke bought a beer and a couple of pies, lined up some songs on the jukebox, and then checked his bank account on his phone. The balance came up as half of what it was supposed to be. He slammed a hand down hard, and the guy behind the bar frowned at him. Peter's number was disconnected. No form of text worked. Luke rang the company number and the site number, even though he knew there would be no one there to take his call. He ate the pies as pathetic consolation, and felt fury flushing through him.

He should have known — did know, in some way. Peter had paid Luke exactly enough to take the fight out of him: Luke would be angry, but soon he would accept what he was given and move on. He wasn't going to go to the media and try to create a shitstorm, all for the sake of a few thousand dollars. His talk about having nothing to lose had been a last-minute bluff. Maybe it had backfired.

There was no other way of getting the money. They had given him so few access points. His original contact had been no more than a friend of a friend. When he had rung the number that first time, he had been nervous, ready to hang up, in case the whole thing was a joke or a set-up.

Now he was boiling, a pressure pot. He'd done what was asked of him, and a multi-billion-dollar company was going to cheat him out of an amount that would be nothing to them. But it wasn't a company — it was people, Peter's, grouped together in their self-serving need, capable of justifying anything. It was the Peters he hated, and the world was rancid with them: stepping on, crushing, undercutting their way through life under the banner of 'winner'. Always shifting the ground, changing the argument, pretending to be righteous. He wanted to smash something, hurt someone, make someone else know what he felt.

He held tightly to the lip of the bar and breathed deeply, silently repeating his mantra: *There is nothing to gain by raging at something you can't fix.* He drank his beer, ordered another, downed it, thanked the barman, and left.

In his room, he flicked through clips and games on his tablet. Nothing held him or distracted him. He knew what he wanted: a fight, using fists, knives, baseball bats. It didn't matter which. But he also knew where that would lead: trouble; a night in jail; a night in hospital; maybe worse. Fighting wasn't the sort of battle he was good at. And there were way too many variables. Who knew who had a knife or a pistol on them, or a group of mates hiding around the corner?

He paced the room, making it his cell, and then grabbed the TV, hoisted it above his head, and stood, poised, his arms shaking under the weight and the rage. He stopped, and slowly put it down. This was not how he dealt with this stuff. He was smarter; he had to be smarter. He took off his clothes, downed two sleeping pills, and climbed into bed.

Luke slept until the early morning, when he woke to confusion and numbness, the anger dissipated by chemicals. He watched TV while the drug slowly left his system, and the shittiness of the world awoke with him. It took some time for him to remember which room, in which hotel, in which town he was in. There was nothing in the room to distinguish it from a thousand other rooms in pubs across the state. He wasn't sure if that was comforting or terrifying.

Down beside the TV cabinet he could see that the bin had

still not been emptied, and was full to the top with strands of something pale like blonde hair. He got up, put his hand into the bin, and pulled out a woman's wig. Then he held it up and shook it out. It was clean and shiny, and certainly not a plastic imitation from a party-goods shop. Underneath it, in the bin, was a collection of make-up bottles and lipstick. He put the wig on the bed, and wondered about the stories behind it: an affair, a cross-dresser, a spy? For a moment, the possibilities distracted him and allowed him to steady his returning anger.

It occurred to him, then, that if someone had left a wig and make-up behind, they might have left something else. There was nothing on top of the wardrobe, but inside he found a dress on a coathanger above a pair of large, flat black shoes. It felt suddenly like there was someone else in the room, or maybe someone had stayed the night without him even knowing. He tried to think if this could possibly be true, and then realised that the hair and the dress and the shoes were all of a part. The dress was a little black number that wasn't little. The shoes were not for a small woman, or probably for any woman. Luke put them back, almost calmed by having encountered something unexpected. Perhaps the owner would come back to claim them. Perhaps not. The wig had been in the bin, after all.

He had breakfast at a fast-food place, and flipped through their newspapers, the anger returning to brew in him like gastro, uncontainable. He walked the streets again, trying to think about other things, looking for job ads and 'staff wanted' noticeboards. But all the time the need for get-back, for violence, was growing within him.

He sat on his spongy hotel bed and ran the pale strands of the blonde wig through his fingers. It was a story in itself, and that might offer an adventure to him, too. There were other outlets in a country town.

He laid the dress out on the bed, and then showered, shaved his body clean, and plucked random hairs from his face and eyebrows. He put the dress on and made it hang the best he could, surprised by the push-up breast inserts, then tightened the belt to its limit, applied mascara and lipstick inexpertly, and pulled the wig into place. The mirror showed a reasonable representation of a youngish woman that probably wouldn't stand up to close scrutiny. He put on the black flats, took one more look, and then shut the door softly behind him.

Luke strolled the street, adjusting easily to a new walk, and doing his best to let the anger go. In the reflection of the shopfronts, he thought he looked hilarious. He watched women across the street walk, and how they moved their legs and held themselves, and he adjusted, making his step shorter and lighter, and pushing his pelvis forward.

At The Royal, he took a seat at the bar, away from the service area, and ordered a gin and tonic. A work crowd was starting to join those eager to get out of the house after Christmas, so he studied his phone as if he had really just come in to make a few important phone calls. He had several drinks, and for entertainment tried to listen in to the conversations around him. There was the usual talk about parties coming up, mistakes made in the office, holidays that people were planning, and bosses that everyone disliked. Behind him, two guys were talking about cars they wanted to buy, and a couple at the table to his right were talking earnestly about some sort of business strategy that involved educating farmers about compost. Then a slim, tall guy in a white shirt and grey trousers that didn't go all the way to his shoes appeared next to Luke and, smiling, said, 'How's it going?' It was a jokey, good-natured opening line. There was no sense that he was taking the mickey.

Luke felt the adrenaline pounding, and thought about his voice. He knew that a crowd like this, with drinks flowing, could turn on you over the smallest thing. Just making them uncomfortable would be enough to set them off, and he could certainly do that. He relished the drama, but not yet. He softened his voice and lifted its pitch without pushing it into a falsetto.

'Fine, thanks.'

'Got some big deals going on?'

Luke nodded.

'You were here the other night, weren't you?'

'No.'

'Oh. Sorry. Someone who looked just like you was here. Anyway, I'm Brett.' He lifted an open palm at her and then dropped it. 'Own the real-estate franchise. Got the office down here for a few drinks.' He indicated a group with his head, 'Get them relaxed and bonding. I think it helps them sell,' and then nodded in support of this indisputably sage thinking. 'It's only a short week. I probably should have shut the office, but I like potential clients to see us open, in action, looking for business.'

Luke stayed fixated on his phone, but he guessed that Brett wasn't the sort to move off just because he wasn't getting a good response.

'What sort of thing are you dealing in?'

'I'm an energy trader. Mostly gas.' Luke waved his phone around.

'Shit. Never heard of it. How do you trade energy?'

'Just futures, really. Always trying to pick which way the

price is going.' Luke had no idea if this might be true, but he guessed he would be unlucky for someone in this pub to know better.

'Wow. Interesting.' Brett moved a little closer, but Luke was ready for him.

'Look, I'm sorry, but I've got some really heavy numbers going on at the moment that I've just got to deal with. Do you mind?'

'No. No. Maybe I'll catch up with you later.'

'Maybe.'

Brett sauntered off, no doubt to inform his workmates of his success. Luke put his phone down, sipped at his drink, and waited.

After a song about truck-driving, another guy, round-faced and round-stomached, accompanied by a wiry, worn woman, leant against the bar next to him.

'G'day.'

'Hello.'

'You've been making friends with our Brett.'

They looked at him, smirking.

'We talked.'

'We were wondering if you could help us out. See, we're having a bet over there. We can't decide, and we don't have any way of resolving the bet.'

They giggled at this.

'Hope you don't mind, but some of us reckon you're a woman, and others reckon … you're a guy.' The woman could no longer contain herself, let out a loud cackle, and when she had finished, said, 'Sorry,' quietly, in more of a snarl than an apology.

'So we figured you could settle it for us.'

Luke had never been bullied—not properly, not with this kind of joyful intent. The opportunity made him happy.

'Well, I hope you don't mind, but I reckon you're a rude, ignorant prick. I think it's a pretty good bet your mother is the star of local gang-bang movies.' Luke felt his nerves sizzling as the thrill coursed through him.

'What? My mother? Fuck you, you fucken weirdo.' The guy was leaping at him, red-faced and choking, the woman trying to grab at his shoulder and hold him back.

Luke stood up and stepped calmly out of his way, looking down on both of them.

The woman put her arms around the man. 'C'mon, Jack. It's a nasty intersex.'

Jack shook his fist, stepping backwards under the woman's guidance. 'You'd better get out of here, you freak.'

They went back to their group, and Luke sat down again. He put his phone in his pocket and finished his drink, figuring he would nearly have time for one more.

His assessment was that Jack would be up for a fight. He didn't have much of a reach, but he would certainly be driven by his emotions: probably someone who would charge in a rage rather than throw punches, but he would definitely be back.

The barmaid came over and said, 'You don't think it's time you moved on?' She had pale, curly hair, and a face that was tired of everything.

'Probably.'

'How about you miss this last drink and save us all some bother?' It wasn't a suggestion. It was a decree.

Luke grinned at her. 'How about you refuse to serve me and write down the reasons, or you pour me a drink?' He smiled as sweetly as he could through his lipstick. She gave him a sour look, and reached for a glass. As she did, four guys, led by Jack, came over and stood close by. Luke pushed 'Record' on his phone.

'We reckon it's time you got out of our pub.' They rubbed their hands together and cracked their knuckles.

'Why?'

'Because you're a filthy freak.'

'Maybe. Is it against the law?'

'You're disgusting. If you don't get out of here, we'll smash your fucken head in.'

'And I'm going to rip that bloody dress off you and stuff it in your mouth, you tranny fruit.'

'And what does the barmaid say to that?' Luke looked to her, pretending he was expecting support.

She put his drink on the bar. 'Not my business.'

A small, compact young woman stepped to the bar, put her foot on the railing next to Luke, and grinned. 'Is everybody okay over here?' No one responded. 'Don't suppose I could get a cider, Linnie?'

The barmaid ignored her, because Luke had put his phone on the bar and begun to play their comments back. The barmaid moved to grab the offending object, but Luke pushed it aside.

'I think I'm justified in defending myself, don't you?'

The men looked at each other, wrong-footed, unsure if Luke was a cop or some sort of vigilante lawyer. Luke looked at them, their impetus suddenly stalled, and remembered his favourite old bouncer's maxim: *Get the jump on them; hit the leader, hard, long before anyone's ready for it.*

He took one long step across to Jack and headbutted him powerfully on the point of the nose, causing him to crumple before the others could react. All they could come up with was to lean down and check that Jack was still alive.

'Bloody hell, girl. You are serious.' The dark-haired woman beside him was almost laughing at him.

He smiled at her, her face alight with pleasure, as if she could see right into him, see everything, and he felt a mad rush of relief at being understood.

Then all there was left to do was upend his drink and leave, head throbbing, heart singing.

7

At midnight, Sweetapple drove to within twenty kilometres of Mountain View, the small farm where Retribution was kept, parked the ute in the trees in a reserve area, and lifted his bike out of the back. He rode east, took the Falls Road turn, and followed it towards Mountain View, the gravel loose under his tyres and the sweat running out of him, even on the flat stretches.

Bob had informed him that Retribution was owned by a syndicate of investors who ran her with several other horses—no camera, no alarms, no spotlights—just like any other mare. It was information that Sweetapple wanted to check for himself, but it was risky. He had driven past Mountain View several times in the daylight, each time at a pretty good pace so he wouldn't attract attention. Mountain View was out of the way, and any traffic on the road past it would probably be noticed and possibly recollected at a later time. One time, he borrowed Carson's car, refusing to tell her why, but still he couldn't go slowly enough to see very much.

Sweetapple had worked out that a pushbike without reflectors or lights, ridden in the dark, would be the best way to get in to have a look. He rode past the Mountain View entrance, up the road, veered into the table drain, and then over the bank of a council roadside dam. He stowed the bike out of sight on the water's edge and then walked out, crossed the road, and climbed over the fence into Mountain View. There were lights on in the house nearby, but there were no security lights or security cars, or even warning signs.

Retribution's mob was still in the front paddock. The strategy seemed to be to hide her in plain view, among everyday horses, and not draw attention to her. Perhaps they were right. Big warning signs and elaborate-looking systems might suggest to potential thieves that whatever was behind the wires had to be worth stealing. The horses took no notice of him as he walked along the fence, looking for anything that might suggest an alarm or a camera, or any form of technology. If there were motion-sensor cameras, he wouldn't know until it was too late, but at least tonight he could only be caught for trespass.

Breeding farms had inspection towers and remote foaling collars on their mares, but Retribution was yet to be put to stud, so none of those things was needed. She was just another mare in a paddock, and, as if to prove it, she arrived with a thunder of hooves in soft dirt, stopping suddenly, crowded by her gang of inquisitive friends. She was the standout in the group, her coat shining in the night light, her shape sleek and powerful. The other horses were no more than hangers-on. Retribution stuck her nose out at him, and he let her smell him. She held still for a moment, maybe in thought, and then spun and cantered away, the mob following, obedient to her example. If he couldn't steal this horse, he would probably have to give up on horses altogether.

Sweetapple had already established that he would be able to park his horse float on the road on the other side of the farm, the road that ran parallel to Falls Road, walk several kilometres in the dark to the mare, and ride her back.

And now a light from the distant house grew brighter as a door opened. Sweetapple hit the ground, unsure what could be seen in half-lit silhouette or what a practised eye might see in an intimately known landscape. The door closed, and Sweetapple got up slowly. Plenty could go wrong on a job like this, no matter how compliant the mare might be. He walked along the fence, past the corner, and up to the gate halfway along. There were no padlocks or difficult catches. He turned and headed for his bike.

Sweetapple doubted that Retribution was really worth stealing. So many big-name, big-price-tag horses were nowhere near as good as they were supposed to be. Their publicity outpaced their abilities, with everyone starting to believe the hype just because everybody around them seemed to believe the hype. Of course, this wasn't his concern, and Sweetapple knew it was best he didn't think about what was going on and what Bob might be trying to do. He just had to steal the horse. He would keep her on his place for a week or so, and then deliver her, whether Bob liked it or not. It wasn't just the risk of the police finding out that he was worried about. What if she injured herself, slashed herself on a fence, put a foot down a hole, or went lame? Bob would be out of the deal as soon as he heard, and Sweetapple would be stuck with very expensive, stolen, damaged goods.

At least a payment of $25,000 (five lots of $5,000) had

rm out behind him in case she might not know where the
.way was. 'Cliffs?'

Oh yeah. Big place.' She scowled unintentionally, and he
d it.

You don't like?'

Nothing to do with me.'

Right.'

she got into the forklift, picked up a couple of slings of
s on the front forks, put them in the ute, then went back
olls of plain wire. In the office, she printed out a docket and
ved him where to sign.

so are you hanging around, or are you travelling or
thing?'

see how this job goes. Might stay for a bit.'

t's harder to get out than you reckon—let me tell you.'

How hard can it be to get on a bus or a train?' And then
w that her assertion was serious and that the casual
ent might cover some sort of anguish. 'You've just got to
rsistent.'

e didn't know what he meant, and he wished he'd said it
er way, but the opportunity was erased by rolling time.
kay, then. Thanks for that.' He moved to go.

ere wasn't anything attractive about his long form or his
ir face, but there were so few interesting, unpredictable
about that she didn't want to let him disappear.

group of us head down to the Bowlo for a drink on
days, a meal sometimes. Nothing special, but it's
ing. You could come if you wanted.'

liked the way she took the risk but made out it was an
ade to any lost dog.

already cleared in his account. Sweetapple had checked the
entries several times, unable to believe that the money was really
there, and convinced that it would be removed or dishonoured
the minute he started to believe in its reality.

He climbed back over the fence and crossed to his bike. At
the bend up the hill, a set of headlights appeared out of nowhere,
removing the darkness and making Sweetapple's every thought
of stealth and subterfuge ridiculous. He dived over the dam
bank, skidded down to the water's edge, and lay still. The lights
roared past, but he stayed where he was, his breathing loud,
the mud sticky and thick under his hands, organic and rich.
Had they seen him out the corner of an eye and then decided
that they should come back and confirm the sighting? Maybe
they had stopped and were backtracking on foot? He waited for
the return of the lights, and listened for the motor, footsteps,
or voices. But there was only the sound of the vehicle growing
more and more distant in the quiet night. He crawled to the
edge of the bank and looked over. There was nothing to see;
even the lights of the house were now turned off. He picked up
his bike and wheeled it over the bank, then got on and pedalled
down the road, his breathing still thick. He would steal the mare
as soon as possible, and get this thing over and done with.

When Luke came into the store and looked around, a little lost,
it took Carson a while to work out what was so familiar about
him. Then something about his nose, the way he tilted his neck
when he was thinking, made her realise how she knew him.

Luke had come in to pick up some extra wire and posts at
the produce store. The fencing contractor who Luke worked for,

Frank Zee, had managed to under-order from his usual bulk supplier, and now they had a sudden shortage. The fact that Luke had been trusted to pick up the extra wire was a surprise, even to Luke.

He had spotted the job on the supermarket notice board. There were truck-driving jobs, poultry-farm positions, and caretaker opportunities on offer, but fencing sounded like it was the best bet for him to get away with giving a false name and asking to be paid in cash. Luke had been hired over the phone, on the spot, told he needed to provide his own hat and gloves, and to bring water and food for himself every day. There would be lifts from town.

Apparently the local young guys thought that fencing in the summer sun was for fools, and chose instead to operate machinery from air-conditioned cabs for better money, or move elsewhere. It made Frank anxious and bad-tempered, prone to yelling at his employees, because he was convinced that they were second-rate, and that his company and his image were diminished because of them. Paying better money for more skilled employees hadn't occurred to him.

Frank was a crisp-shirted guy whose main pretension was that he was a businessman and not a fencing contractor. Staying clean and deodorised were symbols of success for Frank, so he kept away from the physical work as much as possible. When he did have to get his hands dirty, he made sure he had plenty of hand wipes and towelettes to clean off with, and a moisturiser to finish. Luke was glad to have picked up a job so quickly, and Frank wasn't around much, so Luke was prepared to put up with his mean-spirited cantankerousness, for a while at least.

Luke hadn't fenced before, hadn't even w[...] neither Frank nor anyone else working for [...] by his ignorance. It was hot work, involvin[...] which he didn't mind, but most of the har[...] tractors and machines. He felt he could stick[...] The guys were friendly, and when he gave vag[...] questions about what he'd been doing and [...] they didn't seem concerned. They'd only ask[...] time. So the job was peaceful and quiet, and [...] outdoors, which was enough to make him [...] scenery was good, too, and the air was clean[...]

Luke also felt a need to be near the pic[...] case something happened. He didn't know [...] wondered if he was hoping a bomb would [...] or if the police would raid the picket. W[...] stopped off just down the road, in this job[...] Some things you just couldn't know.

He handed Carson a list and a little n[...] walked him out to the yard, where the [...] stored.

'So how's the fencing going?'

'They're paying me.' It came out ligh[...] disbelieving.

'I know what you mean.'

He had a calm about him, as if n[...] important enough to worry him, and sh[...] version of him fit with her memory of h[...] courting danger.

'You working locally?'

'Yeah. On a place off the highway, o[...]

'See if I can.' He held a palm up as goodbye, and she watched him saunter out.

Luke waited for several nights outside the hotel until closing time. He didn't know what shifts the barmaid with the nasty attitude worked, but eventually he saw her leave, walking quietly, head down, kicking at pebbles on the asphalt, sucking on a cigarette. She got into a small green Ford in the half-lit staff car park. It was battered and faded around the doors, and looked like it would remain that way. He watched the car leave, the motor suggesting she must live nearby, a trip of any magnitude obviously beyond it. No wonder she was so keen to take her shit out on someone else who looked an easy target. It didn't give her the right, though.

Two nights later, he walked past and saw the green Ford in the car park. It was dark, but there were a few cars in the street and he could hear the sound of burnouts in the distance. He watched for a few minutes from around a corner where he couldn't be seen, then he pulled his cap down and strode over to the little car, took a valve spanner out of his pocket, and loosened the valves in each tyre. The car slumped satisfyingly down on its hubs, and Luke moved away quickly, confident he hadn't been seen.

In the bar, she looked happier tonight. No cross-dressers, he supposed. All normal people. It had to make you happy.

'Just a beer thanks. New.' The hat was still pulled down too far, but he left it that way, undecided whether he would let her know who he was.

She poured a beer and let it rest, smiling at him. 'Do I know you?'

Perhaps her brain was telling her he was a celebrity of some sort that she just couldn't place. He considered boasting of his significance in a weekly TV drama, maybe a rising star, but it seemed like such a dull thing to say.

'Don't think so. I've never been in here before.' He hid behind the stubble he had grown for camouflage and smiled at her, confirming her suspicions but keeping it as their little secret.

She laughed, in a happy collusion with him. And Luke remembered her name: Linnie.

'You from around here?' he asked, unsure where he was taking the conversation.

She put his beer on the bar. 'Five-twenty, thanks.' He passed her the right change, and she said, 'Born and bred. Never really been anywhere else.' She walked down the bar to a waiting older guy with a bulbous nose and stomach that, if not contained, looked like it might push the bar over. After she served him, she made her way back towards Luke, pretending he wasn't the reason for her move.

'You're a traveller, then?'

'Yeah.' He swirled his drink, trying to contain the fizz he was getting from knowing she might deduce who he was at any time.

'What do you do?' She said it absent-mindedly, over a shoulder, as she put a glass in the washer.

'Muso.'

'Yeah?' She was interested now. 'Sing?'

'A bit. Guitar mostly.'

'You got a band?'

'Yeah, but they're all over the place at the moment. Taking a break.'

'Right. So you chose here for a break?'

Luke conceded a laugh. It was certainly a stretch. Who would holiday in this town unless they had family here that forced them to?

'Sort of. Thought I'd hitch around for a while. Do a bit of work here and there. See the country, for real.'

She disappeared to serve customers, and then returned. They talked about the pub and her boss (a prick), and what she did for entertainment when she wasn't stuck behind the bar. Luke had thought he might enjoy a small gloat by getting her to serve him a drink. Firstly, because she didn't know who he was or who he had been, and secondly because she didn't know what he had done.

But he was finding that he liked her. She was relaxed and even a bit funny. There was an instant warmth about her that he hadn't picked up on the first time. He even considered sneaking out to try to do something about her tyres. He knew he should finish his drink and leave, but her self-deprecating laugh, the soft look of her hair, the faded life in her face made him stay. He decided that if he could, he would walk her home after she saw her car couldn't be moved, even though he still didn't know if she had a boyfriend or a husband or a girlfriend. So first he needed to do some testing.

'I think I'd better get going.' He had slid from his stool.

'You've got somewhere to go?'

'Not really. But I can't be bothering you all night.'

'Oh, I don't know.' She didn't look at him, but he could hear the offer in her voice.

'Well, I'll have another beer, then, please.'

He waited for her outside as she locked up. They crunched

across the car park together, the night air a thick barrier between them. Linnie unlocked the car and got into the driver's seat without noticing anything.

'Linnie? You'd better get back out.'

She put a foot back down on the ground. 'This car seems very low for some reason.'

'Your … ah … tyres are flat.'

'What?' She stood and looked down at the tyres. 'Oh, really? Two tyres? I knew I should have changed them.' She sagged a little. 'What am I supposed to do now?'

He didn't tell her about the other two.

'How far's your place? I'll walk you there, if you want.'

'Thanks. It's pretty close.'

They walked out of the car park, and she playfully took his arm and he let her.

'How did you know my name?' she asked when they'd walked a couple of blocks. 'I didn't tell you.'

It felt for a moment like a small bomb had gone off in his head, loud because of the silence between him and Linnie. Had he been set up by her? Had she known all along who he was and what he had done? He scanned, panicky, through his options. Could he claim she had told him, but she just hadn't remembered? Or explain that someone else had told him before he went into the pub? In his desperation, the man with the bulbous nose came to his rescue.

'Your boyfriend, at the end of the bar when I was having my first beer, with the matching nose and stomach. I heard him say it when he ordered.'

'Ah, Jimmy. We get all the lookers.'

'Thanks very much.'

She grabbed his arm and pulled him closer. 'Not you. Of course not you.'

Her place was small but neat, with two bedrooms and a modern kitchen, flattened pale carpets, and a large TV. But there was colour in the room: cushions, throw rugs, and some arty posters. He felt he could like her in other circumstances.

She got them both a bourbon.

'There's an old guitar there. Out of tune. Don't suppose you want to play me a little something?'

'I won't, if you don't mind. My hands are all cracked and dry from physical work. I wouldn't do it justice.'

In bed, he took her from behind, against her will. Luke didn't think he should have to look into her face after the complexity of the night. She whimpered but didn't resist, accepting her lot, as though what she wanted was never of any consequence. That power excited and then depressed him.

When he'd finished and lay on the bed panting, she rolled away, and after a minute told him, 'Get out.' He obliged, quickly. What else was there to do? It wasn't like he could have a relationship with her. He didn't bother to say, 'Goodbye,' but he did feel faint remorse. They could have been friends — if he wasn't who he was, if the world turned another way.

As he pushed through the doorway from the bed, he heard her muffled voice: 'I'd stick to being a woman, if I were you. You're shit as a man.'

Outside, the moon had risen yellow and overcooked in the black sky, and he felt like it had presented itself just for him. It was good to be on his own with only the moon as accomplice. He could go where he wanted to go and be what he wanted to be, and nothing could touch him.

8

Bob was gone again, north, to business meetings, deal-making, and greenfield sites. The usual. He would return with stories of cruising on some billionaire's yacht or witnessing eye-popping engineering projects in the heart of unseen pastoral country. Caroline wondered how many women would feature in his time away. Everybody loved a rich man, a powerful man. Sometimes they even loved a powerful woman.

She had hoped he would stay around when she really needed him. It would have been nice to enjoy a lazy January together; something they hadn't done since … forever.

Bob would consider that sort of talk churlish, and insist that he had 'made time for her' after the election. Hadn't he cut the Singapore junket? Cancelled a trip to California for a week of electricity-storage talks, and postponed a foray into Russia (whatever that meant)?

Perhaps she hadn't needed him enough in the past few years, and maybe she hadn't shown him how important he was to her. He was gone now, and she wished for him back. She wished mostly for his certainty: the rock of belief that everything would turn out all right, and if it didn't he would make it turn out all right. Problems were just challenges, and he thrived on a challenge. Of course, not every one of them could be resolved by fair play, but you did what you had to do. It would be ridiculous to expect any less. His clarity was still intoxicating: he always knew he could get what he wanted. That wasn't love, though, was it? Nothing like love, but it was something, something she needed, because it felt like everybody else had deserted her and let her down, despite everything she had done.

Long before it all went bad and her heralded popularity went out the window, she had day-dreamed that there would be jobs after politics: positions on company boards, not-for-profit boards, government instrumentalities, maybe even a diplomatic posting of some minor sort. But when it was all over, the phone never rang, not once, except for calls of support from staffers (ex-staffers) and her family. Caroline's clung-to excuse was that independents didn't have anyone — no apparatchiks, no true believers — to organise cushy after-politics positions for them. This ignored the obvious fact that she had done so much for the government: arranging favours, agreeing to deals, supporting their causes, and voting for them when they desperately needed it. Her mother's opinion was that she should be thankful no one was asking her to head up their little committees. She thought Caroline should be glad to be shy of the whole thing.

But what was she supposed to do now? Go back to the Parents & Citizens, where it had all started? Fight, and push, and argue, and lobby, and manipulate? Not bloody likely.

Caroline stretched out on the bed, warm, trying hard at being languid, as even the birds pointed out how pleasant it was. She looked out the large window, and let her eyes run down the ordered lawn over the flower-filled garden beds, under the jacarandas and off the ha-ha wall to the paddock and the creek. Bob's garden. God, he loved this garden. He wasn't around it much, but it was one of his few special things. He had designed and landscaped it himself (with plenty of paid labour), before they were married. He knew every plant, could identify them by their common name and in Latin, and had spent more money on the garden than anyone she could think of. The results were extraordinary, and strangely not gauche. It was one thing he showed taste in: plants. When he got home from trips away, the first thing he did, when there was daylight, was walk around the garden to see what was thriving and what was struggling, and to simply breathe it in.

The two ducks waddled past, too lazy to ever leave the yard. It was still cool, and the colours bright. What sort of person would live somewhere else when they had a place like this? What sentient being wouldn't want to work in that garden, ride horses or bikes in the morning, lunch with friends, cook meals in the evening, have paddock bonfires with friends like they used to, drinking and laughing too much? Laughing. Remember that?

She and Bob hadn't spent much time together in the past few years, not stretches of time anyway—just weekends and nights as he passed through the city, or a day or two in the country when parliament wasn't sitting and she was doing her best to see constituents. He came to some official functions when the media weren't interested, and stayed in the city unit with her from time to time, but it was always weird. Even the sex was unfamiliar, as though they weren't actually married. Perhaps that was a good thing: it kept the spark alive. Caroline was confident he still loved her and often as not liked her. She had to concede that he had been supportive, in his way, even though it wasn't very much. The bit that Bob didn't like was her success. (That obstacle had certainly been removed.) It took her a while to realise that it irked him when her name was in the media, whether it was for good or bad things. When he made it to one of her functions, he was at his most energetic and charming, attracting a crowd keen to hear about his world. The charisma and bonhomie that had served him so well in business were on full, friendly display. Sometimes the function turned into a Bob Statham festival.

He hated people asking him if he was the husband of the federal member for the seat of Lindon, Caroline Statham. She knew he detested journalists, travelling companions, and business mates asking him about her, even if they were just being friendly. But he never actually said it. He was always encouraging, at least in the form of the words he used. Sometimes she caught him saying supportive, touchy-feely things when his attention was really on his phone, the phrases issuing from his mouth as if they were templates regurgitated from that very phone.

Caroline sat up and reached for the computer tablet on the bedside table, and then changed her mind. There was no need. The only thing the media could bring her was more criticism, more lampooning, more bad news. She snuggled down again and closed her eyes, knowing she wouldn't sleep. Sleeping-in was a lost skill; sleep itself, a quarantined luxury. But now she had time to relearn it. In a matter of weeks she had gone from being time-poor to time-filthy-rich. The government had changed, and she had no friends in the new one. Her friends had no friends among the newly powerful. At least her staff had found jobs. Apparently, for them, talent overrode any mistakes of association they had made in the past few years, which meant they were very bloody talented. But Caroline knew she was never going to receive any such concession, never get a diplomatic posting. It was done.

She told herself to let it go. She was lucky, she had achieved things; for one short breath of time, she had even held the balance of power, and what she had done had really had an effect, had really mattered. And now she could enjoy life. Who wouldn't be jealous of her?

Unwillingly, she flipped through an album in her head of all the things she had sacrificed and all the battles she had fought: the endless hours in meetings she'd endured; the doorknocking; the pranks to gain publicity; the recalcitrants she had persuaded; the mountains she'd climbed to reach this pinnacle. All this to become the most unpopular regional politician anyone could remember — and, now, ex-politician.

They hated her, even going to the trouble of sending her threats; clumsy, anonymous death threats. Some of the threat-makers she probably knew, and maybe even knew well. They were members of her own community. All this because she had voted to support the bad guys. Colleagues laughed at her original distress, making comments about it 'going with the territory', and telling her, 'You haven't achieved anything until you've had a death threat from a crackpot.' It didn't help.

Caroline rolled over again, and saw her book on the bedside table. She picked it up: it was serious national literature, specifically chosen because she had known (rather, her minders had known) that one of the major dailies or a women's magazine would do their usual Christmas feature on what politicians were reading. When asked, it was important not to sound like a lightweight or an egghead. Being somewhere in-between was important, according to Janine, her press secretary, now her ex-press secretary. Janine had been very focused on image, easily distressed by media content, and apoplectic about social media, but Caroline had never been convinced by the importance of that stuff to her electorate. No one seemed to be listening either way. How they arrived at their opinions, so tightly held, she really didn't know.

She put the book down again. She still hadn't read it. No one in the world would be ringing to find out what she was reading. The book didn't suit her anyway. It was too unlikely for her to make sense of: a story set in 'the country', where the writer had obviously never spent more than a weekend. Still, neither had most of the reading population.

Her constituents in the seat of Lindon had spent most of their lives in the country, and they thought she had sold them out—betrayed them and treated them like fools. They were wrong. She had done her best for them. How many times had she tried to explain that, because of her decisions, she had garnered more funding, more opportunities for work and business, and more proposed infrastructure improvements than an area like this had ever wished for?

They would never concede this, of course. For them, politics was like supporting a football team. You chose which side you were on, and you stuck with it, whether or not your team was full of bumbling, hayseed idiots. You stayed with them, glued to the refrain, 'There's always next time.' She banged her hand down hard on the springy bed. Next time, bloody next time, was now, after they'd gleefully voted her out, and the electorate was returning to its role as a blank space on the map of the major political parties. Any funding that could be delayed would be, until it slipped off the page in the next budget.

She pushed the sheets back, stood, stretched, grabbed a robe, and headed for the kitchen, musing on breakfast. There was a new yoghurt to savour, and then the promised pleasure of their own farm eggs.

Caroline tried to enjoy the idea of the freedom she now had, that she could sit with a magazine, browse the internet, enjoy breakfast and coffee and time to herself. Instead, the whirl of her life spun back and forth in her mind.

No one could say her career had been an accident. She had craved it, willed it, worked as hard as she possibly could for it. She had thought of nothing else. In the first few years of her marriage, she realised she never wanted to be a chatterer on the sidelines, watching on and wondering what really happened. Bob had so many deals, plans, and things he was *making happen,* she was jealous. She wanted to be involved, close to the action, with her hands on a lever or two. She'd certainly achieved that. The prime minister might have been more powerful, but, held in the vice-like grip of a minority government, he had still had to come cap in hand to her, and not the other way around. It didn't last long, but it was an achievement that could never be taken away.

She stirred yoghurt into a bowl of bananas, and headed out to the verandah to sit in a cane chair before the sun got too hot. The rich scent of the garden beds floated up to greet her. The ducks were now muttering quietly, sitting together in the water that filled the large concrete dish dug in beneath the top-garden tap. You had to be jealous of that kind of contentment.

Of course, she'd done no end of damage to her friendships, her regard in the community, and maybe even her marriage, but she had been one of the most powerful women in the whole country. As far as trade-offs went, that was more than enough.

She ate, trying to let the warmth and the beauty of the garden hold a lid on her angst. Perhaps she could take up gardening. It was supposed to be good for stress relief. Ex-politicians droned about it all the time.

Bob's golf clubs were resting against the cupboard on the other end of the verandah. Caroline guessed he must have a lot of work on, because he almost always took his clubs with him, probably catching up after 'making time' for his wife. But something about the bag didn't match the image of them she held in her head. A club was missing: the longest in the bag, the one that towered over the other less-significant irons. It was his favourite driver, a massive-headed thing that he went on and on about, as if it were an old mate, given to him by a famous professional whose name she couldn't remember.

She was thinking how odd it was when she saw, in the paddock in front of the house, between the garden and the main road, a man in a large, rumpled hat putting a thin rope around a horse's neck, watched by an ugly black-and-white dog. He came in close and patted the horse down the shoulder. Despite the size of the paddock and the ample room to escape into, the gelding seemed convinced that being caught by this man was a good idea. The figure was tall and broad-shouldered, with arms that were almost too long. Sweetapple.

Max, her large labrador, ran down the yard to bark with excitement at the dog. The lean dog ignored him, but Max, soft and kept and as oblivious as a prince, wagged his tail happily.

Sweetapple swung up onto the back of the horse and nudged him forward—no saddle or bridle, except for the flimsy piece of rope over its neck.

Caroline got out of her seat and padded down the spongy, even grass to the edge of the ha-ha, and then down to the garden fence. He noticed, and guided the horse towards her.

'No rest for the wicked?'

He smiled. 'I wouldn't call this work.' He patted the gelding again. 'What about you? You're not having a day off, are you?'

'Uh-huh. Another one.' She finished a mouthful, and added, 'In fact, now every day is a day off for me.'

He nodded and looked away. What else could he do?

Whenever she had the chance, she had tried to get to know him a little, but still found him completely unfathomable. He had no family—only a girlfriend in town, she heard—and no engagement with the community, except for occasional visits to the Bowlo. She knew he lived on his own next door, ran a few cattle and some sheep, kept a tidy place, and stuck to that two-dimensional representation of himself. Sweetapple looked after the horses for them, exercised them, groomed them, drenched them, and guarded them against getting too fat and or foundering, because Joey, the farm manager, was a motorbike-and-machinery man, as was Lance and the other station hands. Bob was very keen on horses, but mostly from a distance. She, Bob, and Joey trusted Sweetapple. He was the first person she turned to, the rare times she was at home, when things weren't right—the one she called on to deal with water problems, sick animals, flooded creeks, and electrical outages.

She turned to him because he was the obvious choice. It was

his country. Even Joey acknowledged Sweetapple's feel for it. He seemed to know every tree and every type of grass, every bird, every beetle. Animals trusted him, and he was always careful with them. He never had a harsh word for Max, despite Max's natural ability for getting in the way or standing in a crucial gateway when a muster was on.

She wondered if Sweetapple was a throwback: if all men in the area were like him in years gone past. Bob and Joey certainly weren't like him. They were 'managers', focused on the dollar, yield, and timing, but ignorant of the small things in their natural environment.

Apparently, Sweetapple's grandfather had owned several large properties in the area, including the one that she and Bob lived on. She'd never learnt how they'd been lost. Bob said Sweetapple's father went crazy after the Vietnam War, and that his mother had struggled to keep the family going. They had both been gone a long time.

Caroline continued spooning up and savouring her breakfast as she stood at the fence. The gelding shifted calmly underneath Sweetapple, its tail independently flicking at flies.

'Season's gone off.'

'It always seems dry to me. I'm never home long enough to notice the changes.' She resisted saying, 'Until now.' It wasn't funny. It was close to pathetic.

He looked out at the skyline and then back, as if he had something important to say. Max rubbed up against her as his second choice, unable to get near the man, or the horse, or his dog.

She was about to change the topic when she stepped onto the edge of the garden bed and her foot stubbed against something hard, hidden by the agapanthus. It was the concrete plinth for a small statue made by Bob's mother: a special favourite that whenever it was periodically overgrown and obscured, Bob would always dig and cut back around so it stood out. But the statue wasn't there. It wasn't the sort of thing someone would steal.

Caroline thought of the golf club, and suddenly felt a vicious, biting cramp rippling through her stomach. She dropped the bowl into the garden, with the spoon flicking off into the mulch.

'You right?'

She held her stomach. The realisation that the favoured golf club and the precious statue were gone was clearer than any written goodbye note. It wasn't shock she felt; it was revulsion. He had moved on without giving her so much as a warning. All of the things she had achieved and endured had meant so little that he had held off for a couple of weeks before bolting, probably with one of his adoring PAs.

'I've got to go, sorry.'

She step-ran over the grass, up onto the wall, hunched over, doing what she could to hold it in. By the time she reached the steps of the house, she was violently ill into the plumbago. And again.

Sweetapple watched her crippled run up the garden, with Max following playfully, and wondered about the right thing to do. It was such a violent reaction that his first notion was to get to her aid, help her to the house. But as he was swinging a leg over to dismount, he realised that it would be too intimate. It wasn't his place.

'You okay?' he yelled after her.

Her pale hair hung down over her face, hiding whatever it was she was going through. She managed to wave back and somehow get out, 'I'll be all right,' before she stumbled up the steps to her house.

Sweetapple turned the gelding away and walked him to the stables. He brushed the horse down, saddled him, and took him out to ride circles. The muscles in the gelding's arching neck rippled in the sun as Sweetapple pushed and guided and demanded. He didn't like to ride the gelding without a saddle, because he believed it taught the horse things he didn't need to know, but Bob and Caroline were keen for visiting kids to have the chance to ride bareback. After the horse had raised a foamy sweat under his saddle blanket, Sweetapple walked him down, unsaddled him, and washed him with cold water. He could see that the horse enjoyed it, just as he'd enjoyed the ride, but was now ready to be free of it all. Sweetapple scraped the water from his back and let him go, and he galloped away, kicked, and raced off, then turned, trotted back, and lay in a bare dirt hollow, rolled onto on his back, flexing his legs and snorting theatrically. He got up and high-stepped away, his tail flicking in the air like a triumphant flag. Sweetapple was impressed, as he always was, by how perfectly horses and dogs could display pleasure.

When the gear was all in its place in the tack room, he made his way to his ute. The light was just starting to fade; it was bright but no longer golden. He looked at Caroline's house with the glow behind it, and thought of how many times, as a kid, he had ridden his own horses out here, unwilling to go home because he was never sure what he might find: a party, a fight, a debt collector, or his parents passed out on the couch. He knew they had tried to hide it all from him. For a long time they had done their best, and then it was too much and the unravelling process began.

Looking back now, he realised that the trouble probably began much earlier. In the 1970s, when it rained often, and grain was worth good money, his father was in Vietnam, through no fault of his own. Where was his thanks? He returned damaged and addicted. Where was the helping hand when he was down? Weren't small communities supposed to rally round? His father couldn't get back to a normal, disciplined life where the work needed to be done, no matter the day or the weather, or how black your depression was. They let him fall. They let him fall because they were eager for his father's country, his grandfather's country.

Bob and Caroline had named their section of Sweetapple's family farm Little Myalls, had spent big dollars on the house, and Bob had turned the garden into a showpiece. Now it looked like a top-end resort, but in the middle of nowhere. Their money had built new sheds, fences, and tanks, fertilised the paddocks, and bought shiny new machines, but the place was the same to Sweetapple. He didn't begrudge them the ownership of it. If he had inherited it, which he never did, he would have had to sell it. They didn't even buy the best country, the low farming country that was so coveted.

Back then, the buyers wanted the soft country on the plain for a price they knew was well below its value. Only the locals knew, or were just realising, how good the country really was for growing crops—how reliable, how productive it was—but they also knew it wouldn't take long for the word to get out. They watched his father go to the wall, and when he did, they stepped in to be the kind of caring, supportive friends and neighbours who rushed in to make the first offer on the best country. When it was bought for a fraction of its later value, they never looked back. They were wealthy now; not just the ones who had bought his father's country, but all those who had profited from the failure and weakness of others. The only one looking back was Sweetapple; looking back from the poorest piece of the country his family had owned. So now, years later, the son, the grandson, was finally going to pay off the family debt by stealing a horse.

When the throwing up subsided and Caroline had had a chance to sit in a chair and think of what she now understood, she picked up the phone and rang Bob. The anger and the pain made her fingers vibrate on the handset.

'You've left me then, have you?'

'Caroline?'

'You've up and left me, you prick.'

'What makes you think that?' He was as calm as ever. It was almost impossible to catch him off-guard.

'Oh, come on, Bob. You could do me the courtesy of talking straight, couldn't you?'

'I haven't left you.'

She could hear him breathing out, preparing to explain something that was obvious to everyone in the world except her.

'I thought it would be good to have a break. It's been a very tough time for you over the past six months, year even. There hasn't been much room for anything except your difficulties. I thought some room would be good.'

'Some room? Some fucking room? That's what you're calling it? Am I a teenager? Are you about to say, "It's you, not me," and you "still want to be friends"?' She could feel her face redden as she walked back and forth, ready to smash the handpiece against the wall or the floor. 'And you couldn't mention this "room" to me? I'm part of it, you know.'

'I was going to talk to you about it before I left, but you were in such a downer I thought it best to keep it for another time.'

Her anger at his prevarication hurt like flesh tearing. She wished he would yell at her, break down, show that some part of what she felt still mattered to him.

'What's her name, Bob?' It came out through clenched teeth.

'It's not relevant. Come on. You've got to admit it hasn't been great between us for a long time. Your love was your job, and everything else was a distant second.'

'You arsehole. Don't you hide your duplicity behind my work ethic. You're just as committed to your work as I've been — the only difference is you're more committed to yourself. The poor little bimbo you're rooting doesn't know she's competing with your first love: you.'

'I've been there for you, Caroline, all the way through. You just didn't notice: you had too many more important things on your plate. You can't expect someone to hang around under those sort of circumstances.'

Caroline was starting to cry, hating herself for it, and hating Bob for being the reason.

'So when are you coming home, if it's just a break?'

'I don't know. When I'm ready.'

'The big man doesn't even have the guts to tell me over the phone that he's left me. What are you planning to do? Send a text? Is that brave enough for you?'

Bob had hung up. She threw the phone across the room, sat down on the floor, and wept.

9

Sweetapple smoothed a flat, shaking palm down her shimmering neck. She quivered under it, her eyes round and shining but yielding, maybe terrified, in the yellow light of the fat moon.

Then, as if to dispute his conceit, she snorted and stamped a foot, holding her position as she'd been trained to do, but whispering rebellion. He swung up into the saddle, his heart booming, and sat down hard, the mare stationary but never still, her energy crackling off every muscle into the still night.

Confident she wouldn't unseat him, he looked up from the withers and saw there was no action from the homestead in the distance: no lights, no inquisitive house dogs, no restless insomniacs responding to goings-on in the paddock. He knew, now, he could do this. If he stayed calm, he could make it happen.

Sweetapple pushed Retribution forward with his legs, and, despite her power, she was soft in the mouth and responsive to the bit. He could feel her, unsure of him, following his direction but not convinced that she should, her feet almost touching the ground. He only had five kilometres to ride to his ute and the horse trailer, and he knew she could do it at pace without breaking into anything more than a nervous sweat. He backed her up, guided her side to side, and then held her in place while the small of her back relaxed and suggested she was starting to trust him. The other horses in the mob returned to watch, jostling each other like curious teenagers, following him as he rode towards the fence.

When he had climbed over the fence into the front paddock, not an hour before, checking for lights in the house, listening for anything unpredicted, he had wondered whether, if things went wrong, she would be able to jump the barbed and hinge-jointed fence, in the dark, with an unknown rider.

That concern was gone. He knew she could jump the height of two fences, flicking her tail disdainfully on the way back to earth. In fact, right now, after riding her for only ten minutes, he knew that Retribution could do almost anything she was bidden. She was a freak of the highest athletic ability—even a pony clubber could see that. He imagined her glossy eyes, rolling back, trying to check on him, wondering who and what he was.

Sweetapple squeezed her into a canter and, to assert himself, shortened and lengthened her stride, then pushed her sideways without her either challenging or ignoring his light touch. But he didn't jump the fence. There was no one around, no trouble to outpace, and the thought of a misjudged foot catching the top barb, and the damage it would do to her, scared him more than the idea of being caught himself.

Horsemen and horsewomen would do anything, would hurt people, for a horse like this. But Bob wasn't a horseman;

he was an investor, a trinket-seeker, a big-noter, and an expert at international one-upmanship. Retribution couldn't be a status symbol. She had to be a deadly secret. What could you do with a horse that was already branded and registered? You couldn't ride her anywhere public. The horse world was small, petty, jealous, and keen to boast of its observations. Entering Retribution in any sort of recognised event would be an impossibility. All you could do was hide her somewhere secret, up some mountain gully, breed from her and then lie about the parentage of the offspring, and avoid DNA testing at all cost. You couldn't legitimately register her offspring either. To Sweetapple, being paid $50,000 for doing this seemed like money for jam. The buyer was an idiot. He would never get his money back.

Retribution moved sideways under him, in response either to a stump or a rabbit hole, cat-like and so suddenly that he nearly didn't stay with her — something he would never confess to anyone.

He was losing his anxiety, enjoying himself too much to care that he was doing the wrong thing, the worst thing, and becoming the kind of person he hated.

And then maybe Statham wasn't so much of a fool. A genuine horseman would pay any amount just to have Retribution in his paddock, to ride her at any time he felt like it. Statham was a mining multi-millionaire, so he probably wasn't an idiot or an aficionado; more likely he was just playing a rich man's game.

They sprinted over the tussock flat together as though they were one animal, her feet certain in the bumpy, half-lit terrain. Together they made their own breeze, but nothing moved around them. Even the cicadas were stilled in awe, the stars bright in their reverence.

Sweetapple could see the trees where he had parked, and then the moon brought up the white panels of the horse trailer. He scanned the darkness, wondering if what he saw could be seen by anyone else. But at 3.30 am there wasn't a light on the plain, not even the meandering glow from a roo-shooter's ute or the shielded light of a fuel thief.

It was going well, better than he had dared to hope, but bad luck could undo him at any moment: a party-goer returning late; a friend or relative turning up from nowhere and seeing him cantering across the flat; an injury to the horse that he simply couldn't walk away from. Even light rain would ruin him: footprints and tyre marks would become his immediate passage to jail. But there was no chance of rain today, and instead of the usual fever of the burglary, he felt joy and even jubilation to be a part of Retribution's pure, natural gift. He could kill for a horse like this. The stupidity of that idea didn't have time to register, because right then a crack like a rifle shot smacked through the night air, deafening and bewildering him. He should have run, pushed Retribution into the gallop she was keen for, but instead he held her with his legs; she barely moved, although ready to launch, constrained only by her discipline. Her ears were straining tautly, and he could almost hear her nostrils flaring. He wouldn't run because he couldn't risk her.

Carson was standing by the horse trailer. She was unmistakeable: compact, short-haired, swaggering even while at a standstill, her teeth broadcasting cheekiness in the half-light, the just-cracked stock whip snaking in one hand.

'Carson! Bloody hell.' He could hear her laughing, excited. 'What if someone hears?'

'Who? There's not a soul awake for ten kilometres, and that little crack wouldn't even carry to the road.'

He shook his head, his fear had burned into anger and now dissipated. Retribution felt it, eased back, and then sniffed at the girl, trying to make up her mind about what was going on.

'Didn't tell me you were a fucken horse thief. This is new territory.'

He swung down, undid the girth, pulled the saddle off, and walked over with it to the ute.

Carson held out a hand to Retribution, and then, being accepted, rubbed it up along the mare's cheek.

'You've got nothing to do on a Tuesday morning?' Only a fool would have told a girl like Carson about stealing the most expensive horse in the business, even if he loved her.

'I was looking for you — thought you'd found another girl.' She waved a hand. 'Turns out I was right. So who is this beautiful lady?'

He snorted and grabbed the horse. 'Never you mind.'

Carson loved her tricks, and this one was probably at the top of her list. Just her presence was enough to put him off balance and stop him thinking in the careful way he needed to. She held his imagination hostage, and she knew it. He'd not been capable of even daydreaming about other women since he'd met her.

'You walked?'

She nodded and then turned to put the whip in the ute. The door was locked, so he threw her the keys. He put the tailgate down and led Retribution up: she was calm now, ears down, head dropped, a pet for a young girl.

In the ute, he asked Carson how she'd found him. He was

trying not to sound alarmed, because if Carson had found him, on foot, then someone else had to have told her—which meant that at least one other person knew, or she had been able to see the ute from some distant point, and in that case it was more than likely that someone else had noticed his vehicle.

'I followed you.'

'What?'

'I was coming to see you. Couldn't sleep. You pulled out of your entrance just as I was coming over the hill. You must have seen my lights?'

'No.'

'Well, don't get tushy. I didn't know you went out on little midnight shenanigans. I thought maybe you were giving Mrs S. a touch-up.'

'Who says I wasn't?'

'Most guys don't take a horse trailer to get their end in. Not even with Mrs S.'

She was playful, but he was reminding himself that the job was a long way from done. Sweetapple kicked the machine over, pulled the ute and trailer forward, then got out with a torch and checked to see if any tyre marks had been left.

When he got back in, she said, 'You're a bit of an expert at this, aren't you?' She swivelled in her seat and examined him.

'Nope. Just desperate.'

They bumped across the grass, staying off the paddock tracks until they got to the boundary gate. She moved to get out, and he stopped her: 'I'll get it.'

When they were through the gate and had pulled out onto the gravel, he checked the road for any lights, and then grabbed a tree branch he had in the back of the ute, went back to the gate, and swept the road with it.

Back in the driver's seat, she put a hand on his thigh, and said, 'Desperate? You look more like an old hand to me.' She squeezed him through his jeans, and he put his foot down.

A few hundred metres down the road, he saw her car parked in the reserve on the side of the road. He stopped and let her out, and said, 'See you tomorrow?'

'You don't want a hand?'

'No.'

'Then I'll come for late breakfast. You better have some food. Nice food.'

He waited for her car to start, waved, and left her behind.

Sweetapple drove past his yards and his little house, up the hill into the scrub to the simple yard he had made out of local timber that was screened by the box trees and their regrowth. He led Retribution down, let her go in the yard, and watched her kick, jump, and then roll in the bare dirt near the gate. She stood and shook every section of her skin, and looked around — alert, expectant, maybe even ready for adventure.

He checked that her water was still fresh, and then threw her a biscuit of lucerne hay off the back of the ute. She sniffed at but ignored the hay, more interested in smelling her surroundings and taking a trot around the new boundary. Sweetapple watched her, filled with simple wonder.

Someone witnessing this might have thought he was making sure she was okay, seeing that she wasn't confused or pining, or that she didn't go crazy in this new space and run madly into the fence. Horses did that sort of thing, but none of these risks was real for Retribution. He was just watching because he couldn't stop himself.

He dragged himself to the ute and rolled it away in the dark. Retribution would stay there for some weeks, till he was ready to move her to Bob's. It was a dumb sort of a deal, he guessed. Others would have insisted that the horse be moved as soon as possible: evidence gone. But the Stock Squad had no money and little support from the community, and Sweetapple wasn't a known thief; without a tip-off, their chances of catching him were very small. All he needed to do was make sure he got paid. Dealing with a multi-millionaire made him nervous. He was certain there were endless tricks that a man like Statham could pull, so Sweetapple wasn't going to try being clever. He was just going to make sure he got the rest of the money into his account, cleared, for goods supplied — as simple and as straightforward as he could keep it.

Once Retribution was out of his hands, whatever advantage he had would go with her. If Statham tricked him or double-crossed him, he would have no form of redress. All Sweetapple could come up with as possible retaliation was shooting him or burning his house down — stupid things, ridiculous things, things he would never do. So if it went wrong, he would simply lose out.

Sweetapple unhooked the trailer at the back of his house and thought about DNA. What if some cop turned up, took a dung sample, and got lucky? He got a dust pan, a plastic bag, and a torch from the shed, and swept out the back of the trailer. Then he hosed the whole thing down. He was keen to hit the sack, but he knew he wouldn't sleep if he kept imagining the police turning up at dawn, having the jump on him. He took the bag to the pit where he took animal carcasses, and emptied the contents there and buried them. Then he burnt the bag. By the time he got to bed, the promise of first light had the birds cackling.

He woke with a black dread, without knowing the reason for it. Then the night returned to him, and the label he had attached to himself: horse thief. The shame bent him double on the edge of the bed.

He had been stealing livestock for a while. Each time, he had been able to justify it to himself: he was taking from much bigger thieves than himself; it was only a few head from a wealthy owner; they had taken from him and all the other little people in the area, so it was only fair that he took back from them. Such excuses allowed him to put his stealing in a dark corner of his mind, where he wouldn't stumble over them. Much of the time, recognition of his own wrongdoing never surfaced. Occasionally, though, something—a memory, a phrase—would bring the truth of what he was doing unavoidably into his consciousness: he stole from people. It shocked and shook him, and forced him to go scrambling back to his excuses.

This time, the excuses didn't work. His slide into becoming a despised person was complete. If caught, he would probably go to jail; more importantly, he would be stained, in his own eyes and those of his community. They would never forget. If it were just a few steers, they might have forgiven him: times had been tough, and he'd made a mistake. Everyone made mistakes. But when you stole a $250,000 horse, there were no justifications. He was a criminal. He had deliberately done the wrong thing, and there was no avoiding that awful fact.

Still sitting on the edge of the bed, he forced himself to face up to the world he had created. There were serious bills he simply couldn't pay without the money he'd get from the Retribution deal. It was nothing sinister, just the normal stuff from utilities, banks, and the council. But if they weren't paid, they would come and take what was owed, which meant a forced sale. He had avoided them, promised, lied, fobbed them off, pretended, but that was over. He was out of time.

After having a shower, Sweetapple dressed, and tidied his room like the self-reliant boy he had always been.

It would be reasonable to ask: could he live with more self-hatred? He'd already survived with plenty of it. Eventually, it faded like everything else. You got used to being the person you hoped you wouldn't be. You adjusted the goalposts and moved on. It was only on those unexpected moments when you looked back at what you had intended to be that it really hurt.

Nevertheless there were bills to be paid. It was the necessity that dominated everything else, and he clung to it. In the future, when he had paid the debt, when his future was secure, he could make things right.

But as he fully woke, he realised there was another feeling creeping around the house, sitting in the cool behind the doors, hanging high in the corners, that he hadn't acknowledged yet: euphoria. It was lifting him and spreading out like a good spirit. Because, despite everything he knew and was suffering, Retribution was out there at his place. He couldn't contest the thrill of her proximity. He was like an adulterer who despised himself for being unfaithful but was enlivened by the infidelity's existence.

And Carson was coming around, probably very soon, which

made the day all right. He swept the kitchen, and distracted himself by thinking about making breakfast.

He got out eggs, bacon, tomatoes, cheese, herbs, and bread, and put them on the kitchen bench. As always, it made him think of his mother in her worn dressing-gown making scrambled eggs at the bench to serve at the rickety-legged table. He could hear her talking about all the work that needed to be done; her slim, brown fingers and fine forearms working skilfully, all the time, placing, moving, combining. That was before things went bad. Afterwards she did her best—he knew that—but it was impossible to do things right when you were trying to stay with a husband who was often on a bender, and the rest of the time was frightened by dangers that hid behind every tree.

If she were alive and knew what Sweetapple had done, she wouldn't talk to her son. She would probably disown him, even as she struggled to believe it. Maybe she would be secretly impressed by his resilience, like hers, and the fact that he was still here on the farm, still fighting. She wouldn't have accepted his solution, but he knew she always felt guilt about what they had lost and what they couldn't do to save his father.

Sweetapple knew you couldn't live by your mother's ideals. Perhaps if she had got help for his father earlier and got him back to being the man he'd been before the war, they might have earned some money and never been put in the situation where they had to sell their land—their best country—to wealthy neighbours after her death, just to survive. And now he was dealing with one of them. Statham had made his money destroying farmland, and now he lived among them with the air of someone who deserved every good thing that came to him.

10

Caroline wandered around her house, looking at it, picking things up and feeling its surfaces. It felt like someone else lived here and she had dropped in for a few weeks, maybe house-sitting. The kitchen, with its broad island and open timber space, was familiar but not personal. She opened cupboards like a guest looking for a glass or a mug. Maybe cleaners had moved everything around. The studies, his and hers, had bookshelves that reached the ceiling, full of books she didn't recognise. She pulled novels and non-fiction works out of their attractive line-up at random, but couldn't remember more than the title pages or the back-cover blurbs. She wondered if she should rearrange the whole house to patterns and a design she could remember. It felt like an awful lot of work. It would be easier to get used to what was already there. Reacquaint herself? Was that the sort of word people used? Acquaint would be the simplest first step.

But she had indeed lived in this house, on and off, for years. These were her things, her mementos, her family snaps: her photos of important politicians she had met on parliamentary study tours; the carpet and the curtains she had chosen; the cushions, the vases, the furniture; even a wooden bowl that a schoolboy from the electorate had made her. She was lost among it all now. The past was washing itself clean, and she was now merely a middle-aged woman with nothing before or after her. She sat on the couch and remembered friends, long since forsaken, who had sat here with her and Bob, and had laughed together at their own vanities and ambitions. And then she began to cry, wet-faced and heaving like someone who had lost a child or a family.

She took the ute, and drove away from the house and the big dam nearby, out across the paddocks, with Max in the back, leaning forward and panting excitedly next to her ear. She tried to remember where the different roads led and which gates connected to which paddocks. She had driven over the country enough times, but usually with Bob, and often with weeks or months between each trip. The truth was she didn't know the place well at all, even though she had used it as political capital for years: she had presented herself as a practical, no-nonsense country woman who knew firsthand the hardship of living on the land — not some party apparatchik with no experience of the real world.

Now she was tired of thinking about Bob, about what might have been, about how much she loved him, how she might chase him down, how it might really be just a temporary separation: a relentless sequence of thoughts that kept rolling around on a hamster wheel, only to come to the same dead-end conclusions.

Bob might have dominated her thoughts, but every morning there was so much for her to hate: so many people to rage against for their bastardry and betrayal; so many who expected everything and gave nothing. She had yelled so much at the windows and the halls, she wondered if they would soon begin to yell back. But in every fully voiced rage, she knew she was giving in to something she shouldn't. It was energy wasted, precious life thrown away, and soon she would have to get control of it. For the moment, there were too many demons to be expelled.

When Bob wasn't appearing in her nightmares, she dreamed, at night, about paddocks, soil, and green plants, and pictured herself in some sort of Second World War time frame, toiling with other women in a lush crop, reaping and threshing, and other things she knew nothing about. This came back to her at breakfast in pulses of emotion and half-coloured-in images, powerful and affecting. Since there was plenty to do, but nothing she cared to do, she decided to take the ute and look for what she had dreamed about. Caroline didn't know what she was looking for, but the sensations were still so strong she wondered if she wasn't experiencing some sort of premonition. Was a disaster about to hit her farm?

The local council had asked her to head a committee on youth crime, and the Department of Education was talking about a position that would oversee rural education. She had declined on both counts. She'd put them off, giving them some old chat about 'loose ends to tie up' and asking whether she could 'come back to them when I have things organised'. They had replied, 'Call us when you're ready,' because that's what you always said in that circumstance. They might as well have said, 'We'll keep your details on file so we can contact you if we need to,' or, 'Of course I voted for you.' It was a long time since naivety had protected her from that sort of disingenuousness.

As Caroline drove through groups of cows and calves and half-grown steers, she wondered whether they were ready for market, soon to be bred, or were being grown out. Around her, the grasses were unrecognised and the birds unnamed. There were so many acres of cattle country—crops, fallow, stubble, and pasture—and she knew nothing about any of it. It had always been her practice, when confronted by a void of knowledge, to fill it. It occurred to her suddenly that dealing with this void could be her way back.

All the farming women she had seen in the media were exemplars: hardworking, fearless, good-hearted, reasonable-minded, intelligent. They stood now as the perfect models for her reinvention. She would farm this place with her bare hands, learn everything she could, and become one of those resilient, windswept women. Her credibility would return with the soil under her fingernails, the sweat on her brow. Joey could teach her, little by little, and Sweetapple, too. She could do a farm-management course and one of those on-farm extensions, and maybe even attend a few field days. She would start by showing the people she was serious, not in it for the publicity. The possibilities were inspiring. She could already see herself giving orders, consulting with agronomists, getting her hands dirty, and surprising everyone.

Caroline sat up straight and looked seriously at the landscape. In the next paddock, a large tractor was dragging a contraption behind it, the dust whisking lightly. She had no idea what it was doing—planting or spraying—but she was suddenly desperate to know. Tomorrow started now.

She drove through the gate and out onto the soft, dark soil, where the wheat stubble lay grey and papery around her. When she caught up with the tractor, their young station hand, Lance, looked alarmed by her sudden appearance. He powered the machine down, and stepped out of the cab and lightly down the steps to her. His face held a presumption that there must be bad news coming for him to be pulled over like this by the wife of the owner, whom he never normally saw. It had to be too important for the two-way.

'Something wrong, Mrs Statham?' He was a short, well-muscled young man, his stubble uneven, and his hair long and curly.

'No. No, Lance. I just wanted to know what you were doing.'

He wasn't reassured. 'Doing?' He flapped his hands a little.

'I mean, are you planting or …?'

His face brightened, and his shoulders dropped as he let out a little breathy half-laugh. 'Crazy, isn't it?'

Caroline nodded unconvincingly.

'We don't normally run equipment over the country.' He wasn't sure if he was answering the right question. 'Joey thought the stubble was getting too thick to plant through, so I'm just running over it quickly to knock it over a bit, help it break down.'

He beamed at her as if it were the best job in the world. When she looked back at him, unable to mask her confusion, he smiled again and took a punt.

'They used to burn the stubble after harvest.'

'Yes.'

'They used to plough it up to kill the weeds and make the seedbed.'

'Yes.'

133

'Over the years, the plough turned into cultivators. Then they figured out it was better to keep the stubble in place to stop erosion, and that burning removed the stubble and a lot of good bugs in the soil. And all that driving up and back with big machinery compacted the soil and burnt a lot of diesel.'

He wiped a fringe of curled hair out of his face and licked at his lips. 'Somebody worked out that if you sprayed the country with chemical to kill the weeds and then just left it alone, the soil would hold more moisture, wouldn't wash away, and would gradually break up and soften of its own accord. So now we try to keep machinery off the country whenever we can — planting, harvesting and spray rigs, that's it.'

Caroline was tempted to say, 'I knew that', because she had known parts of it, but she guessed he wouldn't believe her anyway.

'Amazing, huh?'

She had to agree. 'It is.'

'Anything else I can help you with?'

'No. Thanks, Lance. I'll leave you to it.'

'Righto.' He leapt back up the steps to his cab, gave a little wave, and, when she was clear, powered away.

As Caroline got back into the ute, she wondered if Bob was across all that history. Did he understand the developments in farming, or was he an oblivious landlord like she was? The thought of her own ignorance made her determined to become knowledgeable with a hands-on understanding.

She drove back through the stubble, looking out over vast stretches of her own country and feeling the small beginnings of ownership. The creek that lined the edge of the paddock marked out the blue, bumpy background of the hills. Caroline had never noticed how beautiful the country was. If Bob wanted a divorce, she would fight hard for this country. She found her way back to the sheds and past the stables, thinking that, with the sun sinking, it was the time of day that Sweetapple usually turned up.

Indeed, he had the horses in the yard and was brushing them down, their chestnut coats glowing gold-red in the last light. It was obviously a task he had done many times before, and he radiated a calmness and contentment that she was immediately jealous of. She was paper-thin and insubstantial in comparison. His life held the kind of security and certainty that she longed for. He was not confused by people's opinions, nor swayed by how others thought he should act, and this was suddenly powerfully attractive to her. Caroline had the strange sense that closeness with him might allow some of his assuredness to rub off on her, and she conjured the mad idea of giving everything over to him in the hope of gaining something of his security in return. It terrified her. She had never felt like this; she had always been loudly, forcefully independent, never willing to be beholden to anyone, in even a small way. Her career in politics might have been sustained if she had been less damned independent and more willing to cultivate allies and accomplices — bloody hell, friends even.

But this new sensation was so powerful, her need so strong and shameful, that all she could do was drive past him, smile, and wave. He didn't look up; just raised a hand in the air. A man in his place. She might have been anyone.

At the house, she slowed the vehicle and took a breath deep into her lungs. The dam rose up in the distance like an invitation. If she planted her foot on the accelerator, she could be in that dam and gone within minutes. But the fear quickly subsided, and the need for the man was gone. She quietly ridiculed herself. It had been an impulsive nothingness. She no more found Sweetapple attractive than Lance on the tractor. It was a reaction to being home alone with nothing to do. A withdrawal symptom maybe—didn't they joke about relevance deprivation? She parked and walked to the house, trying to think of ways she might change the garden, how she might re-enter the real world.

In the kitchen, at the fridge, a drink seemed a solace, but it also felt dangerous, as if it might reawaken the silliness. Instead she paced the house, sat at her computer, walked the lawn, cut some flowers, and dug over the garden until it was truly dark. She could really hate Bob at a time like this. And now she could hate almost anyone. She had never felt helpless like this; never relied on other people to handle difficult things for her; never sat back and hoped for good fortune. And now she was some sort of also-ran in a big house on a big farm she knew nothing about. She slumped on the couch, letting the evening news broadcast examples of the awfulness of human beings, and then the politics she couldn't stand to listen to.

After allowing a few days to go by to let her emotions dull, she rang Sweetapple and asked if he would give her some riding lessons. Caroline insisted to herself that this was no more than the first step towards becoming a real farmer, and that there was so much general knowledge about the property that she could pick up from being around him. Her moment of attraction to him had been no more than that: misplaced desire from a woman who was a little lost and lonely. A human being who had suffered the pressures and disappointments she had could be allowed some turbulent emotions. It was to be expected, and she was certainly capable of rising above it.

Sweetapple sounded like he might have been pleased with the idea of teaching her. No doubt it would be easy money for him. He offered to start her off on one of her own geldings the very next day.

In the morning, she scolded herself for worrying about the outfit she was to wear to the lesson, but still she worried. Sending the right message was important, for both of them.

The horses were already saddled when she reached the stables. As his way of saying 'Hello', he led a saddled horse out to her as she stepped out of her car. He suggested they go for a casual ride in the paddock to give him the chance to see how she handled the horse and what he might be able to teach her.

Caroline mounted, desperate not to be ungainly, and sat stiff-backed on the calm gelding, whose name, she recalled, was Felix. As they walked out into the long-grass paddock, she was anxious about riding in front of him and keen to remember her pony club rules, but he hardly looked at her, simply interspersing his conversation with occasional comments like, 'Keep your heels down … Ease the pressure off the mouth … Sit down on your bum bones.'

They rode and talked, and when it was finished, Caroline was pleased with herself. There had been no return of her manic desire, and she had enjoyed his company. Maybe he had even enjoyed her company, too. They organised to meet every week when possible. She hoped there would be a day when she could do without it.

Carson read every local newspaper, scanned local radio stations, and trawled the internet. She found one radio interview with one of the owners of Retribution, and one article in the local *Gazette*. Sweetapple wasn't interested, or so he said. The stories were matter-of-fact, and not of the shock-horror kind she'd hoped for.

'Only two pieces in all of the news. The mare can't be that special. I thought you reckoned it was worth hundreds of thousands?'

'It is.'

'Then why wasn't it front-page news?'

'I dunno. Probably because it's just a horse and not a racehorse, and you've only got the owner's word for what she's worth.'

'So what's all the fuss about? Why's Bob going to so much trouble?'

'He wanted the mare and he couldn't buy her, so he had her stolen. Simple as that. The sort of guy he is.'

'Bit disappointing. Thought you might have been "Wanted" or something.' It was only half untrue.

'The cops turned up, if that makes you happy.'

'Here? You didn't tell me that.'

'Just plain-clothes local blokes. "Checking everyone who owns horses," they said. Had a bit of walk round, looked through the sheds and the yards, got on their hands and knees in the horse float.'

'You should have told me!'

'No big deal. They were nice enough about the whole thing. "Got no leads," they said.'

Sweetapple had been quietly terrified when he saw the police van arrive. He knew he was prepared, but there were too many other things he couldn't know, like what Bob was really up to and who he had told.

'You know what their problem is?' Carson asked with sudden confidence.

'No.'

'They can't establish motive. On those TV programs, they've always got to establish a motive, otherwise they have to go for some sort of mental problem. What's the motive for stealing a horse that you can only use in secret?'

'Maybe he's going to sell embryos or eggs to the sheikhs in the Middle East.'

'They have cutting horses?'

'Doesn't matter. A mare like Retribution, her genetics are good enough for any working-horse sport. Perfect for chasing falcons round the desert.'

'Do you think they'll be back—the cops?'

'Maybe. But they went on like it wasn't an important case for them. Just going through the motions. A day-out sort of thing. I suppose they'll only be back if they find something or hear something. Did the owner post a reward anywhere?'

'He's got a Facebook page. There are a few comments of support, and phone numbers for people to contact if anyone has any info. Were you thinking of putting in for it?'

'It would want to be a bloody lot.'

'How much is Bob giving you?'

'Now, that is a trade secret.'

Luke put a six-pack of beer and two ham sandwiches in a cool bag, and walked out onto the road out of town. He stayed as far from the edge of the road as he could, in case someone he knew or some do-gooder came past and offered him a lift. He didn't want a lift and he didn't want to chat to anyone. He walked along the fence on the other side of the table drain, the thick grass making walking uneven but not unpleasurable.

When the last houses were out of sight, he climbed the fence into the hill paddock that rose above the railway line. The paddock was well covered with trees, but he knew there was a place where he could sit and not be seen while still being able to watch the passing trains. He walked up the hill and along the contour until he found his spot next to a huge white box tree where a fallen log provided a seat and the tree's suckers around him provided a perfect 'hide'. He sat, rested his bag, opened a beer, and looked down over the track. Where else would he rather be?

In no time, he could see the beginning of the silver-jointed spine of a coal train in the distance. He felt a small thrill at witnessing it. The train was long, symmetrical, beautifully formed. It didn't appear to be moving fast, but it was soon right in front of him, the two yellow engines back-to-back at the front looking like dirty, much-loved toys, in no way capable of pulling such massive tonnage. In minutes, the great snake of rolling stock was past him, the graffitied carriages and final engine moving on to the next town and the next step on its way to the coast. It was something between a piece in a longed-for train set and the real, magnificent thing. At least that's the way he thought about it: like an excited boy, something he felt he'd never been. One of the last carriages had the words 'Fuck Zill Coal' spray-painted across its side, and the thought of someone going to that trouble to register their protest gave him a bump of pleasure. Fuck Zill Coal indeed.

He watched the train go, opened another beer, and unwrapped a sandwich. His pleasure at seeing passing trains — the look of them, their power, their engineering — was a mystery to him that he wasn't interested in probing. He didn't even know much about them. He knew about the sleepers that the continuous rail track rested on, and the ballast that supported them both, but he wasn't a spec head or a trainspotter. It was enough just to enjoy a beer and appreciate them.

There were no cars on the road below him that ran parallel to the train track. Luke could hear birds in the branches and a cow calling in the distance. He felt at ease in a way that he never did anywhere else. Nothing could touch him here: Frank, his work, the protest site, what he felt about Carson, what he felt about himself and his life. And he knew that the moment he was bored with himself and introspection, another train would come along to distract him.

Then he began to think about the words written on that carriage. He had never made the association between the trains he loved and the company that had ripped him off. Trains were kept in a special untouchable place in his brain. Just thinking about them could transport him to that place. It was natural that he hadn't allowed the thought of Zill, and what they had done, to tamper with that. But now he couldn't stop it. Everything Zill did was dependent on these trains, and Luke had been a cheerleader for them. Luke was misty-eyed about an arm of a multinational. He was romanticising a machine that supported the existence of people like Peter — as if he was the sort of person who would like something, support something, in spite of the damage to himself. He was not that person, and now Zill had ruined a precious thing. He finished his beer, put the empty cans in his bag, and stood up. It was childish to be upset about it, but he couldn't watch anymore. His peace of mind was gone, and now he was just standing on his own in the scrub.

11

'It's the rich bitch.' Carson said it under her breath and nodded towards a small silver European car that was pulling into Sweetapple's drive. Luke looked at her half-questioningly, not really interested. He now knew there were any number of people who Carson might classify as a 'bitch', most of them unable to match the she-devilishness that the epithet might suggest.

Luke had made it a habit to drop into Ponsford's every few days and shoot the breeze with Carson. He didn't stay long, and he never bought anything, but he asked questions about products that suggested one day he might.

Luke had met Sweetapple a couple of times as a result of Carson's organising: once at the Bowlo and once in the pub. Sweetapple seemed okay, a tough guy in the rodeo mould, and kind of preoccupied. He didn't know what Sweetapple might be preoccupied with, and whether or not it was an act, but you knew that in his presence, other guys would want to put their shoulders back and talk about the risks they'd taken and the daring things they might yet do. Luke didn't share the need to 'man up' in Sweetapple's presence. Sweetapple didn't pay a lot of attention to Luke anyway, which suited Luke. It appeared that Carson had decided that she wanted Luke around, and since he usually didn't have anything else to do in his free time, he didn't resist.

Today the three of them were having a barbecue on the side lawn at Sweetapple's place, drinking cans of beer and cider, and cooking burgers, when Caroline appeared. Sweetapple stood as she got out of the car. 'Shit,' he said under his breath. 'Forgot the bloody riding lesson.'

Luke saw a slim, middle-aged woman with short blonde hair, kind of pleasant-looking, in faded jeans and a bright-green-check buckjumper shirt, getting out of the car. There was something of the matter-of-fact about her as she walked across the uneven ground, smiling happily and announcing, 'Hello,' as confidently as someone who had been invited. He thought he could like her.

Sweetapple sauntered towards Caroline, and Luke heard him apologise with a note in his voice he didn't recognise. It was more than respect. Fondness. This wasn't any employer, any old Frank, which would help explain the 'rich bitch' appellation. When Sweetapple spoke to Carson, it was direct, flat, controlled, but with the sense that the control was only a thin lid over a fat bomb.

'That's okay. I thought I must have got the wrong day, and you weren't answering your phone.'

Sweetapple tapped at a pocket where a phone might have been. 'Sorry. Turned off. We're just kicking back.' He waved an arm at Carson and Luke.

Caroline Statham turning up oh-so-casually while Retribution was in Sweetapple's back paddock made Carson uncomfortable. This woman and her husband now had something over Sweetapple, and here she was pressing the point in a calm, fake-friendly way. Couldn't she have texted or phoned instead of intruding? It was obvious she just wanted to be near Sweetapple and had grabbed at the missed riding lesson as the best excuse. Now she was running the 'sorry to bother you' line, making out she was without an agenda or any guile. Bob Statham was her perfect match.

'Don't let me stop you.' Now it was all a big mistake that could be easily forgotten. 'I just wanted to confirm, that's all. Maybe we could try next week?'

'Sure. But I can do tomorrow if you want.'

'Next week will be fine. Go back to your kicking back. Please.' Caroline would have liked to have lessons twice a day, but she had to resist being pathetic.

'You want to have a drink or something?'

'That's very kind, but I'll keep moving. You don't need me barging in on your days off.' She turned, knowing her judgement was right, but pleased with his invitation.

But Sweetapple had also turned. 'Come on. A beer won't hurt you.'

Accepting the invitation would be an ignorant thing to do. The girl looked hostile; the other guy indifferent. Caroline was invading their territory, and she knew it, but she couldn't stop herself. The chance to find out more about Sweetapple and the girl was something she couldn't make herself forfeit.

'Okay. Just one, and then I'd better get going.' She followed him to the table. No one got up.

'You probably know Carson?'

'Don't think so. Hello.'

'And Luke.'

The young man was lean and long, with a disconnected air about him, but he seemed friendly. The girl simply smouldered, in every sense: with anger, resentment, and white-hot with sex.

Carson looked uncomfortable, but Luke thought Caroline might add something to their three-way. He liked being around Carson, and thought Sweetapple interesting, but he was always aware that he was number three on their territory.

'Hey. You're the politician?' He only knew she had been because he'd heard Sweetapple and Carson say something about it.

'Was.' She said it almost happily. 'I'm a free woman now.'

'You got booted out?'

'Booted?' She thought about this. 'Lost my seat in the last election.'

The other three almost looked sorry for her, even though they weren't certain what the phrase meant.

'So I've decided to be a farmer. The riding lessons are part of the next big plan.'

Luke thought she made it sound half-funny, like farming was one of many costumes she had available to choose from.

Carson bit a lip. She wanted to make the obvious crack about 'riding lessons', but knew it would really annoy Sweetapple, and for some reason she didn't want to piss him off that much today. It felt like it might be a win for Caroline. And maybe she didn't want any attention from Caroline when the horse that Sweetapple seemed so infatuated with was stomping in the wings.

Caroline sat as Sweetapple passed her a beer.

'You want a glass?'

'No, thanks. This is fine.' She sipped awkwardly from the stubbie as if she'd never held a bottle before. No one said anything. Not even the birds.

'What's it like being a politician?' Luke was genuinely interested, and since no one else was bothering, he thought he'd take the opportunity to ask.

'Oh, demanding, exhausting, exhilarating, frustrating, disappointing.' Caroline was struggling to stop herself responding like she would in a media interview. 'Some days you really can make a difference, and you feel like you're doing something important and worthwhile, and other times you're just sitting in pointless committees spouting nonsense.'

'They're always talking bloody bullshit when I hear them,' Carson said.

Caroline took it for the poorly disguised barb that it was. She wanted to tell the girl about the importance of politics and giving a damn, and the significance of representative democracy, but she knew how seriously misplaced that would be. She didn't even know if she believed in it herself anymore.

'What do you guys do?'

'I'm a fencer, and she runs the rural-supplies store in town.'

Carson gave Luke a look that said she didn't need anyone to talk for her.

'Ponsford's?' Caroline was used to people forming a bad impression of her before she'd even met them. She was never ready to leave that impression unchallenged.

Carson nodded.

'They all right to work for? Treat you okay?'

'I guess. Pay isn't great, but the work isn't hard.'

'Good place to meet old dudes, apparently.'

'Shut up, Luke.' She pushed him hard, and he laughed.

Caroline looked away. Sweetapple had not responded through any of it. Maybe this girl slept with older men, but it was also a good bet that she was hassled by men, too. Caroline thought a simple question might be a way to reach her. 'You get harassed?'

Carson's scowl didn't dissolve, but Caroline saw, just for the moment, a lightness, a glimpse of surprised appreciation. The girl hadn't grasped that whatever it was that bothered her wasn't unique to her. You could see she was thinking about shrugging it off, pretending nothing had ever happened. But then she said, 'Yeah. I've had my bum squeezed by a creepy older guy. You'd know —' and stopped herself.

It was a moment of confession, of openness, that was immediately erased by a nasty laugh, making Caroline's question a ridiculous piece of softness from a silly older woman. Luke and Sweetapple laughed, too.

Caroline joined them half-heartedly and said, 'Hope you reported it.'

'Course not.' Carson looked away, barely covering her disgust. It was a suggestion from someone who had power and rights but no understanding. Someone who had no clue that her husband was an abuser. 'He just squeezed my arse. No big deal. Probably part of the contract on his herbicide purchase.'

Now Luke was laughing too hard, too loudly, and Carson hated him for it.

'You should report it, you know.' Caroline had considered keeping her advice to herself. She understood Carson would not accept it from her, but her convictions had compelled her to speak up.

'Maybe someone like you can, but not someone like me. Even if they believe me, they're not going to do anything about it — they'd say a few choice words, and then blow it off.'

Caroline took a deep, buffering breath. She was sitting with people who were the living embodiment of everything she had hated and been defeated by: apathetic and self-serving. She had to stop herself from slapping the girl.

'It's not true. There are laws, workplace obligations, and people who will listen to your complaint.'

'Of course there are. These guys.' She gestured to Sweetapple and Luke, and they laughed again, Sweetapple guarded in contrast to Luke's loud, thigh-slapping response.

Caroline swallowed her failure and smiled at Carson, as sweetly as she could manage. 'So how do things ever change?'

'Things never change for us. Everyone knows that. They change for people with money and power — people with a voice. That's not us. That's you. But you get to say nice, hopeful things, so you feel better about it all.'

'Jesus, Carson,' Luke said. 'Caroline just came over to have a beer with us. There's no need to get stuck into her.'

'That's okay. She's right. But I spent a lot of time trying to do more than just say nice things. I spent years and all my energy trying to make things better. If you're not even prepared to report abuse, then you can't expect anyone else to do anything.' Caroline was in control of herself, placing the words as deftly as possible.

'Oh, fuck off with your smart words. I report it, and they get rid of me. I'm out of a job, and nothing has changed.' Carson stood with her fingers squeezing the drink in her hand. The temptation to tell was almost too much. 'Brilliant piece of thinking.' She walked to the house and slammed the door.

'Sorry I've wrecked your barbecue. I'll go. Thanks for the beer.'

Caroline got out of her chair, leaving her drink behind, as Sweetapple shrugged and said, 'We like a bit of argument over a few drinks, don't we, Luke?'

Luke nodded, surprised by the collusion, but Caroline was already moving to her car.

When she was gone, Luke sat back and said, 'It's true, isn't it? The wealthy and the powerful just get more, while we stay the same or slip backwards.'

Sweetapple nodded without saying anything.

'The gap just gets wider, according to the media anyway, but there's always nice people on the news saying how it needs to be changed, and it's wrong, and something needs to be done. Carson's got a point.'

'Yep. But it's not Caroline's fault.'

'Really? You got a soft spot for the old bird? I mean, it was her husband who put it on Carson, wasn't it?'

Sweetapple looked away. He didn't like debates or silly word games, and wouldn't be enticed into verbal combat. Luke guessed he was like this, but liked to try him out.

'She's certainly got one for you.' Luke wondered if the slight turn in Sweetapple's neck suggested he hadn't realised this and was just a bit pleased, in the way that it takes someone to say it out loud for you to realise something you already knew. 'She's okay, I guess, if you're into older women.'

Instead of telling him to shut up, which Luke had expected, Sweetapple took a swig of his beer and sat back in his seat. 'You know about these things?'

'I've known a few older women, if that's what you mean.'

'I bet you have. I bet you have.' Sweetapple pulled his hat a little lower over his eyes. 'Caroline's a nice lady who's been smacked by circumstances, despite trying to do her best. Makes her more like us than them, as far as I'm concerned.'

'Is that how you see yourself? Smacked by circumstances?'

'Don't you?'

'Nah. I've always smacked back at circumstances whenever they smacked me. I'm a strike-back dude.'

'Strike-back dude, it's your turn to check the burgers.'

Luke stood lazily and stretched his back. 'What about you? You ever feel like getting back at any of the bastards?'

'Nope. And I wouldn't tell you if I did.'

Luke pushed a spatula at the spitting burger patties. 'See, now that's where you're making a mistake. Friendships are made by sharing personal stuff, thoughts, ambitions, experiences. I-give-a-bit, you-give-a-bit sort of thing.'

'Who says I want friendship?'

'No one. I was just saying — helping you out with life's little complexities.'

Sweetapple laughed under his hat, and they were both silent. Then Sweetapple took the hat off his face and sat twirling it in his hands. 'I've got one secret I'll share with you.'

Luke nodded at the barbecue, ready for the joke or the set-up.

'I've got a bomb.'

'Uh-huh.'

'I really do. Came across this girl in a car accident.'

'A girl in a car accident with a bomb?' Luke made the spatula carve a circle in the air. 'All right. Hit me with the punchline.'

'No joke. No punchline. I was coming home late, middle of nowhere, and these two kids had crashed their ute into a tree. Going like a rocket. Lucky to be alive. I got them out, and she had a bomb in a bag.'

'That's a pretty far-out story. I don't think I'm going to go for it.' Luke sat back down, happy to let Sweetapple's story drift off and be forgotten. And then he remembered Ginko's words and his suspicions about Anna, and realised that Sweetapple had painted a possible scenario. 'Are you sure it's a bomb?'

'No, but it looks like one, with all the set-up.'

'Did she tell you why she had a bomb. How?' Luke was trying not to sound too eager to know.

'No. She didn't tell me anything. But it was the middle of the night. They'd just got out of this terrible smash-up. I was more focused on making sure they were all right, and then she pulls out this case. It was surreal. I couldn't make a proper decision about it.'

'But you ended up with it?'

Sweetapple shrugged. 'She said she was in desperate trouble and she needed me to help her.'

'And …'

'And I said I would.'

'You said you would what?' Carson kicked her feet forwards as she stepped across the lawn to them, putting an end to Luke's questions.

Sweetapple was about to say, 'Nothing,' but Luke was too quick: 'Said he would strike back against the bastards, all of them. Strike back at people like Bob Statham like a fucken Robin Hood, to defend the poor and the downtrodden.'

'Yeah, right. And give us the money?'

'He didn't mention the money.'

It was after more riding lessons and enough time had passed for the barbecue disagreement to fade away when Sweetapple said, 'Come with me. I want to show you something special.'

Caroline got into the ute with him, intrigued and a little flattered. He said nothing else as they drove up through the scrub behind his house, past a set of cattle yards and up a steepening rocky track. Eventually, they bumped up onto a flat, grassy area, lightly treed with a small set of yards and neat new paddocks. There were cattle in the distance, shiny and smooth-skinned. In the largest yard, a wild-looking horse paced back and forth, tail out and up in alarm, round hindquarters flashing its contours.

Sweetapple pulled the ute in alongside the yard and grinned in a way she had never seen before. It was the open, easy grin of someone who cared nothing for the past or the future, only this moment: an unreserved display of pleasure that didn't belong to Sweetapple.

The horse snorted and trotted, high-stepping away from them, back across the yard, ears sharp, head proud, mane flowing. Something had upset her, and she was a fierce sight. Her body arched this way and back, each step so lightly sprung you knew she didn't need the earth's support. Caroline was in sudden awe, thinking of mythical beasts like Pegasus and unicorns, and feeling a strange, resonating arousal.

She shuffled on her seat, trying to move away from the feelings the horse had somehow fired inside her. Sweetapple grabbed a rope and got out, his eyes on the horse only. Caroline cautiously followed him to the rail as he said, 'Impressive, huh? Missy.'

Caroline kept her feet flat, legs locked, hoping the bones would keep her flesh in place and not betray her. But Sweetapple saved her by moving to the latched gate, opening it, and stepping into the yard. Caroline nearly screamed for him to stop but caught herself, the risk of seeming ridiculous increasing every moment.

He stood in the yard watching the mare, smiling, as she stayed as far away from him as she could. Then he talked to her softly, firmly, and Caroline thought for the briefest moment he was talking to her.

'Girl. Easy. There are bad things out there? Of course there are.' He kept talking, waiting, watching. Eventually, the mare turned, examined him, and then stepped confidently towards him. He held out a hand and she nuzzled him. Caroline felt something. What? Jealousy? Sweetapple moved alongside the mare, and rubbed a hand up and down her softening neck. She kicked at the air and stamped her feet hard on the ground, but slowly gave in, loosened, calmed. He looped the rope, put it over her nose, and set the lead back at her withers.

Caroline could feel the beast in her blood. She wanted to say, 'Call me Missy,' knowing how melodramatically insane it would sound, but instead whispered involuntarily to herself, over and over: 'I am Missy, Missy, Missy.'

Sweetapple, half-hearing, nodded his head, beamed, and said, 'Yep. That's what I call her,' his response no more linked to the regular world than hers. 'Hop on.' He said it as he turned to look at her. Perhaps he was teasing, but it was possibly the most terrifying thing Caroline had ever heard.

'Me?'

'You. I'll hold her. She's a darling. Go on. You just have to know what it's like.'

'I think I'll wait till there's a saddle.' A small giggle.

'No.'

Now terror piggy-backed in on everything that had gone before. Caroline let herself into the yard, telling herself that this was no greater challenge than the many others she had faced and survived.

Sweetapple guided her, and put the rope in her left hand and placed it on the withers of this prancing firebomb. Then he bent and tapped her on the calf.

'I'll give you a boost.'

Caroline lifted her left foot, and he got two hands underneath it and hefted her upwards. She swung her right leg over and sat down hard, as she knew she should. The mare's back was flat and smooth underneath her.

Sweetapple was watching, holding the rope, and Caroline knew that if she couldn't appreciate this gift she would never appreciate anything, and that was how Sweetapple would always see her: a woman dull to the things that really mattered. Her heart banged for his acknowledgement as the sweat trickled behind her ears, her blood booming, expanding as though there was way too much for such a small body. She let out a small, pathetic, 'Ah,' and then held with her legs and sat straight before he could offer her the way out she knew was coming. It didn't come, and she didn't ask for it. Instead, he said, 'Ride her. Go on. It's a tiny yard. She can't go anywhere. You can handle it. She's not going to buck or anything.'

He let go of the rope, and again she wanted to scream out, but she held on. She squeezed the mare forward and the mare responded, carefully, softly, and Caroline felt her fear ebbing. The mare walked as if she was in a hack class, confident of what had been asked of her.

'Canter.'

'No.'

But she pushed the mare along anyway, and the horse broke into a slow, smooth lope, suitable for ferrying a child. Caroline rode round the yard more relaxed and more confident with every stride as he witnessed her progression.

And then it was over, and she stopped close to Sweetapple and slid down the mare's withers onto him. He grabbed at her, body to body, and rested her on the ground, oblivious to the woman, watching the mare at all times. She stood back, wrung out and shaking, her shirt wet, her energy gone, knowing she was the odd one out, but triumphant nevertheless.

'Who is she?'

'Just a horse on loan, I'm afraid. A brilliant horse on loan.'

It was Bob on the phone from Singapore, matter-of-fact, not keen to yarn, asking if 'the product' could be delivered in the next week.

Sweetapple had been expecting the call, or at least expecting Bob to turn up at the stables to talk about the delivery arrangements. In the past weeks, Sweetapple had seen a lot of Caroline, but there had been no sign of Bob. He didn't mention any of his dealings with Bob to Caroline, and she, in turn, made no mention of Bob.

Sweetapple had been trying to think of reasons he couldn't deliver the mare, but every excuse felt weak: he needed more time to calm her down; he was worried about being spotted; or he thought someone was watching his place. So now all he could say was, 'I'm pretty flat out at the moment. Might have to be next week.'

Bob's response suggested that he wasn't happy with any stalling and wanted the horse now, but he would accept a few days' delay for Sweetapple to get organised. 'I'm not going to be around for a while, so make sure young Lance knows you're coming.'

'Not Joey?'

'Just Lance. Joey's taken some leave.'

'I can look after the mare if you're not going to be about. No worries to me. Horses aren't really Lance's thing.'

'I need her at my place. ASAP.'

This wasn't the friendly, easygoing Bob who would come down to the stables for a yarn. This was another version. Sweetapple wondered how any of it made sense. Why the urgency for the mare, when Bob wasn't even going to be around?

'So let me know when you're ready.'

Sweetapple put the phone down, thinking about the handover day he now dreaded. To have Retribution taken was the worst thing that could happen, and he knew now he would play for time until Bob called again, and probably again, until Bob's demands and threats got serious. Sweetapple pushed his way out the door into the clear night. It was moonless, but the stars were bright and overwhelming in their numbers, assuring him that the only things that mattered were the things he felt right now. Everything else was fantasy and delusion.

If he stalled Bob too long, the second half of the payment would disappear, but Sweetapple was beginning to think that keeping Retribution for a little longer was worth forgoing whatever money was owing to him. The money was losing its meaning.

Bob might threaten to tell the cops that Sweetapple had stolen Retribution and that he had form for stealing stock. But that would be a risky strategy for Bob, because he would lose Retribution and could expect significant scrutiny himself. Maybe that sort of risk didn't bother a high-stakes player like Bob. He was probably a master of brinkmanship. At least Sweetapple could guarantee himself a couple more weeks with Retribution.

Inside, the phone rang, and when Sweetapple got to it he heard Bob's voice again, this time smoother and cooler. 'I know you really like this horse. And you're worried about the stealing. The thing is, she's not actually stolen.' He took a breath, and Sweetapple wasn't sure if this was the sound of someone concocting a lie or making a confession.

'I'm a part-owner. Not a significant part, but a part nevertheless. I set up this really good deal for the mare's eggs, but none of the other piss-weak bastards wanted a part of it. Except for one. One other guy has come in on it with me. We thought we'd just go ahead with the deal before the buyers change their mind. Nobody gets hurt, no harm done. I just need her on the farm for a little while.'

Could Sweetapple believe anything that Bob was saying? He'd probably made it up to keep things calm.

'For a little while? What then?'

'So it's not the big deal you think it is. Don't go AWOL on me, okay? No games, just deliver the animal.'

'Am I supposed to take her back where she came from? You

never said anything about that.'

'Let me worry about that. I expect we'll come clean with the other partners when it's time.'

Sweetapple put down the phone, unsure whether he felt relieved or unnerved.

In the morning, he saddled her and took her out. Together they had covered every part of his place away from the road, so they rode it again: through the slope thick with mature trees and shiny bush, up under the cliff face, then around through the dogwood and the rock slides onto the top of the ridge and back down through the rolling grass country to her yard. It was good just to be with her. She was fresh this morning, her nostrils flaring at every new turn, her ears sharp. He knew she enjoyed it, out of her paddock smelling refreshed smells, watching odd shapes and hearing new sounds. He jumped her over logs, and let her flatten out when they galloped the clear stretches.

As he walked her through the steep country and let her have her head so she could place her feet, he began to think that perhaps he should disappear with her. He could be packed up and gone tonight, and if Bob was away for a while it would take him weeks to find out. Sweetapple could be interstate before Bob worked it out. It was a fine plan, except that Sweetapple had nowhere to go and definitely nowhere to hide a horse and trailer. The alarm would go out, and sooner or later someone would notice him. It would increase his risk, and then he would be caught and go to jail, and the mare would be no more his than it was now.

Retribution found their way onto the flat area above the cliff. Sweetapple could see down across the plain, out along the undulating country to his east. The Stathams' was over the nearest ridge and ran down onto the cropping country as far as you wanted to look. There wasn't much to like about Bob, but Sweetapple had grown to feel something for Caroline. She was a formidable woman, but she listened, and that surprised him. She had really appreciated what he felt about Retribution. She understood. He would have liked to have her as a friend, but that wasn't ever going to be possible.

At the yard, he washed Retribution down and let her go. She rolled vigorously in the dirt, all the way over like a good horse was supposed to, and then got up and pranced away as if it were the first minutes of the new day. Suddenly, a new idea struck him: he should deliver Retribution and then steal her back. He could put another mare in her place. If he could find a mare with roughly the same markings as Retribution, it could work out.

Later, he shared the idea with Carson and Luke over pizza in the town's one-room pizza shop.

'You're crazy over this mare, aren't you?' Carson was always engaged by the possibility of risk and what she thought might be an adventure.

Luke pulled a piece of pizza away and rested it on his plate, too hot for his mouth.

'But are you really going to be able to trick him with a substitute? I don't know anything about horses, but there must be plenty of photos and stuff of a horse worth that sort of money. And what about a brand? Do they brand horses?'

They had become a sort of a team, the three of them. Sweetapple never went to anyone else's place, but he would meet up with them for a meal in town, or a couple of beers. Carson liked to have Luke around, finding him 'interesting' and 'fun', and Sweetapple didn't mind. Luke always had something original to say.

'The brand's not very clear, which is lucky. It'll take a good match to fool Bob, but for the time being, Lance won't know. She'll be just another horse on the place to him.'

Carson watched him, unnerved and excited by his certainty. He was fighting on the side of good, and wouldn't be persuaded that he wasn't. This horse had some sort of magical hold on him.

'It's kind of a cool idea, but you'd better think it through. Unless it's a perfect match, even Lance is going to be able to tell. If he's checking the horse every week, he'd be pretty simple not to notice the difference.'

'He's not going to check her every week. I'll be the one looking after her.'

'Bloody hell, Sweetapple. You're looking after her? Are you a fucking idiot? You steal the horse, take her to your place, then deliver her and look after her at his place. How are you going to plead innocent if someone finds out? No one is going to believe that a horseman like you had no idea he was looking after a $250,000 missing horse. If the shit hits the fan, Bob's going to claim it's all your doing—nothing to do with him. He's been out of the country the whole time, and he can prove it.'

The table was quiet. Sweetapple looked at his drink and accepted, silently, that she was right. He had known that before she said it. Once delivered, he would not be able to look after Retribution. He would have to let her go, to pretend she didn't exist.

'Why don't you just put in a substitute in the first place? Never supply the real thing. Hang on to Retribution yourself.'

Luke sounded like he'd found an interesting game that he'd like to play.

'Because I don't know when Bob's going to be home. And I need time to find a match for Retribution that Bob won't pick up on.'

'When are you supposed to deliver her?' Carson was watching him, looking for evidence that he might want to change his mind.

'Next week. But I'm putting him off. I'll stretch it to a few weeks.'

'Do you think you can find a horse that can fool him?'

'She's a chestnut mare with a big butt. I feel like it can't be too hard.'

12

On a night that Sweetapple couldn't make it for Chinese in town because he was away looking at horses, Carson insisted to Luke that they go anyway. He met her at the restaurant. She was sitting, studying her phone, drinking green tea.

'I ordered fried rice, spring rolls, Mongolian lamb, and crispy-skin chicken. Hope that's all right.'

He shrugged and sat. 'What's going on?'

'Nothing. You?'

'Frank's being a prick, as per usual.'

Frank's business had contracted to the point where he needed to be onsite most days, and it was making him loudly unhappy and nitpickingly frugal. His ranting about the speed they worked at and his insistence that he would dock pay for targets not met (targets that were never communicated) was niggling at Luke like a persistent jabbing in the ribs. He had begun to feel an old anger rising, but had done his best to stay cool.

'Anything positive to report?' Carson knew it was too easy

to fall into the trap of moaning about your life every night, especially when there was group support. And there was plenty to moan about.

'Not really. But I can't stay long tonight. Got stuff I've got to do.'

'What stuff?'

The food arrived all at once.

'It's personal.'

Carson piled her plate. 'Personal? Phone calls?'

'No.'

'Well, then, it can't be personal, can it? You only know me and Sweetapple, and the guys you work with. There's no one to do "personal" with.'

'You're wrong.'

'Must be sex, then. Ooo-ee. The man's got some action.'

Luke laughed out loud, with no suggestion that he'd been caught out. He started to say something like, 'I wish …' but stopped himself and played with the food on his plate.

Carson said on impulse, 'Take me along.' She wasn't sure why, but it was clear that whatever he was doing was probably as wild as what he'd been doing when she first saw him.

He ignored her and focused on his meal.

'I know you'll be doing something crazy. Take me with you.'

'It's not the sort of thing where you take someone along.'

'I bet it can be.'

'It could get you into trouble. More trouble than even you want. I don't want the blame for that.'

Carson gave the waitress a wave and asked, 'Can we get some of this in a bag to take away?'

The waitress reappeared with containers and a plastic bag.

Carson began filling them.

'I think I should come with you. I'm old enough to take responsibility for myself, but I reckon you need someone looking out for you.'

'No.'

'You won't be able to stop me. It'll just turn into a scene. I bet you don't want a scene. Not tonight anyway.'

He had a restlessness that told her he was going to do something really out there.

'I need something, Luke—like what you're going to do. I know it's bad.'

'It's not cross-dressing. Don't blame me if it's not all you hope for. It's just a bit of good old get-back.'

Luke stood up and walked over to the cash register, paid, and then left with Carson following, swinging her bags of food.

She trailed him to the pub where he was staying. It was the least popular in town; the front bar was even emptier than the other front bars. Rumours without foundation circulated about support from bikies and organised crime, because no one could understand how the place managed to keep its doors open. Perhaps having people like Luke as boarders was the answer to that question. Carson followed him up the wide timber stairs to his room.

Inside, he said, without looking at her, 'Take your clothes off.'

'Piss off.'

He threw an old shirt, a pair of shorts, and the blonde wig at her.

'I need you to put these on, and I'll throw them out when we're finished.'

They stripped and changed—nothing said, nothing seen.

Luke grabbed a handful of supermarket plastic bags and some surgical gloves, and Carson followed him back out the door, down the stairs, and out onto the street. They crossed the road and went around behind the shops, away from the small cameras that watched over the main drag. They scrabbled their way along the street, climbing fences and tracking around rubbish and discarded equipment. When they reached the car park that sat across the road from the pub, Luke flattened himself against a wall and looked across at the cars, then nodded imperceptibly and gave Carson two plastic bags, two rubber bands, and a pair of gloves.

'Put the bags on your feet like this,' he said. He put one over his shoe, and rolled a rubber band into place to hold it. 'Then put your gloves on.'

She had to stop herself laughing at his secret-agent intrigues. If she made fun of him, he might send her away.

He reached into his pocket, pulled out a shiny key, and then walked quickly towards a white ute that sat in the middle of the group of cars. The car park was hardly lit, but Carson kept her head down, hoping not to reveal her reflected face to a camera or an unseen watcher.

Luke opened the vehicle with his key, got in, and started it. Carson was beside him, sliding down in her seat, not sure what she was hiding from, her heart pumping. The motor ran smoothly, and Luke pulled out of the car park and drove up the hill, away from the main street and to the protection of houses and their quiet streets. Then they turned back along the top of the rise, made their way through several blocks to the church, and turned left towards the well-lit industrial area. Near the entrance, with its small security car in the distance, Luke took another left and headed down a poorly maintained gravel road to the creek, killing the lights as he did so. Carson was trying not to giggle with the rush and the excitement, but she was starting to realise that Luke had gone to some trouble to find a place to do whatever he was going to do. It wasn't a spontaneous prank, or even something he'd just thought up today. It made her look across at him in the half-light and study the way he stared out into the night as if he had plans for everything out here.

They drove to where the cement culvert crossed the creek, its edges several metres wider than the stream that ran through the middle, and fell in a small waterfall off the edge into a deeper pool. Luke let the ute roll down so the front wheels were sitting just at the water's edge.

'Now we get out. Don't leave anything behind—have a really good check. A lost earring could get you in deep shit.'

When they were both out, Luke leant back in the window and let the handbrake go. The ute lurched forward, and Carson muffled a squeal as the machine free-wheeled smoothly down the concrete, slipped over the edge, and clunked nose-first into the water, sounding like a large fish plopping back into its habitat. Then it sat still, rear wheels off the ground, front ones hub-deep in the water—someone's practical joke gone wrong.

Carson was jumping on the spot just a little bit.

'Man. That is some trouble there.'

It wasn't an accusation. It was praise spilling from liberation. She had found someone who could break the rules and smash through all the things that kept people in their place. All those stupid, unreal things that whispered in your head which you never acknowledged: *This can't be done, no one does that, that will never happen.* Luke seemed unconfined by them, or by anything, really.

It was like rocket fuel in her blood. Anything felt possible. They walked up the road in their plastic-bag covers and then turned off through the grass towards the back of a farm-machinery dealership. A few hundred metres from the creek, he stopped and pulled the bags off. Carson did the same, and he took them from her.

Then they trudged in the dark, up the hill, not looking at each other, but she knew he was smiling. His walk was loose again, the stiffness gone. Maybe he was an alien, a new being from somewhere else who saw no limits, and she was lucky enough to have found him.

'What'll happen?' she whispered between grinning lips.

'Probably nothing. They'll think it's some local kids — Kooris maybe. The machine won't be damaged, so no real harm done.' He turned in the half-light. 'At least that's what I'm hoping.'

'What about all that plastic-bag stuff. Was it really needed?'

'No. Most local cops don't have any DNA experience or any requirements to collect it. I just don't like to test fate, now or in the future.'

'The future?'

'Yeah, well, if I did happen to do something that led the cops to collect DNA, I wouldn't like them to get a match-up, or something that placed a certain person in a certain place at a certain time.'

'Are you planning to kill someone?' She held her laugh, and it fluttered out in a blowing of her lips.

'No, but no one knows the future.'

They reached the back of the dealership, followed the high chain-fence along until they found a gap they could climb through, and made their way to the main road. There were no cars, and they crossed the road to the side where it was dark and poorly lit. Carson could smell the asphalt on the road down to her right, and a dog kennel and cut grass on the other side. Everything was normal, and she and Luke were more than normal.

It took them fifteen minutes to walk to Luke's pub, where she demanded a drink, knowing she wouldn't be able to drive home, and insisting that he sleep on the floor and she in his bed.

At his kitchen table, Sweetapple laid the classifieds section of the newspaper out in front of him, and began circling prospects for horse replacements. Then he rang each number and asked precise questions about the horse for sale. After that, he went through the same process with online ads: sifting through them, then ringing and interrogating the advertisers. Several owners sent through photos. Two of them looked like possibilities, with their horses' colour, age, and style matching pretty well. But the more he looked at them, the less feasible his gambit seemed. Retribution had become such a distinct presence in his imagination that trying to find an animal like her felt stupid and ignorant. There was no horse like her. There would never be any horse like her.

He tried to convince himself that he was being stupid to think like this; his prejudice was creating a model that couldn't be matched, and that wasn't what he had set out to do. His attitude had been that 'close enough would be good enough'. But it was pointless. He could never make himself believe in the substitute. Even if he were to make himself go and look at one of the mares in the flesh, he knew that the minute he saw the possible stand-in, all he would see would be the dissimilarities. They would be so stark that he would be unable to make the purchase, knowing he would be buying a Shetland to replace a thoroughbred. And then there was the problem of the unknown vet who was supposed to check on Retribution. A vet would immediately identify a fake or a replacement.

He put the paper away and gave up. There was no alternative to delivering the mare.

Caroline found some online courses on farm management and basic agronomy. She started studying at night, driving around during the day — seeing what the men were doing, how the crops were developing, how the plants and animals were changing — trying her best to become a genuine part of the landscape. There were birdcalls to identify and the mating cycles of the domestic animals to understand. It encouraged her to start something so new. She felt the thrill of the neophyte.

And still there were the lessons with Sweetapple, which she looked forward to so much every week. Her riding improved with her confidence around horses, and the relationship with Sweetapple developed steadily. At least that's what she felt. Sweetapple probably didn't notice, which didn't matter. Caroline told herself she didn't want anything more from him than he was already giving. But on the mornings of her riding lessons she would always anxiously check her phone to see if he'd cancelled or changed his mind. She had to stop herself sending messages asking if the lesson was on, if he thought the weather was nice, if he'd noticed the box trees flowering. She allowed herself one four-word text: 'Still on this afternoon?'

Caroline gradually cleared Bob's things into suitcases and boxes, and put them into a back room. If he was ever coming back, he could come back with a removal van. She thought about him most nights, replaying times they'd had together, arguments and missed moments, and tried to work out if there was something she could have done or should have known. And there were plenty of mistakes she had to admit to—his birthday celebration missed, weeks with no more communication than texts, laziness about sex and special times together, the phone never turned off—but nothing that she felt was enough to have driven him away if he really cared. It was enough probably for him to demand she try harder, and the same for her about him. There were plenty of easier options for Bob.

No doubt he was shtupping secretaries the whole time. That's what men did, didn't they? There were a number of members of parliament, some of them friends, who had turned up at her office door, late at night, with a bottle of red and a couple of glasses, but she had never done anything more with them than sample the shiraz. Caroline had been tempted, but could never fit that sort of perfidy with her vision of herself. And she had assumed, lazily, stupidly, that Bob was the same.

Sorting through his things, trying not to throw them against the wall, she found a box full of old mobiles. Some of them were old enough to be centimetres thick, and others had only recently been retired. One, in particular, was what she thought was his current phone. He had obviously tossed it out as a remnant of an old life. The angry, dumped woman inside her decided to power it up to see what he might have been talking about. She knew it would probably cause her pain, but she couldn't help it. The desire to confirm her worst, bitter suspicions was too strong.

The phone took some time to boot up, and she thought that maybe it wasn't going to happen, couldn't happen, and then the screen came to life with the words 'Hello Bob'. Caroline suddenly knew this was childish and even a little pathetic. Nothing healthy or healing could come from it. To stop was the best idea. She held the phone above the box, ready to pelt it, but then thought, *What the hell?* There was nothing else going on.

She watched messages come up on the screen. Most of them were indecipherable requests for meetings, or clandestine information, or boys' jokes. 'Camilla' somebody featured a lot, but most of her messages were no more than flirtatious. If Caroline hadn't known Bob was leaving her, she might have been angry and jealous, but now it seemed ho-hum. His texts over the past few years probably would have been similar, and whether he was always sleeping with the recipients was another story that she really didn't care to pay attention to.

There were also quite a few messages from 'Laura' that only mentioned meeting times. But those times were almost always after hours at restaurants, cafes, or bars. Laura might be a very industrious PA, Caroline guessed. And everything about 'Laura' might have been above board, too, because Caroline was allowing her imagination to create nightmares that would cause suffering for only one person. She had promised to be positive, forward-looking, a veritable phoenix, but now she was wallowing—in fact, creating wallows. But she couldn't stop herself.

And then, in among messages she didn't understand, and some she didn't care to, was a letter from a Finnish girl, an Ag student looking to make a connection. It read like a scam, but it was possible that it was a genuine enquiry. The photo looked so innocent, but the letter that went with it was irksome, which could have been explained by the naivety of the writer or even a language difficulty. Caroline thought she would like to find out, because if it was genuine, she might pass it on to someone who could help. An idea was festering in her imagination: if it was a scam, it might be a beautiful opportunity for payback.

Caroline texted the Finnish girl, suggesting that Bob would like to know more about her and perhaps receive some assurance that Felicity was genuine in her interest. If Felicity Sven was a real person, she had no idea what she was getting herself into; and if she was fake, it was just plain funny. Caroline thought Bob might like to give this woman lots of money.

The message that returned read: 'Please. How should I assure you Mr Statham? University graduation certificates? Maybe references? Samples of my work?'

Caroline was pretty sure you didn't get a quick personal response from an international scammer, but that didn't mean it was genuine. She knew she wouldn't be able to tell if the paperwork provided was authentic without going to some trouble, so instead she asked the girl to tell a little about herself.

13

The fourth phone call that Sweetapple took from Bob contained the edge of a threat and hinted at a barely held temper. Sweetapple listened to Bob laying down ultimatums, and realised he had stalled for as long as he could. Pushing Bob further might create other problems that would ruin his plans. So after Bob hung up, Sweetapple rang Lance and told him he was going to ride Bob's horse down to the yard, where it was supposed to be stabled. Lance already had his orders and directions from Bob, and had been expecting Sweetapple's call.

'What's so special about this bloody horse? Boss keeps going on about it. I'm not allowed to talk about it to anyone. It's got to be kept separate from the others, up the back in its own specially built enclosure, and I can't let visitors see it, except for some vet. Has it got some sort of disease?'

'Nah. Just a special horse, apparently. Don't really know myself.'

'Are you going to look after it?'

'That's your job.'

'Bloody mad. I don't know anything about horses.'

'Time to learn, I guess.'

'Why doesn't he pay you to do it? Would only take an extra half an hour a week, wouldn't it?'

Sweetapple thought about Carson's warnings. She had been right. It made no sense to be looking after the horse on Bob's place. But he said, 'I tell you what, I'll keep an eye on her if you want.' He knew he should retract it, say he'd forgotten how busy he was in the next few weeks, overcommitted, but instead he inserted the gambit, 'But don't tell Bob. He gets a bit antsy about these things. He'll think I'm trying to get extra cash out of him.'

Lance sounded like he'd just won something. 'Deal. I'll see you tomorrow.'

Sweetapple rode Retribution down out of her hill paddock and across the flat to the boundary gate. He undid the gate latch, remembering it as a construction of his grandfather's: a now rusted ring-chain that looped over a corroded steel head. Almost everything had changed, but not this one catch—once a gateway amongst hundreds, now holding the entrance to the neighbours' place: Little Myalls.

So much had been given up—taken and lost. But now Sweetapple was at the predators' end of the food chain.

The ride to the yard where Retribution was to be kept took him across the soft black soils that awaited planting: furrowed, weedless, faultless. He thought it must feel good for Retribution underfoot as they strolled, taking their time down the straight lines, enjoying something like freedom. It took them three-quarters of an hour to reach the stables, which were a small, recently constructed complex of timber railyards, a covered stall, a trough, a feed shed, a tap, a trough, and a hose. Lance saw them arrive, and drove down as Sweetapple dismounted. He washed the mare as Lance asked, 'Should I feed her?'

'Just hay.' He let Retribution go, and watched as she stepped away, unaware of his sentimentality. It would only be for a short while, he was sure of that.

'Looks pretty impressive to me. Not that I'd know.' Lance looked to Sweetapple, who was watching the mare discovering her new surroundings. Sweetapple kept staring at the horse, not acknowledging that Lance had spoken, or that Lance had offered to give him a lift home and had a million things that needed doing which were more important than staring at a horse.

'I'll run you home. She'll be right here, won't she?'

Sweetapple scratched his head and turned to Lance as if returning from a trance.

'Sure. Let's get going.'

Lance drove fast, with an arm out the window, his hair blowing around on his face. 'I've never seen so much fuss over an animal that isn't supposed to be anything out of the ordinary. I reckon you and Bob are having a go at me.'

'Sorry, mate. There has been a bit of carry-on.' Sweetapple knew he couldn't have Lance's imagination fired up over who or what Retribution might be. 'I'm afraid there really is nothing magic about her. She cost Bob big bucks and she's extremely well bred, but she doesn't have any of the ability her exclusive genes say she should. She's a dud—a pretty dud, but a dud nevertheless.'

They neared Sweetapple's ramp, and he let his tongue go, spinning a story that he had only just thought of. 'I keep thinking she's going to grow into her genetic potential. Ugly-duckling stuff. Wake up one day and perform like a champion. But it never happens. She just eats her feed and enjoys the day. Like the son of a famous sportsman who you expect to be as good as or better than their old man, but actually they have no interest in sport. Turns out they love the violin or something. You with me?'

Lance seemed convinced and a little relieved by Sweetapple's story. He was grinning and nodding.

'Horse people are mad, eh? They all reckon they've just bought or bred the next big winner. Can't be told. Won't be told. I didn't take Bob to be one of those. I guess we're all soft somewhere.'

Sweetapple laughed, too. 'And your soft spot would be?'

'Women.' He showed his irregular teeth as Sweetapple got out and thanked him for the lift.

Sweetapple watched him leave, feeling dispossessed, and suddenly thinking about Carson and wondering if he could get her to visit. He didn't know what her plans were, or even what she had been doing. Recently, finding a substitute and then delivering Retribution had captured all of his thoughts and emotions. It was a mistake — he knew that Carson disliked being ignored. Now, in the empty space where the mare had been, he felt panic that he had let Carson go, too.

He tried her mobile, but there was no answer, so he sent a text and tried to make it sound casual. It was a normal workday for her. No message came back, which wasn't unusual, but it turned the crank on his fear. She might just be with a client or too close to the boss to be able to take a personal message. He sent a text to Luke, even though he knew Luke would be working. It remained unread, and Sweetapple had a sudden recognition of a feeling he had been carrying but keeping smothered: he was jealous.

Carson and Luke had a friendship that had developed quickly, that was important to both of them, and that existed independently of Sweetapple. They had created a world that didn't include or need any reference to him, but he had pretended, even to himself, that this was of no concern, that he would never think to care about what they might get up to together. What they had was not worth the energy required to care about it. He ignored them when they prattled on to each other about not much; when they shared the weird part of their senses of humour, and made references to music and media he had never heard of. They had forged a bond because they were both young—that was all.

But he had let the mare become his total focus. He had hardly thought of Carson lately. Now he needed to find her. The old feeling that she might have grown tired of him, might be bored by his simpleness and his contained ways, rose up like a demon within him. He got into the ute without bothering to clean up or shower. He would make sure she knew he was still her man, and that he hadn't left the territory open for newcomers.

As he drove, he thought about the mare, using his sense of loss to make sure that his imagination about Carson didn't take the reins and take him on a mad ride that would lead him to places he didn't want to be, that didn't need to have ever been created.

———

In the early morning, Carson had written:

> Moi!
> I grew up on the town of Akaa with my mother and father and older brother Onni. My father is a farmer and we have cows which we keep in a shed over winter time. We also grow turnips and sometimes Brussel Sprouts.

She had to break from her typing, as her laughter was making her fingers type the wrong letters.

> I went to school in my local town and then university in Helsinki where I studied Agricultural Science specialising in Agronomy as well as a certificate on International Supply Chains. It was very interesting. After graduating I got a job in the Department of Agriculture as a junior (not very exciting). Some of my friends from uni got jobs overseas while they were travelling so I thought I might do the same thing (and have some fun too) but I don't know anyone overseas and I don't have any contacts. That is why I wrote to you.
>
> hyvää päivänjatkoa!
> (have a nice day)

The Finnish phrases were a cute addition, but she hoped the rest of the letter didn't make Felicity out to be too straight. She wanted Bob to think it was possible to get into her pants, with a bit of effort; otherwise he might lose interest.

A text returned: 'Thanks very much for that, Felicity. What

is your opinion on terrorists?'

For a moment, Carson wondered if she hadn't found her way into some weird internet place where she might be recruited to fight for the caliphate, and then she worked out that Bob was making sure she wasn't some sort of machine- or template-based answering service.

She wrote, 'They hurt people for reasons I can't understand.'

'That would be an observation, not an opinion.'

'Yes. I think they are bad, scary people. What do you think?'

'When do you want to come to Australia?'

It sounded like a breakthrough. Bob believed she was real.

'In a few months. When I get some money together.'

'Maybe I can help you with that.'

'I saw your photo on the web. You are very handsome! (Excuse me for that.) Maybe I shouldn't come to your place.' That was too much. Olga was creeping back in, but the message had already been sent anyway.

Caroline was enjoying herself. Felicity was smart, but soon enough she would expose herself, whoever she was.

'But I would like it very much if you came to visit. Would you like to come here?'

'Hundred and one per cent. That's the saying, isn't it?'

'Yes. Don't come in summer — it will be too hot for you.'

Sweetapple parked on the other side of the street to Ponsford's. It was nearly her knock-off time, but he didn't know whether she had an after-hours meeting or another job to go to. He could see her car in the car park, so he chose to wait. Harry Taylor, who'd been with the company for years, pulled the gates shut at the enclosure and waved at Sweetapple. He acknowledged him, knowing that Harry would probably mention it to Carson. In a few minutes, Carson appeared and stood there, hands on her hips, staring at him as though he was a stalker she couldn't get rid of. She crossed the road to his window.

'You here to see me, or is your ute broken down?'

'I'm here to see you.' His arm was on the steering wheel, his head tilted towards her. He might have been saying a passing 'G'day' to almost anyone. 'Been a bit off the air … sorry about that.'

Carson had been annoyed at him for his neglect, but even more annoyed that she was annoyed about it. She held onto the gunnel of his ute and thought about not caring, about not giving a shit, the way she wanted to feel. She considered sneaking out the back to her car, and disappearing on him, but she knew it would turn into a something. He would have to track her down, they would fight, and he would know how much she cared, how much she hurt. It had only been a week or so since he'd called, and she was at risk of indulging in girly tricks and tantrums. She did not want that.

'Yeah, well, don't expect me to wait around for you to resurface. Plenty of other fish …'

Urgency was racing inside Sweetapple, new and unrecognised. He was used to strong emotion — rage and even fear — but not this, and not this need to let anyone know, especially her.

He grabbed at her hand, held it, and looked hard at her. 'I'm not going anywhere. Are you?'

It was sort of shocking coming from Sweetapple. Almost a love song. She laughed at him, unsure whether she liked this kind of open expression of his need, but feeling the balance tilt back her way. She only answered, 'Where would I go?,' deliberate in her avoidance of his meaning.

There was no rejoinder to this, except for a joke that he wasn't going to try to make. Instead he just kept looking at her.

She turned, and said to the sky, 'Anyway, I'm meeting Luke for a drink. Do you want to come?'

'Luke?'

'Yep. Luke. Jealous?'

'Maybe.'

She liked this, he could tell. Finally, the right words.

It wasn't just the pleasure at hearing his words that Carson was feeling. She was realising that she loved him. She didn't want to love him, and had done her best not to love him. He was a man going nowhere who could be happy with a horse and an ugly dog. It was not what she wanted. Something had to be done about it.

Luke was already at the pub, playing pool against some locals. He waved 'hello' before his shot. Sweetapple saw that he was good and that his opponents were trying to sledge him out of his form. Carson went to get their drinks, and Sweetapple took a stool nearby, watching as Luke calmly took control of the game. The comments from around the wall became louder and nastier, but Luke wasn't swayed.

As he lined up his shot on the black to finish the game, one of the detractors pushed lightly on the end of his cue and laughed raucously. Luke stopped, didn't look round, but held his place for that moment. Sweetapple saw in the tightness of his grip and the pressure of his lips a fury that he hadn't known was inside Luke. He got up off his seat and walked over behind Luke, smiling at everyone. If Luke swung that pool cue, the night would usher in a lot more trouble than Sweetapple needed.

It caused Luke to swivel, smile, and say calmly, 'You're watching my back? Trust me, Sweetapple, I'm not that guy.' Then he completed his shot.

They drank in a corner away from the pool table, the crowd happier now that Luke had given up his ownership of the table.

'Did you find a horse, or did you deliver the original?' Luke was amused. He watched Sweetapple answer, and thought about the man's obsession with this mare. He didn't get it, couldn't understand why anyone could care that much about anything. Animals were nice, and he didn't like to see them hurt, but they were never worth this level of fuss. Sweetapple was carrying on like he would sacrifice everything for this horse: his girl, his freedom, his farm, and, who knew, maybe even his life. Didn't he realise that he was with one of the hottest women you could ever see? Who was also one of the most volatile and fiery? She was the sort of woman who was only ever a short step away from moving on. The smallest misstep, and she was sleeping with someone else. It was like he was encouraging her to go somewhere else. If Carson ever looked at him twice, Luke knew he would never say 'No'. And even if she never looked at him, he was still willing to try his arm.

'You don't think you should let it go? Just take the money and move on?'

Sweetapple was silent, swirling his finger in the condensation on his glass. Carson's suggestion was one that hadn't arisen among his imagined options.

'She's next door, and I should forget about her? In a paddock on her own, who knows how long till someone rides her, or talks to her, or does more than just chuck her her feed? An animal like that, so close to perfect, within my reach, and I should just wipe my mind of her? I can't do it.' The last of this was said as an apology, not a threat.

Sweetapple put a hand on Carson's thigh, and Luke wondered if he'd read things wrong. Maybe Sweetapple had conceded his foolishness.

'Anyway, Bob says we're going to return her.'

'Bullshit.'

'Back to where she came from.'

'He's only said that to keep you sweet. Who returns something like that?'

'When he's got the eggs and the job's done, he doesn't want the mare around, does he?'

They finished their drinks, and Carson said, 'I got a nibble.'

The men looked at her.

'On my letter. My Finnish girl. You'll never believe who.'

They looked at the ceiling and the floor.

'Your man Bob.'

'Bob Statham?' Sweetapple was open-mouthed.

'Bob Statham. Keen for a bit on the side.'

'He might just be wanting to help a young traveller out. Good Samaritan sort of thing.' Luke didn't believe it either.

'Are you sure it's him? He's not even in the country, you know.'

'Dunno, but it came from his phone. Unless he lost it and someone picked it up. Pretty unlikely.'

'So what'd he say?'

With a giggle, Carson reported the text she had received.

'What did you say?'

:o go without her they would tell her, careful
\ butcher in the big town bought the rabbit
e other man came to the house and bought
dry on 'U's of fencing wire, when her father
n saved up.

o have such an important personal memory
g. Her city contemporaries viewed the death
ore significant than the death of a human
pted to feel the same way, until she thought
s and the closeness with her father, whose
:ed.

she'd discovered in Bob's desk, Caroline
binet and extracted a gleaming .222. It was
her hands, smooth and simple—a barrel, a
as seductive to hold something so powerful,
fective. She considered that it would take
r to kill with it—one round, one trigger
vondered if she could still do it.

was flying business-class, Bob Statham
the Premium Arrivals Lounge in the
nal Airport. There was the possibility that
holder, a journalist, a competitor—would
take the opportunity to ask how things were
it fellow travellers seemed to think they had
asant questions. Fuck their questions.

in one of the long rows that sat across from
to board, and looked down the walkway
art of the airport where the duty-free shops,

'I wrote a message back about my childhood and my family
to show, you know, that I was earnest and kind of naive. I don't
think one of those Russian girls would write back anything like
that. They'd be just saying, *I'm so liking you, you're such big nice
man.*'

'Yeah, yeah, you should go a bit agricultural-scientific on
him. Might put him off, though. Geeky's not that sexy. Maybe
start scientific, and progress to soft and girly at the end. You
know, like *I'm nowhere near as clever as you, but I'd like to learn.*'

'Geez, Luke, you sound like you've done this before.'
Sweetapple felt mild disbelief. Writing things was not something
he wasted energy on.

'Me? Nah. Just thinking. And he's got a holding in the mine,
doesn't he?'

'One of the original developers. Made a fortune, another
fortune, out of it.' Carson was refusing to picture the leer and
the squeezing hand.

'If that's the case, I'd be glad to see someone get back at
him.'

It was something they agreed on.

'You wouldn't want it, would you, Sweetapple? You like the
wife.'

'I do, and Bob doesn't worry me. He does what he does.'

'Oh, come on. He's the same as all those other pricks. He'll
use us, manipulate us, and crush us any chance he gets.' Carson
was annoyed at him now. Sweetapple, unusually, moved to calm
her.

'Fair enough.' He put his arms around her. It was so out of
form that Carson jumped when he did it.

'You all right?'

'Yep. Just being friendly.'

She shook free of him. 'Not sure I'm that over the moon about "friendly". Bob will take you down over that horse. I don't know how, but he will. He'll leave you with nothing, carrying the can, I bet. And you still think he just "does what he does". Like it was the most harmless thing in the world.'

'I didn't say I thought he was harmless. I just stay out of his way.'

'But you'll steal the world's most expensive horse for him, and treat him like he's a good guy? Come on, man. Work it out.' It sounded like Luke was moving to gang up with Carson.

'Look, you're probably right about him, but I need the money, and I've got to stay cool to make this whole thing come off.'

Carson was placated. It felt to Luke like an opportunity had just been lost.

restaurants, and gigantic screens shone and flickered at each other. It was probably a five-hundred-metre walk, all part of the one building, past boarding gates A, B, C, D, and E on shiny polished concrete in air-conditioned equilibrium. Above him on both sides, sky trains glided silently back and forth. There were smoking rooms, resting rooms, prayer rooms, spacious, spotless bathrooms, and escalators that responded to the weight of their workload. It was unbelievable what humans could do if they had enough ambition, if they were tough enough to see things through. Your average person didn't understand that. You had to make the hard decisions and endure the hard times. Which was what he had been telling himself for the past few weeks.

Things were not good with the company, and he had the first sense that the dogs were beginning to howl. Everybody loved an imminent failure. He could handle it, but it would not be easy.

And now the bloody horse deal looked like falling over. His 'man in the desert', who was supposed to be the investor to beat all investors, who had originally approached him about Retribution, had got cold bloody feet. Bob had not kept any secrets from them. When the other owners declined to sell the mare or her genetics, Bob had told the man in the desert the lengths he would have to go to to get eggs from the horse. He had told him it would be risky. The man had just offered more money. But it wasn't about the money, not initially: it was about good faith and the access that good faith could provide. If Bob could give the man's boss something special that no one else could, it would open up a pipeline to investments and opportunities. Bob's companies were in need of both. When Retribution had been stolen, Bob had told the police it was most likely the other shareholders, accusing them of hiding the mare from him and his potential deals. They were farmers and horsemen, and didn't know what had hit them. They couldn't believe someone would steal Retribution. He had threatened court and media exposure to keep them on the back foot, and because he knew they would be intimidated by his money.

But now the deal with the man in the desert was shaky. Bob didn't understand why, but he was certain it would mean that word would leak that he had been involved in the theft of the horse. He knew these people. He knew what they were like. If they were happy with the deal, their lips would be sealed — no risk. Now it was all risk. The eggs had been collected from the mare, so there was still a chance for a sale, but not until things had significantly cooled down. But the holy grail of good faith was gone. It was time to cover his tracks.

He flicked through his contacts, checked the time, and then dialled a number. Craig Reinfleisch was a nasty little guy, but a very useful one.

Craig answered the phone with the kind of confused belligerence that he always displayed. There was a good chance he had been drinking, even though it was only 11.00 am, his time. At least he was the sort of drinker who could turn it off for a few days when needed. Bob explained to Craig the job that he needed doing. He told him he would be paid good money, more than he was used to, to do the job efficiently and to keep his mouth shut. Bob said he would ring Craig again in the morning, and suggested he leave the drink alone for a while. All of this Craig took as unsurprising.

Craig was a local fellow who Bob had employed, years before, to help him with the garden. At various times he had been a truck driver, a fencer, a butcher, and a station hand, but, like all the other men Bob had attempted to recruit, he considered gardening to be work for women or simpletons. Bob had convinced him to take it on by framing it as a design-and-management job, which it wasn't. They had worked pretty well together, and Bob gave him the authority to order the contractors around when he wasn't there. He told the contractors that if they wanted his business they would have to put up with Craig.

One week, Bob got home from a hectic time in the US and decided he needed to do some small alterations to the garden to relieve a bit of stress. Craig wasn't answering his phone, so Bob took the opportunity to pick up some things in town and pay Craig a visit. He knocked on the door several times until Craig's groggy voice called him in. Craig was bleary-eyed and adjusting his trousers as Bob pushed his way into the airless room, apologising for bothering him. A laptop was open on the table, and Bob took an interest in it to avoid watching Craig organising his clothing. On the screen of the laptop were pictures of naked young girls, really young girls, doing things really young girls shouldn't do. When he saw what Bob was looking at, Craig had half-fallen over to the screen, and slapped it shut.

Bob didn't ask for Craig's help that day, and Craig didn't turn up at the farm any other day. But after a week or two, Bob gave Craig a call. He had given it some thought, and reasoned that while the images were sick and disgusting, Craig was really just a pathetic, lonely old boozer. He was only looking at pictures. He didn't have the capacity to make them or sell them. And one thing Bob knew for certain: if you ever got the chance to buy loyalty, you should take it. From that day on, he got Craig to do small jobs around the place, and paid him well. Craig was always very thankful. The job he needed Craig to do now was a kind of peak in their relationship, and restitution for the faith showed in him.

Now Bob put his phone away, stretched backwards, and looked up at the timber ceiling with its small rectangular sky windows. A steel or concrete girder arched its way from the floor. Nothing in this place was small-time, and that encouraged him.

Bob was pleased with his plan and himself. The dogs could howl all they liked. They would not bring him down.

Sweetapple visited Retribution almost every other day. He even took her for short rides on the flat, letting Lance know that he was just keeping her fitness up and trying to stop her foundering. Lance wasn't interested. He was happy for Sweetapple to do what he wanted. After three weeks, it began to feel like a new normal was settling in: Retribution would always be within his grasp, just not on his place. Lance told him a vet had visited several times, but Sweetapple never saw the vet or the vehicles; he only noticed that Retribution was unsettled on certain days.

On a day when Sweetapple was out of phone reception, up on the boundary fence on the hill, Lance had tried to call several times and then left a voice message. The phone came into reception near the house, and Sweetapple pulled up to hear the message properly.

'Lance here. Just thought I'd let you know, even though I

probably shouldn't, there's a fella coming to look at the mare today. Bob didn't say what it was about except I wouldn't have to feed her after today. Anyway, leave it up to you. Cheers.'

Sweetapple checked the time of the calls: three hours ago. Whoever they were, they had probably been and gone. Panic rose in him, and he skidded while trying to turn towards Statham's. He'd known this day was coming, and had pretended to himself that it never would. If she was gone, he would have to chase them down—and say what? They'd got the wrong horse? There'd been a mix-up, and they'd have to come back in a couple of days? There'd been a change of plans, and Bob had decided to keep her? Bob would be furious, but it wouldn't matter, because there wouldn't be a fight to take up if the mare was already gone.

He sped down through the boundary gate, leaving it open, every bump in the track launching him out of the seat as he tried to tell himself that it was probably just a vet giving her a check-up or a blood test for authenticity. Besides, you couldn't just take her out onto the road in the broad daylight—it would be too risky. In the distance, a white four-wheel-drive sedan, which he didn't recognise, was leaving the Statham place and heading out onto the main road. Sweetapple tried to tell himself that he was watching the 'visitor' leave, which meant that everything was okay.

When he reached her enclosure, he could see a small, aged truck with a large, white box on the back, parked next to the fence. He breathed deeply and let his fear go. He had been stupid, jumping to conclusions like the worst panicker. There was no horse carrier or float. Nobody had taken Retribution. It was just some sort of check-up; maybe getting her ready to be secretly exported somewhere. But as he pulled alongside the yard, he couldn't see the horse anywhere. There was an older ginger-haired guy washing his hands at the tap, obviously finished with a job he had had to do. He looked like he had been sweating heavily. A pair of overalls, recently removed, were hanging from the truck gunnel rail.

Sweetapple got out, and the older man looked at him as though he was an intruder. 'Who are you?' he asked.

'I've been looking after the mare,' Sweetapple said. He looked around again. 'Where is she?'

'Mr Statham didn't mention anyone else "looking after the mare".' The man splashed his stubbled face with water and walked to his truck, where he dried his hands on a cloth and ignored the existence of the other man. Sweetapple crossed the yard to him, his anxiety rising. There was a pool of dark fluid that had already sunk into the ground near something that might have been a pinkish sawdust, and a familiar animal smell he couldn't immediately place. He was seeing but not understanding, unable to make the physical facts come together.

'Bob wouldn't have mentioned me, but I'm the only one who knows anything about horses around here. Where is she?' Sweetapple could see that the box on the back of the truck was an insulated container like a refrigeration unit.

The man paid no attention, put the overalls in a box in the back, and moved to get into his cab. Sweetapple half-tripped in the rush to get to him before the door closed, realising that the smell in the air could be that of blood, a body, and death. The man was in his seat reaching quickly for the door when Sweetapple got to him and pushed his shoulder against the trim.

'What have you done with the mare?'

The man kicked a foot down hard at Sweetapple's face, and

Sweetapple fell back but held on to the window winder as the man kicked at him again. Blood from a cut on his face obscured his vision as he grabbed at the foot and hung on to it, pulling the man, who was screaming obscenities, down towards him.

'Where is she, you bastard?' Sweetapple ripped him away from his grip on the steering wheel and pushed him face-down onto the ground, squeezing at his neck.

'Someone came and took her.' He was choking it out. 'In a horse float.' Sweetapple let the pressure off, in relief that she might be still alive.

He took his hands off the man and watched him.

'Flash-looking bloke,' the man said, catching his breath and turning onto his side, 'with all the Western gear, hat and boots and everything. Big rig, too. You know the type.'

'When was this?'

'Couple of hours ago.'

Sweetapple sat back on his knees, wiped the blood out of his eyes, and breathed deeply. Bob had on sold her, but she wasn't dead.

As Sweetapple stood up, the man rolled over and sat up on the ground, his chest heaving. 'What do you fucken care? It's his horse. He can do what he likes.'

'What makes you so sure it's his horse?'

'He said so. I don't want to be involved with anything stolen.' He got up and stood next to Sweetapple, brushing himself down as if a few hand-swipes would make him look respectable.

But Sweetapple remembered the smell, and knew without understanding that a horse float didn't explain everything.

'So what are you doing here?'

The man said something about 'tidying up', and Sweetapple could see the lie immediately. He grabbed him again by the neck, lifted him to his feet, and dragged him to the back of the box.

'Open it.' The man tried to struggle away, but Sweetapple overpowered him and smashed him hard against the box. He could feel his own rage, murderous and unlimited. 'Open it.'

The man flicked at the locks as Sweetapple held him fast at the back of his skull and watched his small, powerful-looking hands in case they struck backwards at him. When the door was pulled open, Sweetapple could see the smooth corrugations of an icebox — not refrigerated, just insulated, designed for short trips or temporary cooling. There were lumpy bags of ice laid across the floor.

Sweetapple felt his legs go, and he reached for the support of the truck. He was making small whimpering sounds that he couldn't stop, couldn't hear.

On top of the mounds of ice were large slabs of crimson flesh, still steaming, carpeted in orange hair, with feet, face, genitals, and tail still attached. Pieces of a jigsaw that might have made a horse.

The man took his opportunity, twisted away, and ran to the driver's seat as Sweetapple crumpled, staying upright only because of a limp hand still hanging on to the tray of the truck. The truck started up and pulled slowly forward as if the driver was concerned he might run someone over, but Sweetapple let go, couldn't care, might even have welcomed the truck reversing over him. It was soon gone, motoring, bouncing across the paddock, leaving Sweetapple behind, a small lump alone on the ground.

15

When Sweetapple got back to his house, hours later, having taken so long to get to his ute and then make the drive back, he pulled a chair into the shade and sat there, mumbling to himself. He hadn't allowed himself to believe that Bob would return the mare, even though he knew it was a possibility. It had taken Sweetapple weeks to get used to the idea that he no longer had her at his place. The thought of Bob or anyone else killing her had never made its way into his fears, so now it was almost impossible to believe. But he had seen it. He had seen the pieces of Retribution with his own eyes.

After some hours, he emerged from a stupor, and his first thought in the real world was of Carson. He rang her and asked if she could come out, telling her Retribution had been butchered and clicking the phone off without waiting for her answer.

For a moment, the desolation in Sweetapple's voice made it impossible for her to move. His voice did not do that. His voice was deep and melodious and predictable. You could rely on a voice like that. Not now. And then she moved quickly, grabbing some clothes, food, a bottle of rum, and then running to her car and driving it at a speed it normally wouldn't allow her to.

She saw him sitting in the chair, a lost child, isolated in his own landscape, and wondered if this was who he really was. If the mare really was dead, it would take a lot to reach him.

She put a hand on his shoulder and asked him, because words didn't supply anything better, 'You okay?'

He nodded unconvincingly, and she sat.

'What happened?'

'He's got rid of her. Got some low-life to chop her up and get rid of her.'

'You saw?'

'After. In his chiller box. For dog meat or something.'

They were in Sweetapple's spartan living room. There was a TV, a table, two chairs, and a lounge—none of them new, but none of them well-worn. There were pictures on the wall of his mother and his father near an empty open fireplace. The carpet was clean, but flattened and hard.

'Oh God.'

'Lance warned me, and I went down for a look. This guy, a little ginger prick, had already done the job, cleaned up and everything. She was just slabs of meat and a bag of offal. Fucken unbelievable.'

He was shaking his head from side to side, and Carson wanted to reach out and grab him on the chin to stop him, but she didn't, and his head kept going back and forth, back and forth.

She'd not seen Sweetapple like this. In front of her he concealed almost every emotion, shook off disappointment, insult, and pain. He was doing his best now, but it was close to pathetic. She was surprised and maybe pleased that he was allowing her to see it. But she didn't know what to say next. It was a shocking final strategy from that bastard Statham, and there didn't seem to be any next step. Could Sweetapple track down the guy who had chopped up the horse? And then what? Tell the police, but to what real end? Bob would have lawyers to protect him from anything. It would just get Sweetapple in trouble, and still not bring Retribution back.

'You want a beer?'

'Might make me worse.'

'Something to eat?' Carson examined him, his face red, his fingers wrapping and unwrapping.

'No.'

'I think I'll do pasta anyway.'

She went to the kitchen for something to do. The sound of Sweetapple in the TV room, pacing up and back, swearing quietly, unnerved her. She knew he needed her, but she wasn't sure how to help. Care and support did not come easily to her. Preparing food seemed like the sort of thing someone better at this would do—something useful, while staying near him but not hovering.

Sweetapple needed to get back at Bob. They both did. Strong and decisive action would save them. Carson thought of Luke and how he would be the person who could take the thought of revenge from an idea to an action. Luke was the experienced man in this field, had probably been doing it all his life, but it wasn't the time to be asking for suggestions from Luke.

'What are you going to do?' She said it in an almost offhand way, trying to keep the anxiety down.

His head stopped moving, and he drew a powerful breath through his nostrils. 'Get the bastard, somehow.' It was what she expected, even hoped for, and the thrill of the idea caused a tremor to pulse through her body. She knew it would probably all just remain as words and rage bashed back and forth between them, but at least there was that. She walked back into the room and took the fingers of his hand.

'I reckon you should, somehow.'

He nodded and looked at her, his eyes blazing. 'I will, I tell you. I will.'

They stood with the thought between them, no sound in the house. She put her arms around him, and he didn't move or respond. She let him go.

'Luke might be good at this sort of thing.'

'Revenge?' Sweetapple appeared to be thinking about the idea, not Luke.

'Yep.'

On her way back to the kitchen, she said, 'I might give him a call.'

'Whatever you reckon.'

Carson rang Luke, and caught him as he was getting out of his lift home from work. He agreed to come over straightaway.

Luke had been considering not answering Carson's calls anymore. He was tired of being the third leg in their trio, and he was restless. Nothing had happened at the picket or in the mine, and he was trailing Carson around like a wishful teenager, the kind who settled for friendship in the hope that it would turn into something else. So he was thinking through where he might go. Perhaps he should track Anna down, or just get on the road and see where it took him. Yet it only took Carson's number to come up on his phone to water down his resolve. She hadn't explained what was going on, but she had made it sound like he was needed—and 'needed' meant something.

In Sweetapple's house, Carson was in the kitchen doing something with food, or maybe not doing anything, and Sweetapple was moving through rooms and doorways: out onto the verandah, back inside to the TV room, the kitchen, the bedroom, as if he was looking for someone to hit. Carson explained quickly what had happened, looking out for Sweetapple as she spoke. She was fidgety and unsettled, and Luke didn't know why he'd been summoned and what he was supposed to do. Carson was no help.

He went to Sweetapple, stopped him, put a hand on his shoulder, and said, 'I'm sorry, mate.'

Sweetapple nodded and swore through his teeth. 'Fucking Bob Statham.'

Luke agreed with him, and thought maybe he would go home. This was nothing to do with him.

Behind him, Carson said, 'How can we get him back, Luke? Any ideas?'

The question told Luke his purpose. This is what they wanted from him: not his friendship or his humour or his company, but his capacity for vengeance. He wasn't hurt by the thought. He was the right man for the job. Immediately, Sweetapple's not-believed secret came back to him: 'The bomb?'

The word was so powerful that just saying it made him half-believe it existed.

'What?' Carson was annoyed at him, perhaps disappointed that the expert she had called in had come up with something stupid. But Sweetapple turned and looked at him with the expression of someone experiencing a Eureka moment.

'Yes.'

'A real bomb?' This was too far out for Carson to believe. No one had ever hinted at a bomb's existence, and she didn't know why Luke knew of it. She looked at Luke, but he shrugged uncertainly.

'Where did you get a bomb?'

'From a girl, in an accident. She made me take it. I've got it hidden in the scrub.'

'Really?' He made it sound like a dream, a fantasy. Maybe he just hoped it had happened. 'What accident?'

'On the road, when I was out in the truck at Christmas. I didn't tell you. I thought it was incredibly bad luck.'

It was possible that he was completely out of his head. 'You actually have explosives?'

'Yes.'

A bomb. It made her imagination mad with possibilities: Mark's shearing shed; Bob Statham's house; the premises of Ponsford's. But even above those targets was Bob himself. The way he looked, the way he smelled, what he had done, made him the number one.

'I'm going to go and get it.' Suddenly he was going to make this mad thing real.

'Is it safe?' She felt like she should be asking more questions, slowing him up, demanding precaution.

'Yep.'

She put down the bowl she was holding and went over to him.

'Just take it steady. We can do this tomorrow, or any other day. No rush.'

'I'm going to get it.'

'Do you want me to come with you? Or Luke?'

'No. Only take me half an hour. Back in a bit.'

He was out the door, leaving the other two stranded in his neat house.

Sweetapple returned after three-quarters of an hour, and walked straight to the kitchen table with a package in his cradling arms. Carson and Luke stepped away from him, because even if it wasn't a bomb, he was radiating enough rage to send off sparks.

He put it carefully on the table and removed the plastic bags it was wrapped in. Carson involuntarily stepped back, but Luke leant forward. Sweetapple released the catches, and opened the top of the suitcase as if he was revealing a load of cash in a heist movie.

Carson felt Luke start, and presumed wrongly it was in fear. Luke moved closer to the laptop bag, rubbing his hands together, his eyes wide and shining. He carefully ran a hand over the contents of the suitcase, entranced.

'It's a complete unit—detonators, computer links, explosives. I thought it was just explosives. Someone in the know has put together the whole package.' He looked at them to share his excitement, but they were blank-faced.

'See? We could do anything. You can blow this up manually through the cords, or do it remotely using the computer codes. There's enough bomb here to blow up a house.'

The reality was hitting Carson in a rush, but Sweetapple was stony-faced, as if it was what he had expected all along.

'But can you do it? Put it in place and make it work?' She wanted to hear him talk practically so she didn't drift off into some sort of thriller fantasy. She was pretty sure she wanted this to be real.

'I think so.'

They stared at it again, together in the presence of the brilliant light of their destiny.

'The girl. In the accident. Did you get her name?'

'Why?'

'This is from a mine, isn't it?'

'Wouldn't have a clue.'

'Straight, dirty blonde hair? Nose stud? About this tall?' He indicated a height with his hand.

'Oh yeah. Suppose so.'

'Was Anna her name?'

'You know her?'

'A bit. She was on the protest. I didn't know she took it. I was going to do it, and she talked me out of it.' Luke took a pace back and looked up at the ceiling, rolling his eyes and arching his neck. 'Bloody hell!'

The other two were looking at him, waiting for something they could make sense of.

'So what do you want to do with it?'

'Not sure.'

'You want to blow up his house?'

'Yeah.'

Carson didn't comment. She didn't like Caroline, but she had no desire to see her hurt. Sweetapple saw the risk. 'But he's never there, and someone else might get hurt.'

'Maybe a car or truck, or something he drives?'

Sweetapple and Carson shook their heads. Making sure you got the right person in the right vehicle was too far-fetched.

'Has he got offices somewhere? Or a special monument or something?'

They didn't know. 'We could check on the net, I suppose.' Carson said.

They searched under people's names and company names, and even though there were offices and many projects and investments, nothing that could hurt him without hurting other people came up.

'I guess we could wait until we know he's home,' Carson said. 'Invite Caroline out to something, maybe a riding lesson, and then blow his house up while we know it's only him there.'

'Kill him?' Luke asked.

'No. Just scare the shit out of him.'

It had become the group's project, not just Sweetapple's revenge. Carson and Luke took small, excited looks at each other. They were now a band of guerrillas united in getting their own back.

'I don't want to kill anyone.' After those first hours of desperation and despair, Sweetapple's thinking had returned to the question of what was practical. There was no myth or romance for him.

Luke stretched, and then got up and poured himself a glass of water.

'All that stuff on his investments says the most important thing he's done, and probably the thing that finances everything else, is the coal mine. So maybe we should blow up …'

'We can't blow up a coal mine. They're too big, and besides that, they work around the clock. There'd never be a time you could get in without people seeing you.' Sweetapple was dismissive and annoyed.

'I was thinking about a coal *train*. The line that runs south-east through here is the only way for his coal to get to port. It's the only way for all those mines to get their product to port. If we blow up the line, we stop the mine meeting its contracts, and we create a bit of doubt in the company—shares slide, investors lose confidence, Bob loses money, big-time.' Luke had been wanting to suggest this since the bomb had been unveiled, but he knew it was smarter to let them spill their first ideas.

The other two were quiet. It sounded clever, but Sweetapple wondered if it was too clever. 'Don't they patrol the railway lines?'

'Not much that I've seen, anyway.'

Carson was amused. 'You've looked?'

'Yep. I like trains. Watch 'em on my days off.'

'Wow. Country trainspotting.'

'Seventy-five carriages at eighty tonnes each one. That's bloody impressive, as far as I'm concerned. Ten trains a day, even at $60 a tonne, is over three-and-a-half million bucks a day. A day.'

Luke thought he might have dumbfounded them with these figures, but Sweetapple wasn't interested. 'So, is it easy to blow up the line? I mean, do we have enough grunt to do the job?'

'You've really only got to move the line a little bit to cause a lot of trouble.'

'We won't derail a passenger train, will we?' Carson was doing her best to hold back a mad excitement, and to attach herself to the real-world possibilities. Her heart was leaping ahead with visions of herself as part of an outlaw group blowing up trains, eluding the law, supported by a cheering public.

Luke looked at her, annoyed and surprised at her expressing

a creeping nervousness. 'We just follow a timetable. We don't even have to derail a train—we can just stuff the line so all traffic is stopped before they even get there. In that case, they put passengers on buses, but they can't do anything about the coal—not in the numbers they want to move it in.'

'It sounds pretty good to me.' Sweetapple sat back. 'We need to get a timetable for the passenger trains, and work out when the coal trains come and go. We need to find a good spot where we won't be seen and where we can see them, I guess. And we need to know how often they patrol the line.'

'You really want to do this?' Luke looked at Sweetapple and then at Carson. They looked at each other and nodded. 'If we get it even a little bit wrong, we could go to jail—would go to jail.'

Luke needed them to feel they had been given every opportunity to back out, until backing out was no longer an option.

Carson examined her hands. 'I don't want to go to jail. But let's see … They can't link the bomb to us except if this "Anna" goes to the police and tells them she had a bomb and she gave it to some cattle thief in the area. They don't even know about the horse, so they're going to have trouble working out a motivation. Unless someone can trace the bomb to you?' She looked at Luke, aware that there was a whole lot she didn't know about him.

'No, not to me. They might blame it on the protestors, though.'

No one proffered sympathy for the protestors, while Luke wondered at the truth of his statement. He might be the first person Peter would think of after an explosion. But maybe not.

The protest group had had one bomb, and it wasn't a big leap to think they might have sourced another one and used it on the line. In fact, they would be a pretty good cover. If Peter tracked him down, Luke could blame it all on the picketers. Militant greenie bastards.

Sweetapple slapped his hands down on his knees and stood up. 'So let's go for a drive.' Carson acted indifferent, stretching and scratching, and implying she would go along if she had to.

In Carson's car, with her at the wheel, Luke said, 'Let's drive all the way to the mine, or close to, then follow the line back till we find what we're looking for.'

They set off silently, unified, looking like farm buyers or picnic-spot searchers. The road followed alongside the rail line and crossed it twice with ostentatious, out-of-place traffic-light and boom-gate constructions, courtesy of too many car–train collisions over the years. The track sat high off the surrounding earth, fully reinforced for the huge, heavy, relentless coal trains.

Halfway to the mine, Luke squeezed forward between the two front seats, pointed through the windscreen, and said, 'Up here. See where the line goes into the Bull Oak and Pine scrub?' On their left, the line that had been plainly visible for many kilometres veered into an alleyway in thick, straight-trunked scrub.

'It's like a secret corridor. You can't see it from the outside, and there's only a couple of access roads through it.'

It looked like dirty scrub to Carson: dusty floor, dry grass, and sticks without greenery. 'You've checked it out? Before?' She asked over her shoulder.

Luke ignored her.

'You must be a train nerd or something.'

'We'll drive in there, on the way back, if we've still got light,' Sweetapple said.

They continued looking out their windows, watching the railway line, the fall of the land, the trees, and the crossroads. Despite his love for the trains, Luke had the sensation that a break in that relentless, faultless line would be a good thing—something that ought to be done. Its fidelity and integrity were almost insulting.

Eventually, the walls of the mine rose up in front of them, grey and mesa-like, a dusty wound in the landscape.

Carson pulled over on the side of the road, then turned back. 'We're too close here to do anything, aren't we?' The men agreed soundlessly. When the mine was out of sight, Sweetapple stopped her.

'Just here, where the track cuts away from the road, into that rise. That could be all right.'

'You want me to follow that dirt track?'

'Yeah. Just for a bit.'

She pulled the car across the road, up a washed-out gravel track that soon found the railway line. They bounced over it and looked back. There were no other cars around. The line was cut into the hill, the rise towering over it on one side and keeping it out of sight on the other.

'Protection from the road and stuff, but you can see all the way through from one end. If any local pulled up here, they'd see us or what we'd done.' Luke was saying it, but they had already made the observation to themselves.

Carson added, 'And the only getaway is at each end, by the look of it,' liking the sound of 'getaway'. She turned the car around and rolled back down to the main road.

After a few more minutes' driving, Luke said, 'I can't see anywhere that's going to be as good as the pine tree place.'

They drove until they saw the trees sticking up like a plantation on the side of the road. Carson turned off and drove in alongside the track. The road was rutted and rocky, and almost not a road. They stopped at a centre point, got out, and looked back and then forward. Because of the way the line arced over distance, the way out and the way in were obscured.

'It's perfect,' Sweetapple said.

'Perfect,' Carson repeated.

Luke walked over to the line, crouched down, and then stood up abruptly, spreading his hands and yelling, 'Boom!'

Carson laughed raucously, head back, open-mouthed. Luke joined her, and they ran around screaming their excitement and eventually falling to the ground and rolling around while Sweetapple looked at the trees and the track and even the sky. Carson and Luke grabbed at each other, joking, teasing, indulging, imagining that Sweetapple might not notice.

'Do we drive in here, or walk through the trees from the other side?' he asked, silently promising himself he would not be goaded by what was going on between Luke and Carson, not have his powerful need diverted or diluted.

Luke gasped through the end of his convulsions, and pushed Carson back down before she giggled and he stood up, brushing himself off. 'I think we drive in here like we just did,' he said. 'Set everything up and then leave. When we come to blow it, walk in from … somewhere.' He looked around. The trees were tall and thick, but the understorey was thin.

'Yes. Yes. From … somewhere. Outstanding observation, Mr Luke.' Carson adopted a Sherlock Holmes posture, and rubbed a hand at her chin. 'Because in the end, we've all got to come from somewhere, don't you think?' When Luke turned, she skittered down the track away from him.

He let her go. 'We need to be at a join, like this one. So we could come through somewhere around here.'

He marched towards the trees, entered the thicket, and kept on going. Sweetapple and Carson watched him go, thinking they might follow and then realising quickly that he had disappeared. They could still hear his feet over-stepping on leaves and sticks, and then they were left alone.

Sweetapple reached out and grabbed her hand. 'You don't have to do this. Luke can show me what to do, and I can do it on my own. It's not your problem.'

Carson couldn't think what to say. Almost nothing else mattered in the world anymore, except blowing up this train line. Was he taking that away from her? How could he not see how she felt right then?

'I'm in it with you, problem or not.' It sounded good and even convincing. It was the way, perhaps, that she should be thinking: go all the way for him, with him. She knew that here was the most exhilarating ride she could ever conceive of, and her one big chance to get back at the pricks, to make a mark and blow all those bastards sky-high.

'Okay.' He looked at her with meaning, and she felt something recoil inside her. He didn't see that the three of them were together in this as one mad team. He thought they'd come along for support, out of some sort of obligation, and would drop him at the first opportunity. She could only think to push him away, joking, as she would have at any other time. And then Luke broke the moment, returning, announcing that it was maybe two hundred metres to the other side, complete with a contour bank where they could hide a vehicle. Luke couldn't believe the whole layout was so good; it was as if it had been set up for them. Even while he announced this, it didn't stop him noticing something about Carson and the way she turned her body side on, rigid, away from Sweetapple. It was possible she was making a new choice. Things were going well.

'I was saying to Carson, she doesn't have to go through with this. Same for you. Once you set me up, I can do it on my own. Cover your arse and walk away.'

'Not a fucken chance, mate. I wouldn't miss this for the world.' He clapped his hands together boyishly, gleefully. 'Although I don't think we can drive in here again, along the track. That clay stuff will hold perfect tyre prints. They'd find us before the week was out. In fact, we'd better not try anything until there's a rainstorm to remove the tracks we made today.'

Carson thought she saw Sweetapple's face show some appreciation for Luke's abilities.

'I don't want to wait that long,' Sweetapple said. 'Nobody's going to notice or care about a few tyre marks out here. It'll be fine.'

They got back into the car as Carson scuffed at her shoe tracks in the yellow sand. She sat for a moment in the driver's seat, wondering if she should turn around and risk making cuts in the sand or driving straight out, leaving a track for a kilometre.

Sweetapple answered her before the question was asked. 'Turn round and go back. If we cut in, I'll get out and cover it over.'

On the way back to the entrance, past the trees and over their old tracks, Carson could feel an odd, contented happiness being shared. It was like finding your destiny and experiencing the kind of peace that came with it.

'"Kumbaya", anyone?'

16

Carson couldn't steady, couldn't sleep. She listened to music, drank another cider, checked her scam page, sang loudly, talked to herself, and eventually went to bed, only to sit up watching movies on her laptop. But they were false to her now: poor representations of what real action would be like, with make-believe stunts and scripts, and huge production crews directing actors to fight their way out of fake trouble in fanciful locations. It was no longer possible for her to suspend her disbelief.

She shut the laptop and thought she should have stayed on with Sweetapple, but that moment near the trees when she had felt something close to repulsion had forced her to make up an excuse: her dog had been sick, and she wanted to see that he was all right, and didn't want him left on his own overnight. She knew Sweetapple was disappointed. She expected him to offer to come to her place instead, but he didn't; which said something, but she wasn't sure what.

It was a peak night for him, for all of them. The intensity made her want to have sex just to celebrate life. But something in her body said 'no', and she trusted her body on these things. If there was anyone she wanted to celebrate with, it was probably Luke. But she loved Sweetapple, that was a certainty, and the only thing she was looking for from Luke was the physical rush that was going on between them, the three of them. But now, standing in her quiet kitchen, the only noises coming from her relentless dog and nesting duck, she thought she would have had either of the men, or both, if they had just taken the moment and showed some sort of shared exuberance that she could have joined in with. They were going to do something huge, maybe even history-making. They would definitely make the news, and the best the men could come up with was a couple of drinks and home to bed. Weird. And now here she was, an electrical charge with no earth, ready to burn her house down. She considered going back out to Sweetapple's place, and then rang Luke's mobile.

'Hey.'

'Hey. Is there a problem?'

'No. Just feeling a bit wired. Big day.'

'Yeah.'

'What are you up to?'

'Walking. Bit wired, too. You can join me if you want.'

'No, thanks. But if you said you were going to blow up someone's mailbox …'

He laughed into the empty, echoing space. Carson could picture the long stride that he bounced into when he wanted to get somewhere quickly. She couldn't think where that could be.

'Do you really think we can do this?'

'If not, I'll dig that line up with a crowbar and a shovel.'

'Where are you walking to?'

'Just walking. I like it when there's no one about.'

He sounded at ease, but whatever she thought she had rung for, he wasn't offering.

'Okay. Thanks. Just wanted to … share. I'll see you.'

When Luke put his phone away, he felt a euphoric lift. There was something powerful going on — she just wasn't ready to acknowledge it yet. And he hadn't told her that he was on his way to visit Jackie, a girl he'd met at the RSL, whom he'd been with a couple of times. Yesterday, he would have told Carson where he was going. Tonight, he withheld. It wasn't a planned strategy or deviousness. It was instinct. The closer you got, the less they wanted to know about the others, but you could share every relationship detail with a mate.

Luke was happy not to be with her tonight, though. If she asked him any more closely about the bomb, his lack of knowledge would become evident. He had a pretty good idea what to do — they had talked about it often enough when things got heated on the picket — but there was a significant difference between thinking about it and doing it. He knew that he couldn't search for 'How to Detonate a Bomb' on his phone, and he couldn't ask anyone what to do, so he would just have to go with the procedure he had picked up. At least there would be time on the night to work his way through it.

He knocked on Jackie's door, and a small, young redheaded woman he didn't know answered.

'Is Jackie in?'

The girl turned and yelled, 'Jackie! For you.' Jackie appeared in the hallway in flannelette pyjamas and a gown. The redheaded girl disappeared without looking back.

'This is a surprise.'

'You got another date?' He hoped it sounded like a joke.

'I didn't know you were coming. It was supposed to be last night.'

'Sorry. Got a bit busy. Have I missed my chance?'

'Yeah.' She was indignant. 'I watch my shows tonight. Girls' night in. Lollies and white wine goon. Not negotiable.'

Behind her, a girl laughed in a loud, unembarrassed way.

'Wow. TV wins. That's flattering.'

'Way it goes.'

'Okay. I'll catch up with you later.' He turned away and waved a hand, thinking, *I'll get you, sometime I'll get you*, and Jackie shut the door behind him, not entertaining any second thoughts.

On his path back down the street, he sent a flying kick into a small mailbox on a thin stem. It went down easily, and he stomped on it as though it was a dying bird. His hands were shaking and his teeth grinding, but the violence gave him release and he began to sing softly, gasping, trying to regulate his breathing and flatten his rage. Vandalised mailboxes would just attract attention. The other two would hate him to do that.

He punched the air and hit a hand hard down his side. And then his tension was gone, and he went back to walking calmly, alone in the night, because there really was no one else about. In the morning, he would watch trains and note the time intervals. He might even take a week off and do it every day, if Frank would give him the time off, which he probably wouldn't. He was still filthy about his ute being stolen, blaming it on Abo kids in town, and constantly phoning the cops, demanding they do something about a crime where the villains were obvious. It gave Luke a special type of pleasure.

In the main street he could hear music coming, distorted, from the pub. He felt like a beer, but he knew himself too well to risk having one at the bar. At this time of night, when he was feeling like this, there would always be someone who could set him off, and he really didn't want to be set off. Perhaps he should go out and visit Carson just for a cup of tea, or at least for the excuse of a cup of tea. It might be the perfect night for it: she all revved up; he suddenly close to her because of what they were about to take on, and he was going to be the star of the show. He thought about her face and the bright fire of her body until his breathing got thick and his chest tight. *Not now, not now*, he told himself. It would create a problem that none of them could deal with; it could ruin everything. A child could see that. They might even end up blowing each other up. Which didn't matter, except he wanted to blow up a train line even more than he wanted Carson. Luke bought a six-pack at the bottle shop and went to his room.

Sweetapple sat in front of his TV watching nothing, replaying the day in his mind. Even after all the plans and little thrills of the past twenty-four hours, he couldn't stop thinking about the mare. The vision of her being killed and butchered was traumatising him to the extent that he thought maybe the bomb should be in his house under his own bed. Now he was at the limits of his imagination. He couldn't think of a future. Even Carson's sudden intention to steer clear of him didn't make any difference to the constant presence of the horse and the bomb.

If Bob turned up now, out of nowhere, Sweetapple couldn't be sure that he wouldn't murder him. Before today, the thought of killing someone would have been a stupid, idle threat, or someone else's mad impulse stemming from an uncontrolled rage. But now he clinically and practically thought through the possibility, and knew that he was capable of it. The death of the mare had given him more than enough motivation and justification for killing Bob. In his mind, he could take Bob's life many times, in many different ways, and be much less horrified by it than he had been by the slaughter of Retribution.

And then he began to sob quietly, painfully, into his chest, hating himself and everything he had become since his parents had died — the thief, the liar, the bullshitter, the sneak — but there was no way back from it. He was at that precipice where every bridge had been burnt behind him. Even Carson appeared to be stepping away from him. So he clung to the practical things: how to make this thing happen; timetables; timing; getaways. Could he trust the other two? This wasn't a choice, because neither of them would give up the opportunity. In the past few hours he had noticed very little outside himself, but he had felt the bond between Carson and Luke. He had seen them communicate without talking, and felt Carson's missing light touch land on Luke's arm. He knew they would betray him, and there was nothing he could do about it.

After two weeks, they met again at Sweetapple's place. Luke and Carson had bumped along in Carson's car. Now Carson stepped out, asking, 'Do you think we should be doing this at night or really early in the morning? We don't want anyone thinking we're some sort of a team.'

Sweetapple figured that it was only the inclusion of Luke

that made it a team. He and Carson had reasons for being together. 'Luke could keep his head down when he's travelling with you. That ought to remove the risk.'

They nodded together sagely, seriously. Perhaps they really were a team. It had been two weeks of checking timetables, and plotting coal-train loadings, and trying to keep calm. They hadn't seen each other, and had avoided talking on their phones, at Luke's suggestion.

'But I want to have one practice in the daylight, and then we can do it at night,' Sweetapple said. 'I reckon we need to be able to see what we're doing for the first time.' He handed Luke a bag like the one with the bomb in it. 'We can take my ute.'

'I'll keep my head down.' Luke laughed, but the others didn't.

They drove to the pine scrub, and turned off when they got close. The track took them in behind where the scrub shielded the railway line. Sweetapple pulled the ute into a gap between a small clump of Angophoras. They squeezed out, Luke holding his bag. Sweetapple led them around through more trees and into the dusty world of pine trees and she-oaks. They tracked through sticks and sand, wondering if they looked as obvious as they felt. There were piles of discarded timber railway sleepers at the edge of the trees. Sweetapple stopped and looked out at the line. The sand was pushed up into a bank at his feet and all along the edge of the trees.

'We go to the nearest join.'

So they stepped out into the bright daylight, one after the other, Sweetapple holding a small spade against his legs, Luke in second place, Carson trailing, looking over her shoulder, listening for sounds of a train or any vehicle. There were magpies and distant galahs. She was aware of the light breeze swishing through the fine pines of the oak trees, and of something rustling though the leaf matter further down the tree corridor. The footsteps of the men in front of her, and their withheld breathing, were the only background to her existence. Her pulse was loud in her ears, and her skin felt gecko sensitive. It was dead dry beneath their feet, but Carson felt as fully alive as she ever had. Her whole life had been funnelled to this wild action. Coming back from the city was just a part of the fate that set her up for this: it was a time she was made for. Carson dared not think of a world of 'after', a time when there was no bomb to plan for, and their purpose was gone. 'Completed' was a concept she would never be able to accept.

Luke knelt at a join and put the bag down. 'We dig in under here, as far as we can go, and then pack the gravel back over it.'

Sweetapple pushed the shovel where Luke directed, dragging the gravel back into a small pile, the shovel hardly penetrating the hard-packed material when he dug again. Carson positioned herself with her back to them, standing sentry until Sweetapple had a hole large enough to fit the sausage up under the line. Luke pretended to place a package in the hole, and then Sweetapple covered it and pushed his foot down on the covered hole. Carson swept the area with an oak branch, and they backtracked to the trees.

Back at the ute, Luke said he thought he could probably set off the bomb from where they were, maybe even further away, but he wasn't sure if the thickness of the trees would affect the signal. This pleased Sweetapple. They stood apart, looking around, trying to imagine what else they needed to do or be aware of.

But after first thinking it was an advantage to trigger the bomb at a distance, Luke realised that they wouldn't be able to see the explosion. 'We need to be able to see it go up. We won't see anything much from here—just some dirt in the air. I've got to see it. I'm not blowing up train tracks and not seeing it happen. If we go further up the line and look back, we'll be able to see it happen and still have the protection of the scrub.'

Now Carson was leading them back to the scrub and then in under branches, walking the diagonal until they reached the other side. The three of them leant out and looked back to where they thought they'd dug under the line.

'Where that tree branch is almost on the ground—that's where we were.' From where they stood, the tracks looked like they might go on forever.

Luke said, 'Can't fucken wait.'

'Your plan is to blow up the line, well before any trains are near it?' Carson was pointing as she explained her question. 'Then the train driver comes along, sees the problem, and stops: all traffic comes to a halt? Coal trains backed up for days?'

Sweetapple was suddenly animated, waving his hands and shaking his head. 'No. No. I want to blow up the line when there are carriages going over it. Halfway along the train, like twenty or thirty carriages in, then boom, and the whole thing derails—carriages and coal and steel and shit everywhere.' He had a gleam in his eye that Carson liked.

'You remember that accident near Wenthom a few years ago?' Luke asked.

Neither Carson nor Sweetapple did.

'Something was wrong with the line, and the carriages smashed in a zigzag because they all have individual braking systems. If one in front derails, the others behind brake and jack-knife: it's a real train-long mess. So not only do they have to fix the line, they've got to right and remove the carriages, which isn't as simple as you'd think.' Luke was now the technical expert.

'And then we say, "If you don't give us five million dollars, we'll do it again … and again."' This was Carson, the big thinker.

'We haven't got any more bombs.' Luke didn't need to point it out.

'I know, but they don't know that.'

'How are we going to get the money from them? I don't think we're going to ask for five million in clean banknotes, are we? And every transfer is trackable these days. We're just not clever enough for that sort of stuff.' The annoyance in Sweetapple's voice was clear.

'I've got Bob's bank account details,' Carson said.

'What?'

'Yep, I do. He gave them to me, or someone did.'

Luke started to laugh. 'That is ridiculous. We take money from him, put it in his account, and then somehow steal it back? Fucken brilliant!'

'That's what I was thinking, but I'm not really sure how.'

Sweetapple face was dark. 'I don't want to do any of that. I just want to blow up his bloody train. I don't want his money.'

'I get that it's your thing, but we're involved too,' Luke said. 'This is a perfect chance to get some money out of these bastards. Big money. You gotta see that.' Luke was suddenly on board. 'I reckon it's worth a shot. We send 'em a note with the demands. If they don't respond, we forget about it. If they do, we worry about it then. Maybe we never even touch the money.'

'I want revenge on this bastard. That's all. If we start mucking around with ransom or whatever it is, we just make it harder and harder to get away with it.'

'You still get your revenge. Maybe you get a little more revenge than you set out for.'

'It's just fucken greed that's going to make more trouble for us.' Sweetapple got into the ute and slammed the door. Carson and Luke grinned at each other, and then got in, too.

Caroline asked Sweetapple to help out with some cattle work. On the pasture country, a gate had been knocked open, allowing the heifers to mix with the steers. They needed to be sorted again, so Caroline had told Joey she could handle the job because she wanted to show she was useful, and she knew it was work that Joey didn't particularly care for.

At first light, Sweetapple helped her bring the mob in and put them in the cattle yards. They ran a group off into a smaller yard for drafting. Caroline selected heifers from the mob and sent them towards Sweetapple, who was at the gate letting them out into the holding paddock. She had done this sort of thing before, and thought it would be a fairly simple process: boys from girls couldn't be that difficult. But as she was taller than the animals and standing close to them, some with their faces towards her and some away from her, it was much harder to see genitalia to tell which was which.

In the drifting dust, Sweetapple asked if the heifers had different earmarks from the steers; as far as Caroline knew, the cattle herd didn't receive that sort of management attention.

The only way to tell them apart was to check their bits. So they proceeded slowly. Caroline would select an animal she thought was a heifer, but if she was wrong, Sweetapple would block it at the gate and yell, without judgement, 'Steer,' turn it back, and they would start again. It took some time, but they managed to get all the heifers in the paddock outside and all the steers in the yard, and then walk them back to their separate paddocks by morning tea.

On her verandah, Caroline served tea out of a teapot and a packet of biscuits on a tray, and wondered if it was okay to serve biscuits that hadn't been baked at home. Sweetapple had declined at first, saying he had things to do, but she 'wouldn't hear of it', so now he sat uncomfortably in her wicker chair, his hair stuck to his forehead where his hat had been removed. They both drank black, sugarless tea while she apologised for her slow drafting, and then they talked about the condition of the cattle, and the season, and the property.

He had been stiff all morning, but now she could see he was relaxing, making small jokes and even teasing her lightly about her new ambitions.

And then he asked, 'Has Bob been around much?'

'Not much.' The tactic of bluntness wasn't deliberate, but she hoped it might put him off.

'That's what I thought. Must have a lot of overseas deals on, eh?'

She had struggled for some time with the topic of when to tell people and how. Initially, she had pretended there was no need because he would be back soon enough. No one would notice because he was always away, just as she used to be. But as time went on and she admitted to herself that his return was a fantasy, she began to realise that holding on to the public pretence of their marriage was stopping her from moving on. If she didn't tell people he was gone, he would never be properly gone. But she still hadn't told anyone — not even her mother. It had to start somewhere.

'We're not really together anymore. We're pretty much split, so I'm not sure when he'll be back, or whatever.'

'I'm sorry about that.' Sweetapple looked much more concerned than she expected. Had Bob and Sweetapple been mates? She didn't think so.

'It happens. Two people with different careers. Never home. You know.' Maybe he didn't.

'It's tough. I think my parents should have got divorced, or at least lived separately. Might have saved them both.'

'They had trouble?' It was a surprise divergence.

'The old man was pretty stuffed up after Vietnam. Drugs and post-traumatic whatever. Had real trouble trying to get his act together, and Mum did her best to fight it with him. They both failed, I guess.'

She watched him saying these painful, powerful things with his usual cool reserve.

'That was when we sold this country to Bob,' he said, making a half-hearted indication with his open hand, 'when he was just getting into the mines.'

Caroline didn't remember. She wasn't even a girlfriend at the time.

'Must have hurt.'

'Yep. It did. But you get that, don't you?'

He had stopped with the revelations. She thought a change of topic important.

'You've always been into horses?'

'Can't remember when I wasn't. Always wanted to be around them. Rode Mum's horses before I had my own.'

'Your mother liked horses?'

'Mad keen. Keener than Dad. But she loved the dressage and three-day events, and that sort of stuff. What about you? Did you have a pony as a kid?'

'You can't tell? No. We had dogs and a cat for a while. Oh, and one time Mum had a bird, a parrot of some sort, but that was it. Have you ever had a horse as special as that beautiful Missy?'

Of all the things they had talked about, she didn't guess that this would cause the greatest reaction. At her innocent mention, his face caved in. He wasn't crying. It was something worse. Awful to see.

'She's hurt? God, Graham. I'm sorry.'

'She's dead.' He began to give some sort of explanation, but pulled himself up.

Caroline put a hand on his arm. 'That is so terrible. Where did it happen? Do you know how?'

'I can't really talk about it, sorry.' Sweetapple stood abruptly, unsure what to do with his hands. 'I'd better get going. Thanks for the cuppa.'

Caroline stood, too, wanting to hold him back, to let him share what he was suffering, but there was no way of doing it. 'Thanks so much for your help this morning.'

He was quickly gone, even as she was saying to his back: 'If you need to talk …'

Left alone with her tea, Caroline put 'Missy horse' in her web browser, and came up with images of a hundred ponies, most of them in different states and countries, being held tightly by small children and doting women. She knew that the mare was special and didn't belong to Sweetapple, but there was no reason to think her death would be any different from so many others. It made her feel like she had lost something, too, and maybe even gained a point of access to Sweetapple.

17

They met at Sweetapple's place at 2.00 am in black clothes and beanies. Luke's calculations had a train going past their blast point at 4.00 am. They would have enough time to get there, set up, and get out of the way. Carson gave them face-black, but then Luke said they shouldn't put it on until they got there, because if someone pulled them over, and they had black clothes on and black on their faces, it would be obvious that they were up to something.

'Who's going to pull us over at 2.00 am?' Carson retorted. So they got into Sweetapple's ute, all in black, Luke carrying the bag, the shovel, and crowbar in the back, their phones charged as torches.

They drove in silence, but the energy in the car was enough to make the windows bulge. Luke fidgeted next to Carson until she had to tell him to be still.

Halfway there, Sweetapple turned his head to Luke and asked, 'You sure you've got everything?'

'I'm sure. Man, we're going to blow this thing up.'

'Yeah. We're going to blow this fucken thing up!' Carson had held her excitement back for as long as she could.

'Blow this fucken thing up!' Luke repeated it joyously, slapping his hand hard on the seat.

They expected Sweetapple to hush them, but he didn't. Instead he nodded his head as if to a song he liked, as Luke and Carson went on whooping and whistling and clapping their hands.

The pine and oak scrub rose up in the headlights. Sweetapple slowed, and Carson and Luke were immediately silent. Sweetapple turned off the road and dropped his lights. They trundled down the track to the appointed site. Carson could hear Luke's laboured breathing. The tyres were noisy, slipping on the stones, and the handbrake was too loud when Sweetapple pulled up at their spot. When the men slammed the car doors shut, Carson couldn't help but hiss at them to be quiet. Sweetapple told her to calm down, and she wanted to hit him.

Out in the night air, standing together, Carson felt like they had arrived at a mighty destiny, and she could see that Luke sensed it, too. He almost glowed, bright against the dark figure of Sweetapple.

Luke knew he was at a great moment in his life, a moment that might shake many others and be remembered by so many more. He was the bomber.

Sweetapple had had misgivings all night. He hadn't slept or eaten, and had barely been able to sit still. His need to hit back was as powerful as ever, but the moral wrong of it had crept up on him: he could hear his mother's voice, and his conscience, pointing out the stupidity of what he was doing, let alone involving two young people in it. But in the car, making their way to the site, he was sure he hadn't convinced or coerced either of them to be involved. They would be involved with or without him. So when they got out together, he felt the pressure lift. He was going to do this for Retribution, and it needed doing.

Sweetapple led them through the trees, single file, aware of every twig and leaf that crackled beneath their feet, because they were the only sounds in the still night. Carson leant forward and stuck a couple of fingers in Luke's belt. He reached back and grabbed her wrist lightly, gave it a squeeze, and let it go.

They were quickly through the scrub, and Sweetapple was on the edge of the sand windrow, leaning out and looking back and forth up the corridor. He was greeted by a distant sound of diesel motors labouring in his direction. 'Fuck—it's the train.' They were still, and listened as the sound rumbled louder, and they knew he was right.

Carson said, 'I thought you had this worked out. Regular as clockwork?'

'I did. Must have changed loading times or something. It's still a fair way off. We've probably still got time.'

And then the glow from a light unseen lit the far end of the track as the low sound slid down the tracks to them.

She put down the bowl she was holding and went over to him. 'Not tonight. There's no rush.'

They retreated into the trees, swallowing the desire to throw rocks or sticks at the train, to do anything instead of nothing.

Luke took a chance, and bolted out of the trees and down to the hole beneath the line. He scrabbled the gravel back with his hand, grabbed the bomb from his bag and slid it into the hole, then packed the gravel and sand back around it. Then he was on his feet running back towards them, yelling, 'Get back, get back.' They pushed each other towards their spot, down the corridor, and Luke caught up with them, knelt down, and flipped open the suitcase. But quicker than they'd thought, the train was on them, clanging past. Luke stopped and gave up fiddling with the laptop. The opportunity was gone. They watched the train like transfixed primitives. This was the great god they had planned to destroy.

As they walked back, Luke stepped closer to Carson and ran a hand down her side. She shrugged him off, but Sweetapple had seen it and was suddenly unsure how to react. It wasn't an intimate touch, but it held echoes of something he had witnessed without knowing.

'Are you right?' He said it to Luke.

'Yep. You?'

'You trying to hit on Carson?'

'No.'

Sweetapple had learnt that with Luke, 'no' was never totally 'no', and that 'yes' was never wholly 'yes'.

'You wouldn't want to be.'

Carson was walking away, ignoring them.

Luke's insouciance could make anything trivial. 'I wouldn't want to be? Relax, man. We're in this together. Yeah?'

Sweetapple pushed him hard with two hands on his chest. Luke fell backwards, surprised, grabbing at a tree branch for support. Carson heard and spun around in the dirt to look at them, wondering if they were going to fight over her. Sweetapple was steaming angry but in control, and she liked that.

Luke breathed deeply, and Carson could see the decision he was making and the self-discipline he was exerting as clearly as if he had told her himself. Instead of stepping forward to challenge Sweetapple, he took a firmer grip on the branch and smiled.

'Just chill. We're friends, and we're doing something big. That's all.' He held his hands in the air as a kind of surrender. He was very pleased with himself. He would have the explosion, and he would get the girl, and he would not let one push ruin that.

Sweetapple nodded and started towards the ute, thinking that when this job was done, he would do something about Luke. Once this job was done, he would do everything for Carson.

In the ute on the way home, Luke said, in a voice that suggested nothing had happened, 'We'll have to give it some leeway. Arrive like half an hour before we think we should be here. Shit happens, things break down, load times get changed. It's probably not as reliable as I thought.'

'We got that.' Carson was annoyed at him, not because he'd stuffed up, but because she was so geed up after the failure that it was difficult to return to inaction and chit-chat.

'Feel free to work out the timetables yourself.'

'It was your job. You just didn't do it.'

'Don't know what you expect. It's not like I've got any inside information. I'm just watching the trains come past.'

'You said you could do it.'

Luke looked out the window at the guideposts ghosting past. He just had to stay calm.

A week later, Carson arranged to drive Luke out to Sweetapple's place at midnight; the plan was to go early, set up, and wait for the train to arrive. She said she'd pick Luke up in town, and he was waiting for her in the dark, leaning against the wall, his beanie in his hands, when she entered his street. Carson had been restless at work, but there had been enough to do to prevent the endless mulling over of the night's possibilities. The hours after knock-off and before she had to get going had been an agony. She couldn't settle or eat or watch TV, and a drink was out of the question. It was a relief to finally have Luke in the car and to be on their way.

And suddenly she felt too aware of him, his breathing, the slight smell of something like fast food, the way his fingers played along the top of his thigh. She looked across at him, and wondered if he felt what she felt. Luke looked back and grinned devilishly, more aware than she had hoped. He cheekily put a hand across onto her thigh and looked away. She pulled the car over to the side of the road, undid her seatbelt, leant across, and kissed him inexpertly, as hard as she could. He grabbed at her body and she stopped, withdrew, righted herself, put the belt back on, and pulled the car onto the road.

'That's it?' He reached out to her again, and found he'd been too slow.

'That's it.' She had the initiative back.

'No way.' He grabbed the steering wheel and reefed it towards his chest. Carson screamed, and he overpowered her as she took her foot off the accelerator and they coasted to the side of the road.

And then they were pulling off clothes and finding each other, the space too small for satisfying anything but the most immediate need.

When they were done and she had finished dressing herself,

she asked him, 'Do I look okay?'

'Oh yeah.'

'I mean, I don't look like I had a fuck on the way, do I?'

'I guess that depends on how observant he is.'

She hit him on the shoulder, and steered the car back out onto the road.

Sweetapple was waiting, and she knew he was impatient. There was no one to remove his tension.

He was refusing to think why they would be late, instead rolling over the logistics and risks of the night in his head. They went in Carson's car this time, with Luke, as always, in the back. No one spoke. The anticlimax of their last trip had made them feel foolish and unwilling to express their excitement. When they reached the pine scrub and got out, the night was still and quiet. It was if they had never left. Only a passing cattle truck distinguished this time from the last.

After Luke had packed the explosive into place, they went back to the car. Sweetapple had a thermos of coffee, which he shared with some chocolate that Carson had brought. They were confident that they had time to spare, and Luke even made a joke about being 'early for our train'. But they were restless, stretching, getting in and out of the car, unable to stay with one line of conversation. Every few minutes they thought they'd heard something, but it turned out to be nothing. Luke and Carson had to stop niggling each other like bored schoolkids on a bus. Then, when another big truck went past, they decided it would be better to wait in place, no matter how long it took.

They sat in the sticks and didn't talk. Their task had become real again. Carson and Luke sat close to each other. Sweetapple crouched away from them in his own dark universe.

And then, finally, they heard the distant sound they'd been hoping for, and saw the glow of a light moving towards them. Luke stretched the laptop out on his knees, the piece of paper with the code sequence in his left hand. He set the delay and gave a thumbs-up. The train showed at the end of the corridor, and Luke pushed the button and said, 'Three minutes.' They waited breathlessly, Carson grabbing at Luke's shoulder, Sweetapple with his hands clenched tightly. The train neared, its light blindingly bright, then tracked past them, rattling links and carriages. Luke said, 'Thirty seconds,' and they watched the clock on the computer count down. As it neared zero, they grabbed each other and ducked their heads, unsure how big the explosion would be. But the train rattled on with nothing to stop its progress. Luke fiddled with the computer keys, leaning out to check as if he might have missed the explosion, while the other two looked at him and back at the train, expecting something to happen at any second. Nothing did.

And then the train was gone, clacking away from them in storybook form, unimpeded, into the night. Everyone was cursing, and Sweetapple was saying, 'It's a bloody dud. I knew it. That's why it didn't go off in the mine. It's never going to go off.'

Luke was still frenetically trying things on the computer, but his limited knowledge only gave him a few options. Sweetapple stomped up and back, himself a bomb ready for ignition.

When Luke had given up hoping, he slammed the case shut, and the three of them were silent until Carson said, 'We can't leave it there. What if a passenger train comes along, and it goes off? We'll be murderers then.'

The men didn't have an answer.

'You've got to keep trying, Luke. Clear it and reset it, turn it off and on, or whatever you do. Give it another order number. There'll be another train before daylight, and we should try to have the line blown by then.'

Luke opened the case again. 'Okay. I'll start again. No promises.'

He tapped away, repeating the firing pattern, Carson's and Sweetapple's breathing heavy in his ears. The wind was starting to pick up around them; a caressing breeze that Luke knew was going to turn nasty.

'Right. Two minutes.' They turned to look where they thought the explosive was.

'Thirty seconds. Ten, nine, eight ...' And then, again, nothing.

'Shit.'

'I'll give it one more try. Maybe this number key is sticking.'

Sweetapple got up and walked out to the track. Carson squashed in close to Luke as he began the countdown again.

'Thirty seconds. Ten, nine, eight ...' This time, the earth roared as rocks, steel, and concrete rent the air. On the moment of detonation, Carson leant in and kissed Luke hard on the lips. Then they were on their feet squealing at what they'd done, the wind blowing the dust from the explosion at them, their ears ringing in triumph. They skipped out of the trees to dance around like pagans, but Sweetapple was not dancing. He was not standing, and, when Carson ran to him, was not moving, except for one leg that twitched out a last few reflexive kicks. He was lying on his back, a small bloody area at his temple. Even in the dark, she could see that his eyes were dull and his chest not moving. She was screaming and pumping at his chest, moving herself to get the regular compressions right as Luke stood over her, saying, 'Keep at it, keep at it, I'll do his air.' Carson pumped as Luke bent over Sweetapple's mouth and made blowing noises. Then Sweetapple's chest heaved—once, twice—and Carson was sure she heard him suck in a breath.

'He's breathing?'

Luke shook his head. Carson continued to pump, mad for a response. Then Luke stopped and sat back, and this time shook his head in a long, slow movement.

He put an arm out in front of Carson. 'Enough.'

She stopped, exhausted, desperate, hoping stupidly that this thing hadn't happened. The wind was starting to swirl around them like a taunting witch.

'We can't leave him here.' There was a pain in her chest that wouldn't let go, and she was shivering so much that her teeth were clattering.

'We've got to get him in the car. I can't carry him on my own.'

Carson breathed deeply and looked around, unsure whether there was another option, then nodded, wiped her face and nose, and stood up. Luke had left Sweetapple's black beanie in place, but shut the eyes so he looked like he might be just sleeping. It made her kneel again and begin compressions.

Luke pulled her away. 'He's dead. He's been dead since it blew. A rock or a piece of steel, or fuck knows, something.'

Carson slumped on the ground, crying. Luke lifted her and hugged her. 'This is bad, but we have to deal with this. Right now. The cops might be on their way.'

She stood straight, shaking, as Luke tucked the computer in under his shirt, and then they both bent and reached for Sweetapple's legs and arms. He was heavy, and Carson could only carry him short distances at a time, sobbing painfully as she did so. By the time they got to the car, she was shaking and gasping for breath. Luke opened the back door, and they manhandled Sweetapple onto the seat and stretched him out. Luke put the computer on the floor, took the driver's seat, started the car, and then stopped. 'I've got to check for blood. Won't be a minute.' He got out and ran off into the trees. Carson sat, her chest heaving. She put her hands back on Sweetapple, and began to pump.

At the place where Sweetapple had fallen, there was no record in the sand. The wind was starting to flick grains in waves down along the train line. Luke grabbed an oak branch and swept the area clean, every stroke causing more sand to billow into the air.

When he got back to the car, Carson was screaming words she was trying to keep muffled: 'He's breathing. He's fucking breathing!' She was manhandling him, unsure whether to put him on his side or slap him into existence. Sweetapple began to gasp like an almost-drowned person, wheezing and gulping, his eyes rolling back in their sockets. Carson shook him as Luke watched, disbelieving, knowing he had wished the breathing away, and that Sweetapple's magic had defeated him.

He got into the driver's seat, turned on the headlights, and the trees came up ominously and ghostly. He drove them out of the trees and back onto the road.

'What are we going to do?'

'All we can do is take him to his place.'

'Oh God.'

'Unless you've got a better plan.'

'Give ourselves up?'

Luke was calm. His hands were trembling on the steering

wheel, but he felt in control. 'If it was just an accident, sure. But it was an accident that happened with our own bomb while we were trying to blow up a coal train. They might even think we were planning to blow up a passenger train—that we're mass murderers. So giving ourselves up is not an option.'

They were silent then, the wind outside like that of an inferno, bowing trees, breaking branches, and rocking the small car from side to side.

Carson turned on a light and looked at Sweetapple. He was holding his eyes tightly, but his breathing was starting to sound regular. She was thinking about brain damage, and how they would know and what they would have to do.

They crossed Sweetapple's ramp, still well before first light. From a distance, they could see lights on in his house, and the blue light from a television screen flickering through a window. Luke killed the car lights and halted.

'Shit. Is someone waiting for him, for us?' She heard herself saying it.

'There are no cars. You don't watch TV if you're lying in wait for someone.'

Carson got out. 'I've got to see.' She walked towards the house staying low, leaning into the wind, scanning for anyone who might be spying on her in the night.

Luke watched, cursing. He should have done it himself. Carson might fold, might even go straight to the phone and ring the cops herself.

She crept to a window and looked in. There was no one inside, and no sign that anyone had been there. Was it some sort of trap? Were they expecting her to walk in, so they could arrest her? The kettle started to boil, and she had to grab at the windowsill as her legs gave way beneath her.

She was crying again, telling herself to just give in and give up, and rest on the soft ground. Everything she did from here on was making it worse. But no one came to the kettle to make tea. The only sounds were from the wind, the low tones of the TV, and her own throat. She forced herself to stand up, pushed along the wall and around to the front door, sucked the air in, and opened the door.

'Hello?'

She waited, her legs shuddering and her hand against the doorframe, supporting her. If there was anyone there, they were asleep or hiding. It was too much to try to understand. She stepped through the door.

'Sweetapple? You home?'

Nothing.

'Anyone here?'

Nothing.

The wind slammed and re-slammed every door in the house. Carson walked to the kitchen and then to the bedroom, and finally understood it was a set-up by Sweetapple, part of his paranoia about visitors and cops.

Luke was anxious, wondering what had taken so long.

'Anyone there?'

'No. Bring the car over.'

She followed the car as Luke pulled it in as close to the front door as he could.

They lifted Sweetapple up, and laid him out like a corpse. Carson watched his chest rising and falling for too long. If she kept watching, it couldn't stop. Luke took her arm and said, 'Come on.'

'He needs to go to hospital.'

'No.'

'What if he's a vegetable and we did nothing?'

'He's not, but if he was it would be too late anyway. The damage would be done.' Luke wasn't sure if Sweetapple being brain dead was a good thing or a bad thing.

'I'm going to ring Casualty.'

'Don't. They'll link it back to you eventually.'

'Doesn't matter.'

'It does. He'll be all right in a day or two. You'll see.'

Carson walked outside and stood in the wind, unable go forward or back. Sweetapple had talked about love, and on an impulse she had betrayed him. She was the worst person — worse than anyone she despised, anyone she could imagine. She had had so much, and yet hadn't had the sense to know it. The thrill of the adventure was well gone. The rebel in her was dead. She was keen now to do the right thing, but she wasn't sure what that was.

She went back into the house. Luke was lying on his back on the couch, his eyes open. She went to the bedroom, sat on the end of Sweetapple's bed, and waited.

Later, hours later, Sweetapple groaned about the pain in his head. His eyes were squeezed shut, and the words were delivered through unwilling lips. Carson went for painkillers, and found them in a neat first-aid box in a cupboard in the hallway. She took them to him with a glass of water, and held the glass to his bottom lip, saying quietly, 'Drink?' He put a hand to the tumbler and, with her help, drank cautiously. She took the glass from him and placed the pills in the soft part of his hand. 'Painkillers. Can you swallow?'

'Mmm.' He put the pills on his tongue, felt around for the glass and, when he gripped it, emptied its contents. Carson took the glass, and he pushed himself into the pillow. Then she was crying softly, the sobs like convulsions she was trying to quell. When her control returned, she ran the back of her hand across Sweetapple's face and he didn't respond, so she left him alone.

Outside, the sun was midmorning bright, and Luke said, 'You be all right if I piss off for a while?'

'Yeah.'

'There's plenty of stuff in the fridge. Okay if I take your car?'

'Yeah. What do I tell the cops?' She couldn't make herself care.

'He was kicked by a horse. In the yards. We figured it was just concussion.'

'What about the railway line? Wouldn't we have left DNA everywhere?'

'I wouldn't worry about that. We probably didn't do that much damage. They'll fix the line in a couple of days. It'll be called vandalism, and they'll be looking for kids. Hardly a need for DNA testing.'

'Right.' She tried to make herself think logically and practically. 'Where are you going?'

'Said I'd be at work. Said I'd be late, but not this late. Don't want to create suspicion.' He strode towards the car, keen to be away.

Within a minute, he was back, holding the computer wrapped in an oil rag. 'I haven't worked out what to do with this.' He presented it. 'I think it would be stupid to throw it in the creek or somewhere, and I can't drive round with it in the car.'

'Give it here. I'll hide it.' This seemed to relax him, and he gave her a thumbs-up and went back to her car.

Carson watched him drive away, and thought without emotion that he was probably going straight to the police to put her in and leave himself in the clear. She put the computer on the kitchen table, wrapped it in the rag, and ignored it.

Sweetapple was groaning rhythmically in his sleep. The room was hot, and she removed the bedclothes and turned the white pedestal fan on. Then she sat on the bed and watched him, her hand on his thigh, matching her breathing with his. She fell asleep, and woke and fell asleep again, only to be roused by Sweetapple suffering in a nightmare. It was late afternoon. She shook him awake, and he looked at her for the first time, his eyes bloodshot, his face suggesting he didn't know who she was. Then he smiled weakly and said, 'Hello.'

'Hello.'

'Guess I lived, then.'

'Guess so.'

He rolled slowly onto his back and winced. 'Jeez, my head hurts.'

'I'll get some more painkillers. Could you eat some soup or something?'

'I'll give it a go.'

When she'd fed him soup in childlike mouthfuls, she left him alone and took a walk around his failing garden. The evening was cool. She turned on hoses and sprinklers, acknowledging the weight lifting at every step.

18

Luke didn't go back to Sweetapple's after work. He lay on his bed in the hotel, eating chips, flipping through videos on his computer. The noise from downstairs suggested a party or a team celebration. It was good to know there were people who didn't give a damn about Sweetapple, or Carson, or Retribution, or bombs.

Luke was confident that Sweetapple had only been knocked out and concussed. No drama there. But now Carson and Sweetapple felt like losers to him. The bomb thing had been an amateurish mess. For all they knew, it hadn't even upset the rail timetable. What would Sweetapple come up with next? Fight Bob to the death? It had suddenly turned pathetic, and even Carson had gone from wild to whimpering.

He considered that maybe he should go to the police himself and say that Carson had hit Sweetapple with a tyre iron or something. There was no reason for him to be implicated; it was her car, her tyre tracks. He didn't have to be pinned as an accomplice unless he let it happen. The soft sand and the wind on the night wouldn't give up too many secrets, but there was the problem of the bomb. Experts would probably be able to identify it as a mine explosive and to narrow it down from there. But that might be giving the police too much credit. Maybe they wouldn't work it out and not even care. As far as they knew, no one had been hurt. No big deal. The State Government Rail would deal with any breakages anyway.

He shut the computer down and put his head back on the pillow. The ceiling was yellowing but clean, and only one spider persisted, its web discreet in the far corner. He might be overestimating the ability and the commitment of the police, but not Peter. Peter would track him down as soon as he read there'd been an explosion. He might not blame Luke, but he'd want information from him. So the best thing to do was to get on the front foot. He would go to the police in the morning and tell them he knew about the bomb. A woman called Anna had stolen it from the mine. He would say he didn't know anything about who had the bomb or let it off. He just knew where it might have come from. If, later on, they pushed and pushed him, he would let slip that he had heard Carson and Sweetapple planning a bombing. Perhaps he would ask for immunity if he provided information, if that was really a thing you could do.

In the morning, he walked through the dark bar on his way to his work lift. Teddy the publican was cleaning windows, with the lights low and the television on.

'Big night?'

'Yeah. Keep you awake?'

'Nah.'

Teddy dropped his arms, shook his rag out, and said over

his shoulder, 'Some kids decided they'd party it up. No special reason. Took me a while to get them out at closing.'

'They're always the best parties.'

'Not if you're trying to stop them.'

The TV news was showing a police raid on a protest camp. Luke stopped to take it in. It was the mine protest camp, and he could see Ginko, Anna, Wedge, and Panda being bustled into police cars. The pull-through claimed: *Arrests over train bombing; explosive linked to protest group.*

Teddy turned to look at him, and Luke realised he was showing too much interest in the item.

'Fucken terrorists,' Teddy said, shaking his head. 'Since when do Australians blow up trains because they don't like something? The world's gone mad.'

'I reckon.' Luke left the bar, shaking his head at the mad world. If Anna had been arrested, his plan to go to the police was dead. They didn't need the information he had to give. He could feel something like panic moving in his chest.

While he was unconscious, Sweetapple enacted vengeance. He dreamed that he cornered Bob and shot him down like a gunslinger in a Western; that he strung up Bob with a rope by the hands and left him hanging from a tree in the heat; that he tortured him in a cell in a foreign country; and plenty more.

He was aware of Carson as a person in the room, but he also felt her as a spirit of goodness close by and on his side. And then he was aware of her distress, and he knew that he could not sleep forever. He had to come out of it, because it was his duty and because good things were waiting for him. At some point, he ate soup and then slept again, returning to a place where he was a member of a community, stoning a helpless Bob.

In the night, Carson's body was beside him, and it filled him with the will to go on.

In the morning, whichever morning it was, she was standing in the doorway when he opened his eyes. The light hurt and his head throbbed, but he knew he was not dying.

'How're you feeling?'

'Okay.'

He sat up slowly and pushed a pillow behind him, the movement sharpening the pain in his head.

'You want to try some cereal or something? Fruit?'

'Maybe a banana.'

As he listened to her footsteps clatter on the timber floorboards, he remembered the things that had happened in the past few days: his rage and his certainty, the explosion, and the knowledge that Carson was moving away from him.

When she returned, he asked, 'Where's Luke?'

'Went to work. Said he didn't want to *arouse suspicion*.'

'You and him together?' It was a question he would never have asked and hadn't intended to ask, but the answer seemed essential if he was to move on to the next part of his life.

'No.' She said it with a certainty which acknowledged that the question was not out of place.

'That makes me happy.' He peeled the banana, broke off a piece, and gave it to her.

She ate it. 'We all went a bit crazy,' she said.

'Yeah. I lost it. Out of my brain.'

'Me too.'

'Well, no one died, I guess.'

'We thought you had.'

'Me too.'

There was only the sound of the struggling sprinkler outside the window between them.

'No more of that mad shit. Please.' She said it while smiling, and the conviction was clear.

'No.'

Luke returned that evening, in Carson's car, with pizza and Stretch. She was so glad to see her dog that she forgot to ask Luke if everything was okay. Stretch ate and then loped around the house for a while before settling at her feet. Carson and Luke ate in silence in the kitchen while Sweetapple dozed. She could feel that Luke was jumpy, and realised she hadn't found out what he had been up to during the day and night.

'See any cops?'

'No.'

'Any news reports about the railway?' She had only listened to the TV and radio news half-heartedly.

He pushed pizza into his mouth and mumbled through the food. 'Arrested some kids on the mine protest. Reckon the explosives came from them.'

'Really? Arrested? The ones you knew?'

'Uh-huh.'

'You happy about that?'

'They won't be able to prove anything. It'll all be circumstantial, so I reckon it's okay. It might give us a bit of time.'

'I don't want them going to jail for something we did.'

'They won't go to jail.'

For the moment, she had to believe that was true. Sweetapple called out from the bedroom. Luke swallowed and said, 'I'd better go say hello.'

Sweetapple was sitting up in bed, some of the paleness gone, and the life back in his eyes.

'Look who's awake.'

'Took me a while.'

'It wasn't good, any of it.'

'Was it deliberate?' The question was conversational, but still brutal.

'What happened to you, you mean?'

'Yes.'

'Of course not.' When Luke heard himself say the words, he didn't believe them. 'I wouldn't do that, and I can't control bits of metal flying through the air. I could hardly control the detonation.'

'Fair enough.'

Sweetapple had obviously made up his mind about Luke. Their team had been broken up. It was every man for himself now.

'You seem to be recovering pretty well.'

'Yeah. I'll be out of bed tomorrow. Back to normal.'

'Just take it easy, eh? There's no rush.'

'Don't want to waste my life lying here.'

'No. Is there anything you need? Anything I can get you in town?'

'I don't think so.'

'Okay. Good to see you sitting up.' As Luke got back to Carson, there was a knock on the outside frame of the kitchen door, and a female voice said, 'Hello?'

Carson got up quickly, startled, thinking of police assault crews, paddy wagons, and violent threats.

She pulled the door back to reveal Caroline in the clothes she wore for riding, looking anxious and apologetic.

'Oh, hi, Carson. Sorry to bother you, but I was supposed to have a riding lesson this week, and Sweetapple wasn't answering his phone, and the horses don't look like they've been exercised, and I thought ...'

'He's hurt himself. Kicked by a horse. Got him in the head.'

'Oh dear. Oh dear. Is he okay? Is he in hospital?'

'He's here. We've had a couple of rough days, but he seems to be pulling through.'

'Can I see him?' It was desperation hidden under goodwill.

'Probably better if you leave it for a couple of days. If you don't mind.'

'That's fine.' Caroline stepped back from the door. Carson could see her ute at the edge of the garden with a man in the driver's seat. She gestured to the vehicle. 'Bob and I will drop in another time. Anything we can do?'

Carson said, 'Bob?' involuntarily. She had had the impression that Bob was gone for good. The thought of his return kicked her squarely in the stomach.

'Yes. He's home. Finally. For a while, this time.' It was an unconvincing performance that was over quickly. Caroline strode to the ute, leaving Carson at the door witnessing her leave.

Luke had cleaned up the pizza boxes, and washed some cups and bowls. He said he was going to head back to town because there wasn't much he could do to help her, and it would be good to know what the gossip was. Carson barely heard him.

She could feel him arcing out away from them, and she didn't care. She took Stretch in to visit Sweetapple.

Bob had called many times — the first time, several days ago, to tell her he was on his way home. She had told him it wasn't his home anymore and he wasn't welcome, and had hung up on him. He had rung back to say how sorry he was, that he had just needed some time, things had been very difficult, and now he wanted to give it another try if she would just let him. She had hung up on him again. But then she had had the night to think about it. How he had said they just needed a break, and how odd she had felt without him around. After all, who she would rather have around than Bob? Sweetapple? That wasn't likely, or sensible. So when Bob rang again in the morning, she decided to hear him out. He talked about the business pressure he had been under for the past six months. He repeated how much he missed her and their conversations, and what a fool he'd been. He told her there'd never been anyone else, and she hung up. By the tenth phone call, she had stopped hanging up, and had decided that even if it was against her better judgement, having another try with Bob was worth it. They'd had good years together, and they understood each other. Perhaps friendship might be enough. There wouldn't be another chance for them.

And then, when the phone calls were over and the house was quiet, she couldn't believe she had agreed to take him back, after everything he had done. She had come home to find him gone, without a word. She had exacted no revenge; she hadn't even sent money to that supposed Finn girl. And now she was welcoming him back. It was an invitation to be treated badly—the sort of thing she had warned so many women about. But she could not make herself pick up the phone and tell him not to come. She wanted to have a partner, and the thought of finding a brand-new one terrified her. It was awful to know that she was willing to choose the devil she knew over a reasonable bloke she might not.

Before she knew it, it felt like she had hardly even made the decision, and he was on the plane and at her doorstep. He slept in one of the spare rooms, and they ate breakfast together the next morning, cautious and contained. Part of her wanted to scream at him, and the other part wanted him to sit on the couch with her and laugh about things they used to laugh about. She told herself to keep her expectations low and her anger in check. If she was going to give the relationship a chance, she had to make room for that chance.

He gradually revealed to her that the business was in much worse shape than he had let on. Commodity prices were down, certain divisions had underperformed, two senior managers had been found to be incompetent. As he talked about the problems in a serious but sort of offhand way, the resentment rose in her. It seemed obvious that Bob had come back to her because he had nowhere else to go. He said that wasn't true, and that he could have sold the farm from under her if he didn't really care about her. Breakfast was finished in silence. She resented him having kept the information from her, and for the fact that if he had told her he was in this much trouble, she would have let him come back anyway.

Caroline kept away from him during the day. She took a long walk through the paddocks, and spent more time than she wanted to in the garden. Sweetapple didn't reply to her texts about their riding lesson, and she began to get agitated about it, because a riding lesson with Sweetapple was the one thing that could take her out of herself and away from the complexity that was Bob.

That night, he made dinner and chose some nice wine, and went into his spiel again about the mistakes he was sorry for and the good between them that they just couldn't throw away. She enjoyed the dinner and having someone else in the house, and began to relax around him. She felt things for him, and decided to step around her rage at him for as long as she could. The next day, they kept well clear of each other, and Bob spent most of his time remonstrating on the phone. But the following morning, when there had still been no communication from Sweetapple, she suggested they drive up and see what he was up to. For a moment, Bob looked like that was the last thing he ever wanted to do, but then appeared to change his mind, and offered to be her driver.

Afterwards, as they drove away from Sweetapple's house, Bob said, 'You're really into this riding thing, aren't you?'

'I guess I am.'

'Should we get a proper riding instructor?'

'Sweetapple is very good teacher.' She knew she needed to be careful not to be too defensive. It was just horseriding.

'Okay. But if you wanted to compete in, like, a three-day event or something, he wouldn't know about that side of it, would he?'

'I'm really not thinking about competing. I'm just trying to enjoy myself.'

'Yeah, but he's not the sharpest tool in the shed, is he?'

'I beg your pardon?' She blew it out like a fruit pip.

'I mean, he can only talk horses. And he doesn't do that much. Any other topic, he's a dead area.'

'Fuck you, Bob. At least he's honest and decent.'

Bob raised his eyebrows and looked away in mock surprise. Caroline also thought she saw the half-curl of a smile, as if she had just verified something for him.

Carson sat outside on a kitchen stool and kept an eye on Sweetapple as he walked the garden, still unsteady, breathing the air as though someone was trying to steal it from him. He hadn't spoken much, and there was a new sort of serenity about him. Maybe the accident had put a stop to his desire for violence, just as it had for her. He circled back towards her and said, 'Retribution. She died, didn't she?'

She jumped a little on her stool. It scared her that he might not remember the most significant event in his recent life.

'Yes.' Carson didn't bother to add the painful details.

But Sweetapple wasn't remembering. He was confirming. As if he had hoped it was just a nightmare that had come with the knock to the head.

'Bob?'

She nodded, but didn't look at him. 'Had her butchered.'

Carson could see a droplet run out of the corner of Sweetapple's eye and slip down his cheek.

'That was a terrible thing to do.'

'Yes.' There wasn't any way of adding comfort.

He continued to walk, and she let him go. She thought how painful it must be to have to confront such awful things again.

Sweetapple sat on a homemade bench in the garden for

a couple of hours. Every so often, Carson put her head out the door to check on him. He smiled at her and gave a small hand-signal, like an elderly gentleman enjoying his last days of sun.

The next day, they drove down to the horses, and Sweetapple was strong enough to walk out to them, bring them in, and brush them down. They were happy to see him. She sat in the ute watching, letting him have the time to himself. It was as if she wasn't there.

Bob and Caroline arrived. They had turned into the lonely couple next door, desperate for an outing.

Bob got out of the ute, heh-hehing and saying Sweetapple's name as though it was a favourite old word. Carson gripped the seat, fearful of what Sweetapple might do, and of him hurting himself trying to throttle Bob. But Sweetapple did not react. He kept brushing, patting, and admiring the horses. Bob leant on a railing and told Sweetapple that there was no need for him to be working when he wasn't 100 per cent.

'It's okay. I want to.' He didn't look up or allow the words any emotion.

Bob prattled on about the horses being in good shape, and Sweetapple looking much stronger, and how good it was to be home. Sweetapple didn't say anything, didn't pretend that he saw any value in having a conversation with Bob.

Bob ran out of chat, and, after a moment's silence, said sombrely, 'I made the final payment.' Two breaths. 'I can tell you she went to a good home.'

Carson watched as a tremor feathered its way across Sweetapple's hand. It was hardly discernible and quickly covered, but she saw it. She could only guess that Bob's men had not told him that Sweetapple had turned up at Retribution's butchering. But then again, Bob was not above a double bluff. He might pretend that he had no idea what had happened and that he honestly thought the mare had gone to a good home.

Carson looked across at Caroline sitting in the car. Did Caroline know nothing of the death of Retribution? Could she be that ignorant? Carson had to stop herself from walking over and slapping Caroline, let alone slapping them both, for having done this terribly cruel thing to Sweetapple and then fronting up as if it didn't really matter.

When he continued to get no response, Bob said a happy 'Goodbye' and 'Look after yourself', and they were gone. Carson lay back on the seat and screamed. Sweetapple let the horses go, and got in alongside her. He appeared unaffected by what had just happened.

They drove back to his place without speaking. Carson thought if she started to speak about it, she would end up yelling and bashing her fists on the dashboard. As they neared his house, Sweetapple said, in the tone of someone who just had the nicest thought, 'I think I'll get into the knackery business.'

It was another line added to the list of things she couldn't comprehend or deal with. She blew the air out of her mouth, hissing through her lips. 'You want to go round picking up sick and injured horses?'

'I think so.'

Maybe the fire had gone out of him. Perhaps he would remain this shell, moved by nothing. A kind of doddering horse-idiot.

'And take them to the pet-meat abattoir? What an awful job. Why would you want to do that?'

He pursed his lips, screwed up his nose, and shrugged. 'Someone's got to do it.'

'Jesus, Sweetapple, that's the worst idea you've ever had.'

To the window, he said, 'I think it's one of my best.'

In the morning, the media reported that trading in one of Bob's companies had been halted. Carson wouldn't have paid attention to this news, except that when he heard it, Sweetapple slapped his thigh and laughed in a way she hadn't heard since the accident.

'That's why he's home, the prick. I wonder if Caroline knew.'

'What?'

'He's in financial trouble. Suddenly, the farm has become super-important to him. And so has Caroline. I'm guessing the farm is about to be transferred into her name very, very quickly.'

'You do have a thing for Caroline, don't you?'

'No.' He was surprised. 'But I thought they had moved on. He doesn't give a shit about Caroline. Bloke like that can only care about people if they're doing stuff for him or telling him he's great.'

'Well, then, him and Caroline. Perfect match.'

19

A call came up on Luke's phone while he was running barbed wire through a fence line. He ignored it. It was the number that Peter had given him for their covert communications. He had been expecting Peter to make contact, but he hadn't made up his mind how to respond. Information was Luke's only bargaining chip, and he could supply it, but there would have to be protection. And if protection wasn't provided, Luke would go to the media about his spying. His thoughts rattled out in time with the wire-spinning. He reached the post where he was to tie off, stopped, and looked back down the line. He knew he was never going to tell Peter anything. Peter was too tough and had too many resources for Luke to try playing games with him, demanding protection, threatening action.

Lunch was called, and he sat in the shade of a ute eating his sandwiches, trying to think what to do. The weather was kinder. The onset of autumn made an outdoor job almost a pleasure. But it was his only pleasure. The media kept on about the 'ongoing investigation' into the bombing, so it was impossible to push it from his mind.

He knew that nobody would believe he had nothing to do with the theft of the explosives and that he just happened to know the bloke who had received the stolen goods. If he thought about the information the police might have, it all pointed at him. Sweetapple's motive for blowing up the train line was a nonsense to anyone outside their little threesome. Which meant that Carson had no motive either. Luke was the one who had been on the picket, supposedly with hatred for the mining company that ran trains on that line. He began to thump his fist hard into the dirt alongside him. He was in trouble. He thought about Anna and her downcast face on television. She was in trouble too. Somebody knew she had got the bomb out. If Ginko knew, then others must too.

Luke had Anna's number. If he could convince her that Sweetapple, the guy she'd given the explosives to, had done the bombing, it might just get him and her off the hook. He rang the number.

'Hey.'

'Luke?' There was surprise and pleasure in her voice.

'Can you talk? I mean, are you out?'

'Yeah. Guys in the group bailed us.'

'You okay?' He wanted her to know that this was the real reason for the call.

'Yeah. Fine.'

'They didn't rough you up?'

'Nah. Country cops. Nice as pie.'

'How did they link the explosives to you?'

'The mine got the guy who smuggled the bomb out in the first place. He told them who he'd given it to. They haven't got anything on us except his word.' She was calm, almost bored. 'Where have you been? You disappeared. Not even a text.'

'Sorry about that. Lying low. Just travelling about. My mum got sick, so I spent a bit of time with her.'

Anna was quiet. Luke stood up and walked down into a gully, away from the other workers.

'Look, I know who did the bombing.'

'What? How?'

'I know the guy you gave the bomb to. He did it.'

'So how do you know?'

'I was there.'

Anna gave an excited exclamation. 'You did it? That is so cool. You're a fucking hero round here. We were worried the hardcores would hurt someone with the explosives, but we didn't dare hope they could stop the coal trains. That is just fantastic.' She was slapping a table or something with her hand. 'I knew you'd do something special.'

The conversation was getting away from Luke. He couldn't allow himself to be turned into a hero of the protest movement. 'I didn't do it. I didn't even want to do it. I just happened to be there. He did it: Graham Sweetapple and his girlfriend, Carson.'

He could hear her trying to make sense of what he was saying. 'You should be proud. Finally, we get to strike back at those bastards.'

'They're trying to incriminate me. You've got to tell the cops.'

'I'm not telling the cops anything.'

'If you don't tell the cops who really did it, then I'll go to jail for it.'

'No you won't. As far as I can tell, they've got nothing on anyone.'

'I'm asking you …'

'I'm not dobbing in a hero to the cops. This is, like, the protest movement's biggest deal.' She was distancing herself. The movement was more important than anything they'd had together. The emotional thing hadn't worked. If it came to it, she was ready to let him fall.

'Anna, I'm not even a real protester. I couldn't give a shit about the coal mine.' He was admitting they were no longer allies, but he couldn't see another way.

'What do you mean? We were together. We spent weeks on the picket together.'

'I was paid.'

'Someone paid you to protest?'

'Yes.'

'Well, that is fucked. That is really fucked. But you know what? You earned your money. There'll be ships that should have been loaded days ago but can't be because of the explosion. That'll cost the company big bucks, and they might even lose a contract. And now all the buyers are going ask if Australia is the reliable, safe place to buy coal from that they thought it was. It's bloody brilliant.'

He listened to her rave, and knew if he didn't stop her she would create a legend out of him, and the cops would come straight to his door. 'They didn't pay me to protest. They paid me to keep an eye on you.'

'No they didn't.' He could hear her gasping at breaths. 'No they didn't. Wait. You're a fucking spy?'

'Nothing sinister. Just to make sure you didn't do anything stupid … blow anything up.'

'You were a spy all along?'

'I didn't tell them anything they didn't already know.'

'They? The bloody mining company? You were spying for the mining company? You absolute low-life.'

'I didn't mean it to —'

'You'll get yours.'

There was no more he could say. Anna had hung up. Back at the vehicles, the others were getting back to work. He had made everything worse. He was swearing out loud, cursing his situation, himself, and his incompetence. Nobody paid any attention.

Caroline turned off the tap at the base of the tank, took a shovel from the ute and walked to where the ground was wet from a leak in the pipe, and began to dig. The water had made the ground soft and the digging easy, and she soon uncovered the pipe and the hissing leak. She cleared around it, her breathing loud, and then got a poly pipe fitting and a hacksaw from the ute while she waited for the last of the water to run out. She had listened carefully to Joey's instructions for repairing a pipe, and she knew she would repeat this job until there was no chance of a leak being found later by the men.

With livestock, there were always troughs and tanks to check, and pipes to fix or upgrade. Caroline found herself spending most of her time on work related to the stock. Joey was happy to cede control of those parts of the operation, and managed to make it sound as though he was allowing her to take on a huge responsibility. Perhaps he thought she hadn't had much responsibility in her life. But she wasn't gaining much access to the machinery and crop-growing side. Caroline had consumed as much farming-management theory as her brain would allow, but putting it into practice was a long way off—unless she decided to pull rank. Getting to drive the larger pieces of machinery and do something important on the farm like planting was being made impossible by Joey's obfuscations. She was happy to do stockwork, but she knew that if she was to be taken seriously she would have to force her way into the cropping side. Caroline had put pressure on Joey to give her opportunities, but he had outmanoeuvred her with his benign vagueness. He would organise for her to drive a piece of equipment, and then at the last minute would claim he'd forgotten, or tell her that the day's program had changed because of the pressing nature of something else that needed to be done.

She knelt at the hole and cut the pipe with the hacksaw where the split had opened up. Then she roughly measured the amount of pipe that needed to be taken out to allow the hose fitting to be put in place. She cut again, removed the piece, and sat back. If she had cut too much out it would be a mess, and she would have to put two fittings in and a piece of pipe to fix a leak that had only needed one.

Soon she would have to confront Joey and tell him that if he continued to avoid including her, she would have to do something about it. There were other competent farm managers around who would be able to work with her. Caroline was sure this was true.

She undid the nut on one end of the fitting and removed it with the split ring and the insert, and then put them on one of the ends of the pipe in the order that Joey had told her was so important. She screwed the fitting on, and then put the nut and split ring on the other part of the pipe she had cut, and banged the insert in. When she brought the ends close and pushed them together, they joined with the kind of firmness she had hoped for. She screwed the second nut on and sat back. Everything looked like it should. She rested on her haunches and sighed. Self-knowledge was slow in coming.

She got up and walked to the tank, turned the tap on, and then picked up the tools and the cut piece of pipe and put them in the ute. While the water built up pressure on the connection, she leant against the ute, shovel in hand. Somehow it took fixing a broken pipe to make her face things she had known for some time.

The problem with confronting Joey was that she didn't care enough to do it. Even he knew that whatever threats she made, she would not follow them through. She didn't care enough to fight him. She didn't care enough to deal with the scepticism of the men the way she had done in other places, plenty of times before. The idea of reinventing herself as a farmer had been a clever one, but the wrong one. Farming was hard work, satisfying and enjoyable, and it was great to be learning new things. She could go on doing it and have a good life, but it would always be a job and an interest to her, not a vocation. The truth was, she could be a farmer, but she wasn't meant to be a farmer. As she watched the fitting hold, with no drips or leaks, it amazed her that it had taken her so long to understand this. She covered the hole with the dirt she had removed, and put the shovel back in the ute.

Bob dismissed the trading hold on his companies as regulatory nonsense. The exchange was being overly cautious, and things would be back to normal very soon. But he was on the phone from early in the morning until late at night. Caroline didn't eavesdrop. She didn't care. She knew that even if Bob went broke, he would have money stashed away in places that creditors couldn't access. That was the way he was. If they had the farm and a few dollars, that would be enough for her. She had no need for his symbols of wealth and power.

Sweetapple had sent a message that he was healthy enough for a riding lesson that afternoon if she was available. But when she arrived at the stables, she was disappointed to see that the girl was saddled up and coming, too. Sweetapple looked almost his old self. Carson was civil.

They rode down across the flat on the track they always took, three abreast, the smell of the horses rich in the air, Sweetapple smiling as though he had just reached a holiday destination. He got her to canter ahead and circle, talking her through communications with her horse, and suggesting small adjustments. When she returned and took her place alongside the other horses, Carson said, 'Do you know what happened to Retribution?'

'I don't think I know what you mean.'

'The mare — Sweetapple's special mare, Retribution.'

'Carson,' Sweetapple cautioned.

'I haven't heard about her. I know Missy died, but I don't know about Retribution.' But even as she said this, Caroline had a faint recollection of having heard that name somewhere.

Carson cocked her head at Sweetapple. 'You called her Missy?'

Sweetapple widened his eyes in response.

'Well, then. Did you hear how Missy died?' There was a

pointed, controlled nastiness in the question.

'No.' Caroline felt a sudden terror. Was she somehow responsible for the death of Sweetapple's beloved horse? She tried to think what the link might be.

'That's enough, Carson. It's nothing to do with her.'

Carson shrugged it off and turned away. She put her horse into a slow lope and left them behind.

When she was far enough away, Caroline asked, 'What happened to Missy?'

'She died. You know that.'

'But how? Tell me.'

'She was a stolen horse. I stole her. The bloke who asked me to steal her had her butchered. Never told me what was going on.'

And now she knew. From the way he didn't say it, Bob had to be involved.

'Not Bob?'

Sweetapple simply said, 'Come on,' and pushed his horse into a canter, leaving her on a precipice of understanding.

They rode for another hour, and neither of them said anything about the dead horse. When she tried again to ask the question, both of them turned away. She would have to find out for herself.

'Sweetapple had a special horse at his place. He let me ride her.'

They were watching TV together, perusing social media and drinking tea after dinner, like a comfortable married couple.

'He told me she died. Do you know anything about that?'

Bob had finally finished with his phone calls for the day. It could have been their time of harmony. She felt it was the best time to catch him off-guard. He looked thoughtfully at the ceiling. 'A horse? No, 'fraid not.'

'A stolen horse?'

He made out it was a silly question. 'You know me. Lucky to be able to tell the back end from the front.' Good-natured and carefree.

'Called Retribution.' She was sure there was a subtle movement in his body.

'Darling, I swear I don't know anything about a dead horse or any live horse called Retri-whatever.'

She took a breath, and told herself she had to manage this carefully. The next few questions would reveal how little trust had returned.

'But you had a share in a quarter horse called Retribution, didn't you?'

He knew she had looked it up somewhere and already had the answer to her question.

'Oh yeah, that's right. I did. A tiny share. Not worth worrying about.' He wasn't engaging with her, his body language indicating that her questions were of no concern to him.

'Retribution died, and you don't know anything about it?'

'Oh, come on. Let's not get all conspiracy theory. I just forgot I have a very minor share in a Woodhill horse. A horse I've never even seen. I have lots of shares in lots of horses.'

'Is the horse alive?'

'Far as I know. I believe that is something they'd tell me.' Derisive now.

'She was reported missing months ago. That's not something they'd be required to tell you?'

'Well, according to your story, this horse was at Sweetapple's.

I don't see how that involves me.'

'You didn't know she was there?'

He put his computer tablet down and swivelled to look at her. 'If you're going to do witch-hunts on me, ambush me over tea in the evening, then we're not going to get very far, are we? Sometimes things happen in business that you can't do anything about. They're often pretty unpleasant, but you just have to suck it up. But, you know, they're not always as they seem from the outside. When someone dips into something they know nothing about, they can draw some dramatically incorrect conclusions.'

'So explain it to me.'

'No.'

'Why not?'

'For the same reason I'm not going to explain what's been happening with my companies over the past few months. It serves no good purpose, and it will only upset you, even though I know that it'll turn out to be a storm in a teacup.'

'Ah, yes. Don't bother the little woman with it. She won't understand, and it'll just upset her. What a load of patronising crap. You're not going tell me, because there are things you don't want me to know. You got Sweetapple to steal a special horse, then you had it killed without even telling him.'

'That's what he said?'

'Not in so many words.'

'Well, it's bullshit, whatever words he used. He's just trying to split us up so he can get into your pants.' He was facing her now, being earnest, maybe even wronged.

'No, he's not.'

'Are you sure?'

She was sure, but she still felt guilt over her feelings for Sweetapple, which was something Bob had probably understood. She realised she was playing a kind of chess with him, moving, strategising, and trying to guess how many moves ahead he was. That he had done this terrible thing was clear. Any normal person would call this an unpleasant game between them, not a relationship. She was kidding herself.

Caroline stood and took her cup to the sink. A frying pan sat on the stove, its handle pointing towards her provocatively. She reached out and put her fingers around it, and lifted the pan. It had a nice heft to it. Its potential balanced powerfully in her hand. Bob had gone back to checking emails or something, and the back of his head looked enticingly bare and vulnerable. One hard hit would be justifiable. She lifted the pan high, hammered it at the air, and then stopped, turned, and put it carefully back down on the stovetop, frightened by herself. Letting him back in had been a bad mistake, and she could not live with that mistake anymore. If she left now, she would never gain possession of the farm. But if she stayed, she would never be able to get rid of him, short of drawing a rifle on him.

Still at the stove, she asked him, 'How could you kill that horse? You've done some shitty things, but that's got to be the worst … I've heard of.'

'I didn't kill any horse.' He didn't look up from what he was reading.

Caroline packed a bag in her bedroom. She selected only the basics. Sentimentality had to be put to one side. All of this had to be left behind. She needed to make a new life and stop clinging to the old, finished one. It was something she had known, even during that first phone call, but it took the lies about Missy for her to face up to it.

She went out the back past the laundry so he didn't see her leave with her bag; he probably wouldn't know she was gone until he heard the car. Maybe it was what he wanted. He would think he was free now to play his many complex games. But she would stake a claim to her share as soon as she was able to contact a lawyer in the morning.

For a moment, at the front ramp, she stopped the car and considered turning back and storming in to tell him all the things she knew and felt about him—get them off her chest and let him know she wasn't fooled. But sitting in the dark, Caroline realised she didn't care enough about him even to do that. She had been through this rage, and it refused to return with the same heat. She just wanted to be free of him and the stupid happy-home fantasies he'd brought with him.

20

Bob rang Sweetapple and told him he didn't need him to look after the horses anymore. He said he was getting rid of them. Sweetapple didn't ask about the riding lessons that Caroline seemed to enjoy so much. He guessed Caroline didn't know about Bob's decision.

'They'll be going interstate, so you won't be able to use them as an excuse to be with my wife anymore.'

Sweetapple was still looking after the horses, because he guessed no one else would. The thought of not having to see or talk to Bob again was an agreeable one. But Bob had more on his mind than the horses.

'You want to be very careful, you fuckwit. Stirring up trouble for me wherever you can. Setting my wife against me. All because you couldn't part with the horse you bloody stole. It wasn't yours, you self-righteous prick. You fucking stole it. I could turn you in to the cops at any time.' The phone clicked off, and Sweetapple felt nothing.

Luke was watching him when he put the phone down.

Sweetapple guessed that Luke had heard the conversation. Bob's voice had been loud enough for anyone in the room to hear.

'Everything okay?'

'Yep. Just my friend Bob telling me he doesn't like me anymore.'

'I figured that. He doesn't know anything, does he?'

'No. He just thinks I'm trying to get one away with Caroline.'

Luke snorted and turned away. Sweetapple waited for him to say, 'He wouldn't be wrong, would he?' but there were no more words. Luke was pulling back, visiting less and confiding not at all. And Sweetapple hoped Carson had made her choice clear to him.

The cattle trucks were rolling out of Bob's place constantly: B-doubles full of cows, calves, steers, and heifers. The noise from the cattle yards had been loud and insistent for days. Sweetapple guessed that Bob was cashing in his cattle because they would be worth a bit and would pay a few bills. Or maybe he just didn't want cattle anymore.

Sweetapple put ads on trading sites and in the rural media, seeking wounded and rejected horses. He rang the knackery in a town an hour and a half to the north, told them he was in business, and asked about their rates. He rang racehorse trainers and spellers he knew, camp drafters, pacers, eventers, cutters, showjumpers, and miniature-horse breeders to let them know he could take their old and injured stock. The phone began to ring, and Sweetapple began to hit the road in his truck, morning and night, bringing home the crippled, the lame, the old, and the simply unloved. For a week, he drove night and day to pick up horses. He would unload one lot, examine them, feed them, water them, then get back in the truck and drive to pick up another lot. He only put the worst back on his truck, and took them to the knackery. For most, he did what he could to make them comfortable. He fixed feet and ground back teeth, showed kindness to the nastiest, and kept the foundered hungry. There were suddenly hundreds of horses on the farm. It didn't make any sense to Carson.

'Have you gone a bit soft-hearted on all these old nags?' she asked him. She was guessing that guilt had overtaken him and that he was trying to save many lives in recompense for the loss of one. But it was obvious he couldn't keep it going for long.

'No. Why?' He was sitting on a shiny, dark gelding he had called Jimmy, one of the few that had arrived not bone-poor and spiritless. He rubbed a flat palm down its neck, and it seemed to appreciate his touch.

'Well, you're buying way more than you're selling. It must be sending you broke.'

He laughed in the happy, contented way he had developed in the past few weeks.

'Our friend Bob paid me plenty of money to do his stealing. I'm not broke yet. His money will buy a lot of horses.'

She walked over and stood there, marvelling at the smooth health of the horse. 'Eventually you'll run out of feed, won't you?'

'I'm never going to let that happen.'

Carson had felt close to Sweetapple since the accident. As he recovered, she sensed a calmness about him that she liked, and she felt some of the same peace in herself. Her hot-bloodedness had been removed by his near-death experience. But now she was beginning to feel that his calmness was the sign of a lack of something important. It was possible that he was not the man he used to be, and it worried her. He did not speak of Bob or of taking revenge on him. Carson wasn't sure how long she could stay with someone with so little fight in him.

'I saw Caroline in town.'

'How is she? Did you talk to her?'

'She was strange. Really nice. Like I was a friend or something.'

'Well, you could be.'

'Wanted you to know how terrible she feels about what happened to Retribution. Said she's left Bob. Apparently she's living in town.'

'Shit, really? Bloody hell. That is good news.'

'Why?' She was suddenly stupidly nervous.

'She needed to get away from that evil bastard before she became like him.'

The words grabbed Carson, and she hoped they could hold her for a little while longer.

Left alone in Sweetapple's house, Carson took Stretch for a long walk out across the flat, which was now green and thickening with grass. The rain of recent weeks had produced fresh growth that was as high as her calves, undiluted by older dry feed. There were horses in the paddock in front of the house, but most of the others were spread out over different sections of the farm, making the most of the feed that was available. Stretch ran figure-eights, ears back, body flattened, returning at intervals to demand that Carson's enthusiasm match his. As she neared the boundary, she could see in the far distance the Statham house, a rectangle of greens on top of a small rise.

Carson understood how Sweetapple might have lost his fire for revenge. Initially she had, too. But she would never understand how he could look out and see that house and not feel something. Instead he would not talk about it, and wouldn't even allow a conversation about Bob to begin.

She couldn't leave Sweetapple now. The near loss of him was still squeezing her heart, but she wasn't sure she could remain sane living in the shadow of the Statham operation. Retribution had been slaughtered within walking distance of Sweetapple's house. Carson refused to believe that he could accept this. Soon enough, it would return to him, and bring with it all the pain and rage that it had brought in the first place. She was certain of it. Or at least she had been certain. But weeks had gone by, and there had been very little to encourage her.

Carson leant on the fence and let Stretch burn energy. The Statham farm looked empty. There was no livestock in sight. The only animals were opportunists like rabbits, kangaroos, and lizards in the grass and along the fence lines. The farm appeared to be waiting for something: for the next move made by humans. The farm could wait for action, but she knew she could not.

Stretch skidded to a halt alongside her and nuzzled his head at her thigh, and she could only be thankful for the relentless goodwill of dogs. But she didn't want to be a dog. The price of staying with Sweetapple would be the promise to herself to take some initiative. She could not go back to being the person who just let bad things happen to her. She would get Bob Statham somehow. There had to be a way to hurt him, for Sweetapple's sake and for hers, and that was her responsibility.

Carson strolled back to the house, kicking at the dirt, calling up the memory of receiving the response to her letter to Bob. It was a sweet memory. Nobody she had ever known could have conjured up Felicity Sven. No one else could have crafted that letter. It was proof that Carson had imagination — something her dull contemporaries had never had. She walked back into the house with her spirits lifted.

Sweetapple was still away, so she took out her computer, placed it on the kitchen table, sat down, and flipped through her files. The letter to Bob came up; the photo of Felicity, large and pleasing.

But when she read the letter, her elation left her, like every other good thing always had. The writing was inexpert and the intention transparent. What she had thought was a clever adaptation of a scam letter was no more than a copy. It was small-town and stupid, like she was. No one, especially not Bob Statham, would ever fall for something so obviously amateurish. She could almost hear Bob laughing. Whoever had received the text was not Bob, and was most likely a scammer, too.

As she looked more carefully, even the photo of Felicity that she was so pleased with looked like it had been stolen from someone's yearbook. She had to stop herself from throwing the computer across the room.

Carson shut the computer down and sat staring at the kitchen floor. She had made a mess of everything, and so had Sweetapple. The future was jail, or facing up to how small and defeated they were, or both. She should have accepted who she was long ago, understood that her best chance was getting her gear off for those men in that bar, taken the money, and got on with her life. Who was she to deny that? Nobody, simply nobody.

When he returned, Sweetapple asked her if she wanted to go with him to pick up some horses that had been identified as suffering badly from malnutrition. 'It won't be pretty, but we might be able do some good.' If he'd noticed how low she was, he didn't mention it.

'It's one of your more romantic offers.'

They got going in the truck at sun-up. The call had come in from the RSPCA. Some neighbours had reported a farm where a number of horses were badly underfed. The RSPCA vet, Johnny Duncan, thought it was a case for having all the animals put down, but he wanted Sweetapple to have a look at them first to see if he could save them. Over the noise of the truck engine, Sweetapple explained to Carson that the owner had too many horses and had run out of money, and had then run out of feed and hadn't known how to tell anyone or ask for help. He was ashamed, distraught, and possibly facing charges. 'If they put them all down, it's going to be much worse for him.'

After an hour's drive, they turned in a gateway where the gates leaned back off their hinges and the last of the grass finished at the boundary. They drove past a small square house with a garden that looked as if it had been eaten by desperate animals. Sweetapple stopped the truck behind a clean white ute at a set of tumbledown homemade yards, and got out. Johnny was waiting for him in his vet overalls. On the other side of the yards, standing on his own, was an older man who watched them, closing and opening his fists, occasionally kicking at the ground, making the dirt puff up around him.

The main yard was full of horses eating recently delivered

hay, so starved that they looked like they might have been cartoon animals. Their heads were too narrow and dominated by exposed teeth; their spines and ribs covered by thin rugs of skin. Carson looked away at the paddocks, which were bare of grass and greenery. On the loose fence lines, chewed shrubs battled forlornly. Around them, the grass that remained had been half dug up and pounded by insistent hooves. Sweetapple walked among the horses. They hardly bothered to acknowledge his presence. They didn't have the energy to be restless. Carson got out and watched as he ran his hand over their bumpy sides, checked their teeth, and looked closely at their feet. She was certain he would tell Johnny that there was nothing he could do for them. It was an awful, desolate place, and she wished to be elsewhere, with other people. After a long while, Sweetapple walked over to the vet, and Carson heard him say he thought he could look after them. Johnny was obviously very pleased, but asked Sweetapple twice if he was sure.

They put halters on the worst of the horses and led them slowly, carefully, up onto Sweetapple's truck. Then a bigger truck arrived, and they herded the rest of them on, careful not to pressure them or push them for space. Johnny and Sweetapple shook hands, and Johnny thanked him again. From the other side of the yard, the man raised one hand with spread fingers and waved it once at Sweetapple. He waved back and got into his truck.

The big truck followed Sweetapple and Carson. After they unloaded in Sweetapple's front yards, he set about sorting out which animals needed what sort of care. Carson wanted to say, 'I hope you know what you're doing,' but it seemed a dumb sort of statement. If he didn't know what he was doing, the consequences were obvious. She helped him draft and organise the horses into grades: nearly dead; injured; underweight. Sweetapple commented that it was like drafting in an old people's home.

They let the underweight animals out onto the pasture near the house, where they immediately put their heads to the ground and started eating. Carson realised why Sweetapple wanted her to be involved. The feeling of giving feed to the animals was powerfully uplifting and sort of restorative. She wanted to yell with little-girl pleasure. They got hay for the injured, put them in a small paddock at the back of the yards, and then hand-fed the nearly dead, giving them a multivitamin injection and making sure their water was clean and plentiful. Sweetapple explained that he would get them on to a solid feed like grain when their bodies were able to adjust.

When they were done, Carson walked back to the house with him, feeling like someone wealthy who had been handing out money to poor children in the street.

Caroline saw Sweetapple walking in the street in town, saying hello to people, looking healthy and like a man at ease. When she looked across the wide street, and recognised the walk and the way he nodded his head when he was happily engaged, she had the warm sensation of seeing an old boyfriend and enjoying the pleasure of knowing it had been nice when it happened but had always been the wrong thing. Except, of course, he was never close to having been a boyfriend. She crossed the road to catch him, and he smiled brightly when he saw her first.

She had been in town on her own for several days, staying

in the motel, with its chenille bedspreads, tapestry print, exposed brick wall, and the owner who looked at her with a slightly pleased questioning smile: the whole box and dice. When she'd packed her bag and walked away from Bob, she didn't need a second thought to know what she was in for. It would be humiliating and lonely and miserable. Town gossip would be hot. *Caroline Statham's been kicked out. Not even Bob Statham could love her. Living in the motel. She's hit rock bottom. Serve her right.*

It was all this and not. The first moments when she put her bag down in the musty-smelling room with orange as a feature were bad ones, really bad ones. But after that it was like watching an expected violent storm pass quietly with light rain. It just wasn't that bad. She was already experienced in gossip, humiliation, and loneliness. They had become empty threats. Strangely, she felt euphoria instead of pain or self-pity. She felt the glorious rush of *Fuck the lot of them.* She was stronger than all those whispering people out there, and much stronger than the woman she had been on the farm.

She talked to lawyers about a split of assets, and did a property search on what was in her name and what activity had been going on. Apparently, Bob had been attempting to transfer ownership of the farm to a woman called Laura. Since the Little Myalls farm was held in both Bob and Caroline's names, he had to have been forging Caroline's signature. She had to restrain herself from kicking the solicitors' table over in her anger. They immediately challenged the transfer, and began to dispute Bob's paperwork. Now the solicitors were hard at it, making sure that what was left didn't disappear.

Watching the nightly news and displays of the damp

incompetence of local politicians, she understood that she had to go back into politics. Probably state, but if not, then local. She wanted recognition, and she needed to get things done. Not all of it was for the greater good, or for anyone's good except hers, but it was the way she was. So she began to think about where she should stand and what issues might be most powerful. Her greatest weapon in politics would now be the blissful power of being unembarrassable. She could focus on what was right, because even though the personal attacks would come, they could not wound her. Caroline sat back on her motel bed and felt the energy surging. She wanted to start right now. There was plenty to do and plenty to prove.

But there were still things that needed to be put right—for Sweetapple and for Retribution. So when she saw Sweetapple in the street, she asked if he had time for a coffee. They took their seats at an outdoor table at the coffee shop in the main street. If Bob saw them, it would make her happy.

'Carson probably told you, but I've left Bob. For good.'

Sweetapple pursed his lips and scrunched up his nose.

'And I've decided I'm going back into politics.'

'Good for you.'

She had intended to start with small talk, but somehow the need to get on with things overtook her.

'So, weirdly, I'm in a good place. I know where I want to be and what I want to do. How are you?'

'I feel the same, sort of, as you do. Like, all of a sudden, I know what's important.'

They looked at each other with their surprised happiness. Caroline took a sip of her weak coffee and said, 'I still feel terrible about what happened to Missy.'

Sweetapple's face darkened. Caroline knew he would prefer her to leave the topic alone, but she needed to express her remorse. 'If there was anything I could do to make up for what happened, you know I would do it.'

Sweetapple sat forward, the darkness gone. 'I had an idea. Something I was going to do, but if you could help me out with it, it might be so much better.'

'Whatever I can do.'

21

Luke spent his time—whether at work, in the bar, walking the streets, watching trains from his spot on the hill, or lying on his bed in his room—arguing with himself. It was time to leave. Disappear into the outback or somewhere. Maybe get a fake identity. No, it was best to go and see the police, and tell them that Anna had given the explosives to Sweetapple, who had blown up the train line. How did he know? Because he was there. He had been an innocent fool dragged along by a manipulative couple. But he didn't have anything concrete to offer them. No proof, and it would just bring him into the police spotlight.

One afternoon when he came in from work, feeling too crazed to stop for a beer in the front bar, Teddy called him over. He took him behind the counter of the bottle-shop section and said quietly, 'Cops came in looking for you today.'

Luke did his best to show he thought such a thing was funny or weird. 'Yeah? What did you say?'

'Said I hadn't seen you for a few days. I couldn't pretend you weren't staying here. All your details are in the ledger. Are you in trouble?'

'Nah. Probably an old parking fine or something.'

Teddy looked disappointed. 'Mate, one of the cops is a cousin of my brother-in-law. He told me they wanted you in connection with the rail bombing. Said members of the protest group had put you in.'

'Seriously?'

'Yep. They said they were trying to get rid of the bomb, and you stole it. Reckoned you were a hardcore — an extremist in the group who was always planning to blow up a train.'

'What? That's just stupid crap. I hope you didn't believe them.'

'No.' Teddy sighed. It wasn't the sort of story you made up about an innocent.

'Man, I swear I had nothing to do with that shit.'

'I hope not.'

Luke rubbed his hands through his hair, closing his eyes at the ridiculousness of such an accusation.

'I used to go out with the girl who leads the protest group. Then I did some work for that mining company, and she hates me for it. Really hates me. I guess she's decided to get back at me.'

'You weren't involved in the bombing in some way?' Teddy now looked like he might grab Luke and take him to the police station himself.

'No way. Don't know the first thing about it. I don't know anything about explosives.'

'Yeah, but you like trains, don't you? People say you go out and watch them, for hours on end.'

Luke had the sickly sensation that for the past few months he had been pretending to be unseen when he knew, like everyone else, that no one was invisible in a small town.

'I just watch them. I don't want to blow them up. You've got to believe me.'

Teddy sighed, and opened the door for Luke to leave.

'I thought I'd let you know, because they'll be back.'

'Thanks. Appreciate it.'

'If you were involved in any way, I suggest you give yourself up. You can't run from this sort of thing.'

'I'm not going anywhere.' Luke left Teddy, knowing he was definitely going somewhere.

He packed up his things, walked to the end of the second-floor corridor, and opened the window that looked down over the empty beer garden. He threw his bag out onto the grass in the dark, and then ran down the stairs as lightly as the worn timber stairs would allow. Teddy was at the bar pulling beers, facing the other direction. Luke stepped past the bar door and walked quickly into the beer garden and to his bag. He could see Frank's recently repaired ute in the pub car park. It looked brand new in the street lights, and Luke knew the local insurance repairer had taken the opportunity to blame Luke's prank for every dent and mark that had ever existed on the ute. Luke had actually done Frank a favour, which made everything that was already bad worse. On the dark side of a tree in the car park, he rifled through his bag and found Frank's keys. He still had the wig and the dress and the shoes, too. It was childish keeping these things, but having the keys would help him this time. He hoped Frank hadn't gone to the trouble of installing a new ignition switch, but the door unlocked, the ute started first go, and Luke was on the road out of town before anyone cared to notice.

He took the road towards Sweetapple's place, because it was either that or Carson's house, and Carson was almost always at Sweetapple's these days. His heart was big in his chest as he thought about visiting them, and how pointless it was. Neither of them was on his side anymore. He had the police looking for him, and he needed to look after himself. He was the one being followed by the police while the other two played happy loving couples. They had made it clear they didn't need him, and now he was going to take the fall for the lot of them. He would fucking show them. Somehow.

He thought about seeing Bob and Caroline at Sweetapple's that day. The relationship was a strange one, made even stranger by that visit — Bob, the man Sweetapple hated most, visiting Sweetapple with his wife to check that he was okay. Bizarre didn't begin to explain it.

When Luke reached Sweetapple's mailbox, he slowed but kept going, looking down towards the distant lights of Bob's house, mouthing words that might create the magic spell he needed. He pulled up outside Bob's garden fence and sat looking at the house. There were a lot of lights on, and someone moving around behind blinds. At least they were home. A woman appeared at a glass door that faced the broad verandah. She was young and slim. He didn't think she could be Caroline — a daughter perhaps. Either way, he needed to talk to Bob alone.

He knocked on the glass doors and stood back, as casually as he could pretend. The young woman covered herself up, came to the door, opened it, and said, a little hostilely, 'Yes?'

She looked too old to be his daughter, but not by much.

'Hi. Sorry to bother you. Luke's my name. I was wondering if I could have chat to Bob?'

She was unconvinced. 'Sorry? What about? This is kind of a weird time for a visit.'

'Oh, he knows me. I'm a friend … was a friend … of Sweetapple's.'

She thought for a brief moment and then said, 'I'll see if he's available.' She pulled the door shut behind her.

Luke waited for maybe ten minutes, standing on the verandah, trying not to be caught peering inside. Eventually there were shuffling noises, and Bob appeared on the other side of the glass door, looking at him. He was in a worn tracksuit, his thinning hair awry, his glasses on his head—not expecting or wanting visitors.

He pushed the door open. 'You're a friend of Sweetapple's?'

'I was. We had a kind of falling-out.'

'That's what I thought she said. What do you want?'

'I have some information, about Sweetapple.'

'Yes.' It was said with the impatience of someone who was about to slam the door shut.

'Information you need to know, and that could put him in jail.'

Bob folded his arms and leant his head back. 'Put him in jail?' It was obvious he didn't believe it.

'But I need you to help me.'

'Oh, fuck off. Who do you think I am? Jesus bloody Christ.' He turned, but Luke made his words catch him.

'He did the railway-line bombing.'

Bob swivelled back. 'Who says?'

'I do.'

'How the fuck would you know?'

'I was there … when he planned it.'

'Why on earth would I believe you?'

'Because he wanted to get back at you for butchering Retribution.'

Now Bob was drawn in. He stepped outside and pulled the door to.

'Who says I butchered Retribution?'

'He did. It broke him. He wanted revenge, bad revenge.'

'Have you got any sort of proof?'

'I do. But I need an alibi.'

'For the night of the bombing?'

'Yes.'

'Bloody hell. You're pretty far out there, mate.'

'I know how he got the bomb. I know who he got the bomb from. I know how he blew up the line, and when. But you've got to help me.'

'What's your name again?'

'Luke.'

'Your full name.'

'Luke Griffiths.'

'Right, Luke Griffiths. You are going to fuck off out of here right now. If I ever see you again, I'll call the cops — again.'

Bob stood staring, not moving, and Luke wanted to smash him with something, take him down and really hurt him. But he nodded, and stepped off the verandah and down the stairs. He knew Bob was still watching as he opened the door to get into the ute. If he hit the accelerator hard, Frank's ute would go straight through the garden fence and probably knock the beams out from under the verandah when it hit. Luke talked himself down, remembering his rules. *Don't give in to the bear.* Nothing he could do to Bob would make things better. He gripped the wheel, and told himself to hold on. Bob now held all the cards. This was a fuck-up, and Luke was in a stolen ute.

When he knocked on Sweetapple's door, Carson answered. She looked at him and the bag in his hand, and said, 'Hi?' as a question.

'I need to stay. Cops came looking for me this afternoon.'

He pushed his way in.

'But they'll just come out here, then,' she said to his back as he put his bag on the kitchen table.

'Just one night. I'll stay somewhere else tomorrow. If I talk to them now, I'll say something stupid.'

Luke was hyped. Maybe he'd taken something. 'Are you all right?'

'Yeah. Fine. Just a bit of an adrenaline rush.'

'The spare room is yours.' They could hear Sweetapple receiving a phone call, saying little. She led Luke to the spare room. He put his bag on the floor, and they pulled a sheet tight on the bed. Sweetapple was waiting in the kitchen when they returned. She wondered if she saw something sweep across Luke's face.

'That was Bob on the phone. Again.'

'You guys are really working on your relationship.' A joke from Luke, delivered inexpertly.

'He says he knows what I did, and he's going to put me away for it.' Sweetapple was unmoved. 'I haven't told anyone what we did, and I'm sure no one saw us. So how does he know?' He looked at Luke.

'Could be just bluffing. Like an educated guess.'

Carson saw that Luke was calm now, as if he had moved into a role he was comfortable with.

'Suppose so. I saw that Anna girl was arrested,' Sweetapple said. 'Maybe she told the police, and they told him that I had the explosives.'

Luke nodded. 'Yeah, maybe.'

'Or maybe you told him, Luke. To give yourself some sort of protection.'

'Fuck off. Why would I do that? I don't even know the bastard. How's he going to give me protection?'

'You tell me.'

'Mate, I'm innocent. I swear.'

'Why don't I believe you?' There was precision in Sweetapple's coolness.

'Sweetapple, we're all a bit rattled. Take it easy. This is how things fall apart: we get suspicious, we start accusing each other, then somebody cracks and does something that gives the whole thing away.'

'What if someone already has?'

Carson left them and went to the spare bedroom. Her guess was that Luke would not stay now, and that he would be dangerous wherever he went. It was like she and Sweetapple were drifting along waiting for someone like Luke—probably Luke—to put them in jail. Carson could not let that happen. She burrowed into the linen cupboard and pulled out the laptop, now in a plastic bag but still wrapped in the oil rag. She opened Luke's bag, moved the wig and his things to one side, put the computer at the bottom of the bag, and zipped it back up. She carried the bag into the kitchen and placed it at the foot of the table. Sweetapple and Luke were still arguing, and when Luke saw her carrying the bag, he said, 'So you're kicking me out, then?'

'I don't think this is the place for you. You can stay at mine.'

Luke shook his head, focused on the bag. Carson tried not to believe that he could see the contents.

'Fuck the pair of you.'

'Make sure you feed the duck.'

He took the bag and left, slamming the door.

Sweetapple put a hand on her shoulder and squeezed.

'Do you think he told Bob?' she asked him.

'He's told someone.'

Carson chewed on her lip and thought about Bob.

'Let's go and rough Bob up a bit. Bash the prick. I'll help you. I can do that stuff.'

'I don't want to bash him.'

'Shit, Sweetapple, you do remember what he did to you? And after all he did, he still came over to visit you, sweet as apple pie. The guy is a monster. He had Retribution chopped up, and feels nothing. He could have you and me chopped up, and not bat an eyelid.'

'I don't feel that anymore.'

'And what about me? Do you feel anything for me? Or are you just some sort of limp impersonator?'

'I love you.'

'That's not what I wanted to hear.'

Carson had to get out of the house. She asked Sweetapple if she could take his ute into town. He asked why, and where to, and when she couldn't think of an explanation she simply said, 'You don't need to know,' and he accepted it.

She drove directly to the police station, passed it, and parked around the corner. The station was closed, and the only light came from the street and the police sign. She pulled her hoodie up in case there was CCTV, and walked down the street around the corner and to the front door. She took a note from her pocket and slid it under the door, and then turned and walked back out and up the street.

In the ute, her breathing was heavy, her heart banging in her chest. There was nobody about. She knew that Luke had sacrificed them somehow; she just wasn't sure how. Somebody had to stop him, and Sweetapple no longer appeared to have the heart for it. It almost felt like he would accept being arrested, with that serene smile intact. Her note should do the trick, she thought, as long as someone found it in the morning, which wasn't a certainty. The police station wasn't always manned.

22

Luke drove to Carson's house feeling like he was driving into a dead end. The stupid idea with Bob had failed, and now Sweetapple and Carson weren't even pretending to be on his side. He took the ute around the side of the house, where it couldn't be seen from the road, and parked in among some trees. The duck was waiting, honking, appearing none the worse for its time alone. Luke skirted it, carrying his bag, as the duck made more noise than a guard dog might. The house was clean and only a bit musty. He opened windows and doors, and prowled around as though he was doing a security sweep. There was food and drink in the fridge. He flopped on the couch with a can of cider, and turned the TV on. *Fuck Sweetapple*, he thought, *and Carson*. They were the enemy now. They had kicked him out to save their own skins. They deserved what was coming to them. Bob would tell the police — nothing surer. When Sweetapple and Carson were arrested, Luke would go to the police and answer all the questions they wanted to ask, and then he would disappear. He had spent too much time in this area, and too much with these bloody people.

The weight of exhaustion was pushing down on him. At least he could relax here for a little while. He would deal with the ute in the morning. The duck had lost its enthusiasm for being a warning system, and was making soft clucking noises near the front door. Luke dozed in the light of the television.

At first light, the duck woke him, annoyed at the arrival of yet another stranger. Luke sat up abruptly, not certain where he was or what he had done. The duck was getting very upset. There was a firm knock at the front door. He could see the ghostly apparition of a policeman and policewoman through the frosted glass beside the door.

He was caught. His heart was pounding him awake, and he had no idea what to do. If he ran, they would see him move. He hit the floor and let them knock. They were looking for Carson now, too. Who had dobbed her in? Then they called his name, saying they knew someone was in there, and asking if it was him. Carson and Sweetapple had betrayed him. They had fucking betrayed him.

Luke lay on the floor, scarcely breathing, wondering how he could get away if he was able to get out of the house without them seeing him. He had to have faith in himself. He had bluffed his way out of many situations before. This one was no different. Luke stood, straightened himself, and went to the door, demanding his brain think of something to say. But as he put a hand out to the door handle, he saw the top of the wig through the open zip of his bag.

'Just a minute,' he said, in a not-quite falsetto voice. The wig and the dress had worked before, and they could work again. His instinct told him he was right.

'I'm just getting dressed.'

Luke took the wig and the black dress into the next room. He removed his clothes, slipped the dress on, and put the wig on. In the mirror he looked a little rough, but he had got away with it before. Surely he could now.

Soundlessly, he walked barefoot back to the front door, opened it, and put his head around the side. 'Can I help you?'

'Good morning. We're looking for a man called Luke Griffiths. We have information that he might be staying here.'

They had sold him out. Told the police where he would be, and when.

'Luke? I'm sorry, there's only me here. This is … ah … Carson Wright's place. She's staying over at a friend's.'

The policewoman looked at the policeman.

'Are you okay?'

'Me? I'm fine. Just a little flustered at having the police on my doorstep.'

'Would you mind telling us your name?'

'Lea. Lea Turner. I'm not a local. I'm from the city. Just visiting.'

'Do you mind if we come in?'

'I'm not really organised to have visitors. The place is a mess.'

'You really don't know any Luke Griffiths?'

'Never heard of him. Is he a friend of Carson's?'

'Possibly. Are you aware that you have a stolen vehicle at the back of this house?'

'Oh my God, no! Carson gave me a lift here. I didn't even know there was a car out there.' Luke was steaming at his own carelessness. Why hadn't he ditched the ute when he had the chance?

'If you won't let us in, we'll have to ask you to come down to the station.'

'Just give me a second to put some proper clothes on, and I'll let you in.'

Luke shut the door, decided that locking it would make them suspicious, picked up his clothes, and walked back into the bathroom. But as he stepped in the doorway he saw someone in the mirror he couldn't recognise: a crazy man. A man who had lost his grip. And now the man looked afraid. Luke looked away. Things had gone very wrong. His attempt at appearing female wasn't even half-hearted; it was insane, a badly done parody. He was struggling to breathe, his chest compressed, his lungs too small. He searched desperately for calming words, mantras that had helped him before, but he could think of nothing except *Run—fucking run*. He threw the wig on the floor, ripped the dress off, pulled on his clothes, and bolted out the back door.

Luke sprinted down across a wide, open plain, with hardly even a tree for cover. He could hear the police, probably still at the front door, calling his name. But there was nowhere he was running to. The soil was soft underfoot, and there were large cracks in the ground where it had dried out and contracted. He kept running without a plan, thinking that when he heard the police car he would work out what to do.

The paddocks in front of him spanned out, the stubble pale and bright green. And now he could see that the green rectangle in the distance was irrigated corn, tall and thick, a sanctuary of sorts. He sprinted towards it, the sweat pouring down his face, his breathing loud and desperate. He hit the edge of the stubble, and leapt into the corn crop and crawled over the irrigation ditches until he was far enough in not to be seen and not able to see out. He lay on the dark, damp soil, breathing in gasps and wondering what the fuck he had just done.

He had sent a message, and then turned his phone off and crawled through the soft earth over irrigation ditches further into the crop. It was hopeless. Carson and Sweetapple would not come to his rescue. He knew that. He had burnt every bridge available. Above him, the corn leaves rustled like streamers in the breeze, and he had to resist the idea that he could be safe here in this private, green world. There were no human sounds now, but the police would be here soon enough, in numbers, with loudhailers and maybe dogs. They would flush him out like a fugitive in a Deep South movie. He lay still and caught his breath. Sugar ants found him immediately, and the mosquitoes arrived for a look. It forced him to stand up and shake himself. If he waited, it would be as good as giving himself up. If he made his way out of the crop to the road, he would be picked up even more quickly. His best hope, if there was one, was to make his way to the southern end of the block, where the corn met old wheat stubble. Perhaps he could crawl his way through the stubble to a house or a car he could steal—something.

He walked on, holding onto stalks, listening for sounds of vehicles and sirens. Nothing yet. At the end of the crop, he stuck his head out to see what he had to work with. In front of him, a head ditch full of water a couple of metres wide ran perpendicular to the crop lines. Maybe he could swim his way to freedom. The wheat stubble was grey and tired, and maybe a metre high. It would be a very long crawl to the next crop and the farm sheds in the distance. He crouched and looked to his left, ready to run, leap over the head ditch, and dive into the stubble. But further down the head ditch, next to a small pump shed, was a red quad bike parked on the road. He watched and listened and waited. No one emerged from the crop or the shed. There was no human noise, no sound of phones being talked on.

He ran down alongside the head ditch to the bike, and planted himself on the seat. But he couldn't find the key or the gears. Panic made him bounce in the seat, trying to remember or work out how to drive the machine. And then he found the starter and gearshift on the handle bars, and had the bike purring, ready to take him away. No one came running out or yelling at the noise from the bike. He would stay off the road, go cross-country, and make it to Sweetapple's or Bob's, and they would either help him or pay for it.

Luke crossed the road, took the corner of the paddock, and then crossed the road again. He guessed he had about ten kilometres to cover, and he hoped the bike had enough fuel. When he looked back towards Carson's house, he could see what might have been police cars coming down the road towards the corn.

A text came through on Carson's phone from Luke. He said he was hiding in a corn crop behind Carson's house, and needed help.

She showed it to Sweetapple, and he gritted his teeth and looked at the phone for a long while. 'Surely the police will be all around that crop, waiting for him to come out, or getting ready to flush him out?'

'We'll look like we're his getaway car.' Carson didn't want to save Luke, and didn't want to be anywhere near him.

'Yeah.'

They were quiet.

'If we drove past, we could see if there was anything we could do to help,' Sweetapple said.

Carson couldn't understand Sweetapple's loyalty, but she knew he would go to Luke's assistance no matter what she said.

'We wouldn't stop—just drive?'

'Yeah.'

'Okay.'

They took the ute towards Carson's house, then turned off towards the farming plain. They could see a couple of police cars pulling up at a green patch in the broad spread of paddocks. Sweetapple looked across at Carson with a question.

Her answer was, 'Let's drive straight down the road, no stopping, no turning.'

So they drove past the paddocks and the irrigated corn and the police cars. The police were walking into the crop, three of them abreast, with several rows between them. They did not look back at the ute going past. There was no sign of Luke.

'If he's in there, they'll find him.'

'Let's go. There's nothing we can do here.'

It took Luke most of the day to get to Sweetapple's. He took the quad into gullies and scrub thickets to hide from farmers and vehicles on the distant road. He had to find ways through fences and washouts, and stay off the open plain. For several hours he rested in a tumbledown shed in the lee of the hill not far from Sweetapple's farm. But after a while his imaginings of who might have seen him or was about to ambush him got the better of him, and he took off again, deciding that the scrub near Sweetapple's other yards was the best place to hide and to think about what to do. Finally at Sweetapple's, he drove the bike into a steep gully and pulled shiny bush branches over to cover it. Below him in the distance he could see hundreds of horses, and he wondered what that meant. He walked further up the hill into the trees, sat down, propped himself against a large kurrajong, and fell asleep against the scratchy bark.

When he woke, it was dark. His phone was flat, but he could tell darkness had not recently fallen. It was late. He was jittery and unsure. There was no plan, and his brain could not come up with one.

He sat trying to lay out the facts and to assess his options, but nothing was clear. Everything was a mess; no matter what story he told, no one would believe him. Anna would not help him. Bob would not help him. The police were chasing him. Sweetapple and Carson had betrayed him. How had this happened? He was always the clear thinker. He was the one with the plan. The bombing wasn't his idea, was it?

When they were fooling around with the bomb, Luke felt that he had Sweetapple's measure, and that Carson was going to swap sides and desert Sweetapple for him. But now there was nothing, and he wasn't sure how it had turned out this way or why. He bowed his head and squeezed his eyes shut tightly. There had to be a solution. There was always a solution.

After a minute, he stood up, brushed himself down, and began to walk down the hill to the house. The solution lay with Sweetapple and Carson. Any fool could see that. He was going to surprise them, and demand they explain why they had set him adrift. He would tell them he was not going down alone, and if they wanted to save themselves, they'd better do their best to save him. The night was clear-skied and cool, and there was a light breeze.

As he walked, his fury stirred. They were in the house, in bed beside each other, comfortable and asleep. No police were chasing them, while he ran for his life in the dark in the scrub. He had done no more than they had. He had helped them with their mad idea. That was all. But he was copping the consequences. He was the fucking scapegoat. The sound of his tromping feet gave him strength. He knew where he was going. There were no other noises in the night except an owl, close by, hooting of persistence.

He imagined them listening to his demands, giving in to what he asked, and even begging him to team up with them again. They couldn't do without him. He was the brains of the operation.

And then Carson's face came to him, the last time they met: beautiful but distant. She would send him packing. Nothing he could say would change her mind. They would tell him to go, and would kick him out like they had before. They had used him, and he had been simple and naive in ways he had never been before. And, worse, Carson had rejected him and seemed to have forgotten they had ever been together. He knew he was kidding himself, and the bear rose up in him with fury at the injustice and the treachery. They had to pay. He would make them pay. He kicked his way down the hill, his hatred increasing with every brutal step.

The house was dark, and there was no sound—not even Sweetapple's television on its timer. The ute was in the garage, with Carson's little car next to it. At the front door, Luke raised a clenched fist, ready to hammer his arrival. But he stopped himself. He had already accepted that they would not listen to words. If he was going to confront them, he would need a weapon—a rock, or a stick, or something.

He made his way around the edge of the house, trying to look in the window and make sure they were there. The bedroom blind was drawn, and he couldn't risk them making out a shadow or a silhouette trying to see in. He thought he could smash the window and then set upon them, if only he could find something to hit them with.

At the back of the house, a group of eucalypts had dropped branches thick with now-dry leaves. They should have been cut up and burnt. Sweetapple had obviously been too busy to do this, but the branches gave Luke the answer he didn't realise he had been searching for. He began to drag branches down to the back wall of the house and to stack them in the corner that marked out the bedroom. A house like this could go up in minutes. Even if they got out in time, they would get the fright they deserved.

When Luke had several branches interwoven in place, he realised he didn't have anything to light them with. He crept back to the front door and opened the flyscreen slowly, ready for it to creak and betray him. But it made no sound, so he stepped lightly into the kitchen, listening to his own loud breathing and remembering that the matches were kept on the bench next to the fridge. As Luke's hand closed around the box of matches, there was a noise from the bedroom, and he squeezed the box tightly. Then nothing. Sleep talk. He had to fight the fantasy of entering their bedroom and smothering one of them, both of them, with a pillow. He left the room carefully to stop the door banging shut.

But when he had pulled the door to, he saw in the half-light a pile of wound-up used baling twine. Another step in his plan presented himself, and he couldn't help smiling in recognition that he was thinking and planning again. He pulled several lengths of baling twine from the pile, took one of them, and secured it to the door handle. Then he tied the other two pieces to it, and wrapped the greater length around the base of a nearby sapling. He put a truckie's hitch in the twine and pulled it tight, the pressure on the door handle enough to make it creak in its screws. He tied it off, and then happily bounced his hand on the taut line. At the side door, he did the same thing, pulling it tight until the door wedged hard in the doorway. But then he slackened it off until it allowed the door to open a small amount—enough to make them think they'd have a chance to get out. Luke knew from childhood research that you couldn't smell smoke while you slept. Even if they did happen to wake, the smoke would kill them in a matter of minutes, especially if they were distressed and exerting themselves. They deserved a chance. His desire was for them to suffer, not necessarily to die. He would wake them when he was ready. They would get air through the door, and then they could smash a window and get out. By then, the house and the baling twine would be obliterated.

After he dragged a few more branches to his pile, he scrunched up a heap of dead leaves and pushed them together, placing fine twigs on top. He lit the first match, and a light breeze blew it out before he could put it to the pile. The second held its flame, and the leaves on the edge at the bottom ignited, pumped out smoke, and then died. He cursed softly, and told himself there was plenty of time. No rush. The third took, and the leaves began to crackle here and there, and then burst into a unified chorus.

Carson woke, not having been properly asleep, and sat up. Sweetapple had promised he would do something about Bob soon, but he wouldn't talk about it. Not even a hint. It was so frustrating, she felt she was ready to tell him that either he shared whatever idea he had, or she was out. It was his choice. No more bullshit. He was pretending to be someone who could take action. She should have left already. None of it allowed her to sleep.

And then she smelled smoke — just a faint trace, but distinct. Sometimes when the bushfires were bad, the smoke blew in from miles away. It would be as thick and acrid as if the fire was next door. But there had been no news reports of fires that she could think of. And this smoke was rich and sharp, as if it might be not too far away. She got out of bed, her nose telling her the fire was somewhere in the south. The front door was jammed again, and she yanked it hard, hoping she didn't wake Sweetapple. The door wouldn't budge, and suddenly the smoke seemed thicker, and she thought for the first time that the fire might even be on Sweetapple's place.

She grabbed a fire extinguisher from inside the kitchen door and walked towards the side door. It opened a little and then stopped. The door usually swung easily in its frame. She put the extinguisher down. Carson knew that dry or wet weather could change how a door fitted in place, but this door didn't seem to be sticking anywhere. She reefed at it again, and felt the springiness of something like a rope holding it in place. Was the door tied up? Panic scenarios wheeled through her head. Had Bob locked them in the house in a form of revenge? Were the local police holding them inside until they could surround the house? Was Luke involved?

She slid a thin arm through the crack in the doorway, and

felt for the handle. There was rope or twine knotted at its base. She pulled her arm back inside, scraping the skin away from her forearm without even noticing. Her heart was hammering. The smell of smoke was persistent, and she knew someone was trying to kill them. She took a carving knife from the cutlery drawer, and went back to the door and slid it through the opening, the blood starting to run from her wrist. After several sawing attempts, the twine gave way and the door opened. She ran to the bedroom and roused Sweetapple, telling him to get out of bed quickly, and when she saw him sit up and rub his eyes, she left him, grabbing the fire extinguisher as she ran out the door.

Outside, the sky was clear and starry. There was no lightning, not even in the far distance. Perhaps a power line was down somewhere, hit by a sleepless truckie or a fed-up farmer. And then behind her the smell was suddenly strong, and she turned back towards the source, seeing smoke spiral upwards from somewhere at the back of the house.

She quickened her step, turned the corner at the back of the house, and saw Luke kneeling in front of a pile of dry leaves and branches, muttering to himself as the smoke began to rise around him. Then the leaves leapt from smouldering to brightly alight. Struggling to believe what she was witnessing, she stepped forward and hit him hard across his back with the fire extinguisher. He rolled and sprang up, squealing in surprise, and she swung the extinguisher into his midriff, knocking him to the ground, and leaving him in a foetal position and winded. She began spraying the fire back and forth, covering the whole pile. As she did so, Luke got to his feet, hunched over, and managed to grab at her shoulder. Carson swivelled, and smashed the extinguisher into his face. He fell back, clutching at his injuries. She was screaming at him, uttering obscenities and accusations, blaming him for things he had never known about. She raised the fire extinguisher above her head, ready to make Luke take the final blame for others who had refused to. Then she heard a voice behind her say, 'Carson. No.'

It took the stiffness from her spine and the strength from her muscles, and she dropped the cylinder and looked hard at a smashed-up Luke. 'Fuck him.'

Sweetapple was at her side, putting his arm around her.

'So what am I supposed to do with him?'

'Ring the ambos.'

'That'll just put us in the shit.'

'There's no choice.'

'Well, if you want to put yourself in jail, go ahead.'

'I will.' He turned and was gone.

By the time Sweetapple got back after making his phone calls, Luke was sitting up, bloodied, nursing his head.

'The ambos are coming.'

Luke tried to get to his feet, but only staggered a few steps and went down again.

Sweetapple offered him some water. Luke declined, and said into his folded arms, 'I'll fucken kill you both.'

Nobody spoke until the ambulance arrived.

In the morning, a policeman and policewoman were at the door. Carson watched Sweetapple as he opened the door to the neat, fresh pair. The woman seemed to know Sweetapple, and appeared a little embarrassed. They took the trouble to chat about the weather and the season. Carson pushed spoonfuls of cereal into her mouth and made herself chew, but swallowing was an act of will.

Then the policeman asked Sweetapple to confirm that Luke had been picked up at his place the night before. Sweetapple said it was true. He said he had knocked Luke out because Luke was trying to burn the house down.

'He was trying to burn the house down?'

'Yes.'

'Why would he want do that?'

'I don't know. Jealousy? He's pretty unstable.'

'Did you know he was wanted by the police?' The policewoman asked this, almost concerned for Sweetapple.

'No. What for?'

The police looked at each other as if asking the other to allow them to share information.

'We've charged him with the theft of a ute in town, and there are accusations that he was involved in the railway-line bombing. Do you know anything about that?'

'No.'

'Can I ask how you know Mr Griffiths?' The policeman had dropped his friendly tone.

'Just met him round town. The Bowlo, I think.'

'Do you know him well?' The policewoman, too, had given up on her neighbourly approach.

'Not really. Hung about with him a bit. Only known him a few months.'

'He's claiming you were the mastermind of the bombing, and that you forced him to go along with it.'

Sweetapple was quiet, and Carson took her plate to the sink, and, out of view, silently spat out her mouthful.

'Why would I blow up a railway line?'

He held their gaze, and as she sat back down at the table, Carson had the feeling they thought it might have been a good question.

'You're welcome to search the house, the vehicles, the sheds, wherever. I'll come in and answer any questions you want to ask. But I don't reckon you should be taking Luke's word over mine.'

They left after that, saying they'd be in touch and suggesting he not leave town.

'Are they going to arrest us?'

She stood by his side, grabbed his arm tightly.

'Not you. Eventually they'll come for me, I suppose. I don't know what Bob told them.'

She could feel his heart beating, but his voice was without fear.

'Should we make a run for it? Head north to the Territory, or something? You could get station work easily. Some of those places don't ask questions.'

'No.'

'So we just wait?'

'No. We've got important things to do.'

23

In the middle of the night, Sweetapple, Carson, and Caroline saddled a horse each. The moon was bright enough for Sweetapple to see the excitement on the faces of the women. In the afternoon, they had mustered every horse on the place into the paddock that adjoined the Statham farm. Sweetapple explained again that he wanted Carson to take the southern flank, Caroline the north, and he would lead and then circle back to push from the west. The horses and humans were all breathing heavily as they walked out of the stables and stood in a line in the silver light.

'Keep the noise down, and if any animal really doesn't want to come, then leave them behind. We'll come back for them. I'll whistle when I'm ready for you to start.'

Caroline mounted her slim, aged thoroughbred, and followed Sweetapple and the reflections of his gelding's shiny new shoes. He opened the gate into the bigger paddock and held it while Caroline and Carson, both on black mares, went through. Then they split up and rode around out the edge of the mobs of horses.

The sound of her own horse's feet crunching on the dry grass and twigs didn't block out the whinnies and nickering that rose up from the many horses crowded into the paddock. Most kept their heads down, eating, but some watched her go as others teased and annoyed their nearby mates. In a matter of weeks, Sweetapple had got together over five hundred horses. They were still thin and damaged, but no longer weak. She could see him making his careful way through the mob. They might not trust him, but they were accustomed to him. Carson had told Caroline that when he wasn't away picking up horses, Sweetapple was riding through the mobs, checking and watching them to confirm that they would be able to make it on their own.

To be with him tonight on horseback was something that Caroline would remember for a very long time. He had invited her, and she had offered her help, and together with Carson they were doing something worthwhile and more than an act of simple vengeance. And it forced her forward. After tonight's action, she had no choice but to go back out into the world. The farm would no longer be a respite; not for her, anyway.

Sweetapple leant down and unhooked the rusted gate-catch. He lifted the gate around until it held, fully open, and then looked back at the mob. As he hoped, the nearest horses were watching him — some openly, some pretending not to. A pale mare shone ghostly in the light and sniffed at him, its bowed legs almost concealed by moon shadow. He urged Jimmy forward several steps, and then got off and let the horse examine and then take a few bites of the lush grass. The pale mare took a few steps forward, and the nearby horses watched her and Sweetapple's horse.

Sweetapple led Jimmy forward, and several metres back the

pale mare followed, her head low and her nostrils spread. In the gateway, she stopped and looked around. Gates could mean a trap or freedom, or at least as much freedom as a horse like this could ever have known. Then she made her decision and stepped through the gate, and began taking mouthfuls here and there as she walked briskly further on. Her companions watched her go, prepared for her to be sacrificed, but when she seemed safe, they cautiously followed her lead, sniffing at the grass and the gateway until they were on the fresh pasture. Three of them took the opportunity to break into hobbling, unsightly canters, wobbling down the flat to what might be a kind of paradise. Sweetapple led his horse further forward and out of the way as other horses began to trickle through in ones and twos, never certain they were safe until they felt it for themselves. He knew there would always be animals that would refuse to go through without being pushed, unwilling to trust the unknown or anything that a man had had a hand in.

When a good number had started making their way through, he mounted and took his horse back through the gate, delaying some of the number in transition. When he was through, he whistled a long, powerful note, waved a hand in the air that they probably wouldn't be able to see, and rode to the back of the large mob. He could pick out Caroline in the north, plodding along on her wing, back and forth, as the horses slowly moved away from her. In the south, Carson was into a trot, even though he'd told her to take it as easy as possible. But Sweetapple was pleased at her wilfulness. When he had set out his plan, she had jumped at him and hugged him. Now she was excited. He knew he had tested her in the past few weeks, and he also knew how disappointed in him she had become, but he had been unable to do anything about it. The plan hadn't come together properly until now, and only Caroline's support had made it permanent. He also needed to let Carson make her own choices about him and Luke.

He rode along the western edge, encouraging the stragglers and keeping an eye out for bolters. Then, like Caroline and Carson, he stopped and watched. It felt like there were thousands of horses in front of him, rumps and manes and heads filling the space until eyesight could no longer do its job. They were moving well now, a derelict group of hacks that had somehow got the message: life was better through the gate. They didn't need to be pushed anymore. In the light, hundreds of horses passed through the small gateway, the fitter ones jostling and nipping, the weaker ones keeping an even pace, unable to waste energy on fighting or socialising. It was a sight without comparison. Some of the animals even had the beginnings of a shine in their coats, and all of them realised when they got a few metres into the paddock that fortune had turned their way. In the new paddock, the energy of the mob lifted, and Sweetapple could almost hear the sounds of a party—a horse party.

They met up again at the gate as the last few horses passed through. Carson was exhilarated. She wanted to laugh and yell out at their triumph and Sweetapple's return. In the dark, she could see the horses spreading out over the pasture, finding their way through another gate at the other end, and generally making themselves at home. When the last horse was finally through the gate, Carson asked the one question that Sweetapple hadn't answered.

'What's to stop him putting them straight back onto your place?'

'It's still Caroline's place, too.' In the pale light, she caught what she thought was a smile on Sweetapple's face. He said, 'And she's also got something up her sleeve,' and the silhouette of Caroline's head nodded.

'Tomorrow morning,' said Caroline. 'So I'd better get myself to bed.' She turned her horse towards the stables. 'That was lots of fun, though. Thanks.'

'Thank you. Good luck tomorrow.'

She walked her horse away as Sweetapple and Carson sat together, not speaking. Carson wondered what Caroline would be doing in the morning, but she knew this was one of the important moments, not to be brushed over or missed. They were pleased with themselves. They had done something good, got a little of their own back, and hurt no one.

When the humans were gone and could no longer bear witness, the pale mare found a garden gate left open, and bravely pushed her way through. Again, her mates watched pessimistically, and might have considered her a fool. But she quickly showed them that through the gate was a cornucopia for horses of any kind: watered, fertilised plants of every type. The pale horse savoured the sweet, even lawn as she bit and stepped her way to the ha-ha, and then up onto it and across to the garden beds along the verandah that presented like a smorgasbord. There were soft rose leaves and delicious seedlings, tender shoots, young shrubs, and everything that a starving horse's imagination could have conjured up.

Her friends followed. Those who were capable jumped up onto the wall to be with her, knocking rocks down and causing a collapse, while the others perused the garden beds that lined the fence. If there was a sound, it was simply the chomping of teeth and the groaning of stomachs. Quickly, perfect human order became a mess of nature, shrubs rubbed on and broken, plants pulled up, the planned gradations of height and colour levelled, and the careful selection of varieties that would flower in turn, each month of the year, indiscriminately removed from the calendar. Sculptures were knocked over as hooves sunk deep into the soft lawn and moist soil, while manure was spread about like the calling cards of vandals.

The next morning, the media assembled at Caroline's front gate, as she had requested. In the days since speaking to Sweetapple in town, she had sent out press releases to anyone she thought might come, telling them of a major announcement by the previous federal member for Lindon. Two TV news vehicles were there, as well as reporters from the area's weekly papers and a couple of bored politics bloggers with cameras.

Caroline opened by thanking them all for coming. Behind her was a shimmering cloth draped over the front gate of Little Myalls.

'Ladies and gentlemen, I have two very important announcements this morning. If it is all right with you, I would like to make my two announcements and one unveiling, and then I'll answer questions.'

The gathered media nodded their heads. It was a bright, clear morning, and in the paddocks behind her there were many horses grazing quietly. A journalist commented that the horses looked a little the worse for wear.

Caroline said she wanted to officially announce that she was returning to politics and would be standing as an independent in the state seat of Mockbar. She gave her reasons, and outlined the policy areas she would be pursuing. She told them she was aware that she had received much poor publicity and that her popularity wasn't high, but she looked forward to changing people's opinions of her.

And then she turned and said she was glad they could all be present for the official unveiling of a brand-new Statham project: a home for rejected and neglected horses. Her husband, Bob, had been made aware of the poor state of animal welfare on some farms and in some horse businesses, and he had decided to do something about it. Caroline leant over and removed the cloth on the front gate, revealing a wooden sign with chiselled letters that read 'Horse Haven'. There was even a light clap from some of the onlookers.

In his ute, on the other side of the road, Sweetapple slapped a hand down on the seat in between himself and Carson.

After the throng had dispersed, Caroline walked across the road to them, beaming.

'That seemed to go well.' Carson's smile was that of a friend.

A TV news car pulled away from the side of the road.

'Yeah. I felt like it did.'

'Do you think you can get re-elected?'

'I don't know. The election is still a year off, and the standing member is an idiot, but then that never stopped anyone, did it?'

'You'll be right,' said Sweetapple. 'People want someone courageous and forthright, and you've got that down.'

'Maybe.' She laughed in a light, happy way. 'I've learnt a lot about myself in the past few months. Hope I can put it to use.'

'Thanks for all your help with this.' Sweetapple indicated the horses and the sign behind her.

'My absolute pleasure. I'll let you know how the next stage goes.' She began to walk away. 'See you soon.'

They watched her get into her car, and they waved goodbye again.

As Sweetapple drove off, he looked past Carson at the paddocks full of contented horses, and saw a pale, bow-legged mare grazing in the distance. Carson followed his gaze. 'It can't last, you know.'

'I know. But I'll keep the pressure on him as long as possible. The minute he thinks he can close it down, we'll have the media and the animal activists on his case.'

'That won't stop him, though, will it?'

'It will for a while. At the very least, these old horses will have had a nice holiday. They look fatter already.'

Carson looked out her window at the horses grazing on the lush feed. They did look better somehow. Perhaps it was just the daylight.

'What are you going to do now?' Sweetapple asked.

'I'm going to enrol in a uni course.'

'You're leaving?'

Now the paddocks were slipping by: green crops and grey stubble, and fences in need of work.

'No. I'll do it from here.' She had not said this out loud. She had hardly even said it to herself.

'Good for you.'

'Are you going back to stealing?'

'No.'

'No?'

'Those horses still belong to me, so when he sells them, I'll get more than my money back.'

'Guilt-free?'

'I don't see why not.'

'No. Neither do I.'

She put her hand out the window and let it ride the wind.

'I wouldn't want you to leave.'

'No, I don't suppose you would.' She turned and smiled at him, and slapped him lightly on the shoulder, and he drove a little faster, not turning his face from the road.

ACKNOWLEDGEMENTS

I would like to acknowledge the work of my agent, Jane Novak. Without her diligence and optimism, *Retribution* would have remained just another file in my folder of failed endeavours.